DOOLEY

is

DEAD

Diana Rittenhouse Mystery 4/5

Kate Merrill

This is a work of fiction. Names, characters, places, and incidents are either the product of the author's imagination or are used fictitiously, and any resemblance to actual persons living or dead, business establishments, events or locales, is entirely coincidental.

DOOLEY is DEAD
COPYRIGHT 2016   by Kathleen E. Merrill

Cover photo: Marek Novak

MJS

Merlin-Janus Studio, Inc.
Mooresville, NC

Publishing History
First Edition 2016
Second Edition 2022
Print ISBN

Published in the United States of America

For all my dear friends who,
like Diana Rittenhouse and me,
have left the cold northeast
to live in awesome
North Carolina.

PROLOGUE

May 1, 1868...

The sun of high noon beat golden on Tom Dula's curly black hair, but his angry anthracite eyes remained hidden in shadow. Every muscle in his stooped, twenty-four- year-old body trembled as he stood on a horse-drawn cart, which also bore his coffin. They carried him into the Statesville town square, where a record-breaking crowd was assembled—men, women and children, black and white, rich and poor—all eager to watch him suffer a terrible death. Tom's old mother sat beside him on a hard wooden bench at the rear of the wagon, along with his devoted sister, Eliza.

Someone placed a noose around his neck, but Tom remained defiant. He spoke for over an hour, warning those assembled against the wages of sin, insisting his friends and neighbors had borne false witness against him. Finally, his hangman asked Tom's relatives to move off the cart.

A reporter from the *New York Herald* wrote:

"Turning his dark eyes upon them, he spoke in a loud voice which rang from the woods, as if a demon there was mocking the tone and spirit of a wretch who well knew he was going into eternity with an unconfessed murder upon his mind and falsehood upon his lips.

"At twenty-four minutes after two PM, the cart was moved, and the body of Thomas Dula was suspended between heaven and earth. The fall was about two feet, and the neck was

1

not broken. He breathed about five minutes and did not struggle, the pulse beating ten minutes, and then he was dead."

ONE

May 1, present day

"What a depressing story." Diana captured Matthew's hand as they exited the small rustic cabin that replicated the schoolhouse Tom Dula had attended more than a century and a half ago. "Can you imagine? Three women fighting over that man?"

Matthew shrugged as they stepped into the bright August afternoon. "Well, he was a good lookin' young fella, a Confederate war hero with his own little plot of land."

"Yes, but Laura, the girl he supposedly murdered, was actually carrying his child. And what about Laura's married cousin, Ann? Everyone knew that she and Tom were lovers. Then Laura's cousin, Pauline, showed up and started sleeping with the guy. I don't get it."

Matthew chuckled and squeezed her hand. "What I don't get is why both those other women tried to confess to the murder. Tom had already admitted he'd done it."

"Well, do you think he did it?" Diana asked.

"I reckon we'll never know for sure."

She sighed and lifted her eyes to the hazy foothills looming beyond the gravel parking lot. It was hard to believe that Tom Dula, whose grave was nearby, once beheld this exact landscape. Little had he known his bizarre love triangle, his sensational murder trial, and his brutal public hanging would become a national folk legend. The Kingston Trio would write a famous folk song about him, and the older woman inside the schoolhouse, who had just given them the tour, would make chronicling Tom's story her lifelong mission. "The woman who gave the talk really knew her stuff. Isn't she a descendant of the Dulas?"

"Yeah, I think so." Matthew paused to pick a yellow daisy from the edge of the lot. He tucked its stem behind Diana's ear. "The old gal's family built this place, Whippoorwill Village, and it's supposed to accurately reflect life at that time. She painted all those watercolors depicting Tom's life, too."

"Like an obsession," Diana mumbled as they drifted towards Matthew's truck." Remember that ballad, "Hang Down Your Head, Tom Dooley?' My mother played that record all the time, and the song always made me feel sad. I can't believe it all actually happened right here."

"And I can't believe your mama never told you how the famous legend unfolded in her own backyard. After all, she grew up here."

Matthew was right. Although Diana was a Yankee born and bred, her mother was an honest-to-god native North Carolinian. She had married Diana's father and followed him north, but her heart had never adopted the land of cold and snow. When Diana left Philadelphia almost four years ago to make a new start, her elderly mother, Vivian, had moved along with her. For Vivian it was a homecoming. Now Mama lived at Shady Oaks, an assisted living facility in Statesville, only blocks from where Tom Dula was hanged.

"I wonder why the song calls him Tom *Dooley* instead of *Dula*?" Diana said.

Matthew laughed. "Aw, you know how it goes. I guess the folks in Caldwell County pronounced it that way, and it stuck. What difference does it make? Dooley is dead, hanged for a crime he maybe didn't commit. Don't matter what you call him now. Dead is dead."

Diana stopped walking and stared at Matthew. Sometimes she swore she'd never understand these Southerners. They took everything in stride. It would sure as hell matter to her if posterity got her name wrong. Maybe this place felt like home to Mama, but to her, it often felt like a foreign country.

"Mama never talks about her childhood," she conceded, linking her arm around Matthew's waist. "It's a good thing I have you to teach me local history."

"You bet you're lucky to have me, Diana Rittenhouse." Matthew's warm brown eyes crinkled at the corners as he hugged her back. "Otherwise you'd be just another clueless Yankee interloper."

"Oh, yeah?" She squinted up, but his rugged face was shadowed by an aureole of sunshine behind his head. Diana was tall for a woman, but at six three, Matthew towered over her. He would never lord it over her, however. She hooked her fingers in his belt and gave a playful tug. "You're the lucky one, Matthew, and we both know it."

"Amen, you can say that again. You're my one and only, Diana. Look what happened to poor Tom Dooley when he tried to balance three women at once."

"They should've called him *Tomcat*." She laughed. "Laura, Ann, and Pauline…three cousins. Like juggling three balls in the air."

"You're right, young Tom had balls. But he couldn't keep it up." Matthew offered a suggestive grin.

5

"Seems like *keeping it up* was the root of his problem." An unpleasant surge of heat crawled up her neck the moment the words left her mouth.

Matthew stopped walking. He held a calloused hand against her forehead. "I can't believe you actually said that. Are you sick, Diana?"

She was known far and wide for her prudish objections to sexual innuendo, but sometimes a girl had to break loose and have some fun, especially with the man with whom she intended to live in sin. "Not sick, just crazy," she said as Matthew pulled her close.

She closed her eyes when he kissed her. She heard flies buzzing in the field and felt the warm sun in her hair, but she also heard kids giggling. When she looked again, a gang of teenage tourists were laughing at them, the middle-aged couple necking in the parking lot. The surge of heat became a full-fledged blush as she pulled away from Matthew and fled to the safety of his ancient red and white Ford pickup.

She slammed the door and sank low in the passenger seat, while Matthew lagged behind to fiddle with bungee cords. Her first load of earthly possessions—one suitcase of summer clothes, a cosmetic bag, and her beloved cappuccino machine—were packed in the truck's bed. Indeed, this was the weekend she was moving into Matthew's home on Lake Norman. After all the hemming and hawing, C-Day was at hand. Cohabitation Day. She fought off another panic attack, her third of the afternoon, and told herself for the umpteenth time she was doing the right thing. God knew she'd had plenty of time…years…to think it over.

She figured if they could get this initial bunch of stuff into his place without her freaking, they would return to her condo tonight for Perry, her foul-mouthed parrot, and move him, too. Then if they got through the first week, if Matthew's Doberman, Ursie, did not eat Perry, they'd move more of her things. If they survived a few months and were still talking to one another, she'd put her condo up for sale. If it sold, it would be time to take the next step. God help them all.

"You okay, Diana?" Matthew slid into the truck beside her.

She noticed he looked a little flushed around the gills as the teenagers continued to gawk and point. They backed up, left the Whippoorwill Village complex behind, then turned onto a country road leading away from Tom Dooley's domain. She reached across the seat and shyly took his right hand, which he had deliberately made available by steering with his left.

"I guess we're the original odd couple," she told him.

"Why? 'Cause we're old?"

"Because we're old enough to be those kids' parents, and we're kissing like teenagers."

"What's wrong with kissing? If those kids' parents never kissed, then those kids would've never got born."

"True, but those kids don't want to know their parents keep doing it."

"Reckon you're right."

She scooted closer to Matthew and they moved down the road in silence, leaving the Piedmont foothills behind. They were a strange pair to be sure, but Diana had loved Matthew Troutman since the minute she laid eyes on him. He was native as grits and redeye gravy, while she was as Philly as cheese steak. The little town of Troutman, just north of where Matthew now lived, had been named for his great granddaddy. Matthew was all about fishing, fixing cars, and helping his neighbors.

While Diana loved art, classical music, and didn't know a soul in her condo complex. Go figure.

They picked up Route 16 and dropped south to Interstate 40 heading west towards Statesville, where they'd pick up Interstate 77 heading south to Mooresville.

"You sure Liz won't need you at the office this weekend?" he asked.

"I cleared my desk, and she knows the drill."

Matthew owned and operated a traditional hardware store and garage called *Trout's Place*. Through the years it had expanded to include a mini mart and gas station. He served the lake folks and tourists who traveled back and forth on River Highway. Diana was a real estate broker in the little college town of Davidson. Along with her younger partner, Liz, she tried to sell those lake homes to customers who kept Matthew's business booming.

"So you're completely free." Matthew smiled. "That means we can make as many trips as necessary to get you moved in."

She gave his hand a reassuring squeeze. Ever since they'd decided to take the plunge, they'd been jittery as kids on a first date. No one could accuse them of rushing into this relationship, however, because they were both old-fashioned when it came to living together before marriage. It had taken weeks before they committed to their first kiss and months before they had sex, so today's move was huge for them.

"You won't change your mind, will you?" Matthew's eyebrows creased in a frown.

"Hey, not unless *you* get cold feet."

It was an old joke, since it was Diana's toes that always chilled his warm legs between the sheets. Point was, they were both gun-shy. Matthew had been a widower since his wife died eight years ago, and Diana was the survivor of an ugly divorce. She knew Matthew was ready to tie the knot, but she couldn't quite go there yet.

"Does Liz know what you're up to?" He winked.

"Not yet." Her business partner, who was much more modern than Diana, would tease her mercilessly when she found out they'd moved in together.

"What about Vivian? Did you tell your mom?" Suddenly Matthew was serious. He was quite fond of her mother, but he also knew Mama could be a judgmental old bat.

"Nope, I haven't told her. I don't know what to say, Matthew."

"We should tell her together, but I bet she'd be more receptive if you'd let me slip a ring on your finger first."

Diana refused to be pushed. She took a deep breath and stared straight ahead. They'd been down that road so many times, she almost wished they'd reach a dead-end. Her every instinct cried out to say *yes*, so either she was a sniveling coward, or else she had a tragic flaw that kept her from accepting happiness.

"You're deliberately leaving the door open, Diana," Matthew accused. "You haven't told Liz or Viv. You're covering your bases in case we get it wrong."

What could she say? Best to say nothing. Thunder in the distance kept time with the irregular thudding of her heart. Sudden storms were commonplace here in the summertime. They usually hit about five PM, sending boaters speeding home to their docks and outdoor dogs scrambling to their shelters.

"Should've covered your stuff with a tarp," Matthew muttered.

Diana glanced at her watch. The seconds ticked off in sync with her racing pulse. "No, I think we'll beat the rain."

"Promise?"

"Yeah, sure."

But it started to sprinkle as they pulled off at Exit 36, Mooresville. The drops got fatter as they drove west on River Highway.

"Let's buy barbeque takeout," Matthew suggested. "We should celebrate." He made a sudden turn into the lot at Lancaster's restaurant, parked under the gas pump canopy, and then ran between raindrops to place their order.

"Hey, don't bother to ask me what I want," she called grumpily into the wind.

It wasn't like he didn't know what she would order, it was always the same. And while he was gone, she realized she was wound tighter than a yo-yo at this crossroad in her life. Her moods swung down, then snapped up, but Matthew insisted she was as steady as a dripping faucet and twice as hard to shut off. Was that a complement? Who was right?

Mama said Diana was focused, hard- working, and stubborn as the rust stain under that leaky faucet. Who knew? Liz claimed Diana was afraid to take a chance on love. Maybe they were all right?

Matthew seemed to notice her worried expression when he returned. "What's wrong?"

He handed her a big white paper bag with hot sauce spreading like a bloodstain across its bottom. She eased the takeout into one of the plastic grocery bags Matthew kept stashed in the glove case. He was conscientious about litter, she'd give him that.

"I guess I'm scared," she admitted.

He tilted her chin and searched her eyes. "Me, too. Let's just take it one day at a time, okay?"

Her gut said *how 'bout one minute at a time?* And when they moved back out on the highway, her sense of foreboding intensified. A clap of thunder boomed and hit something close by. Soon they passed an old oak stranded in the middle of a field. It had just been split down the middle by lightning. Diana smelled charred wood and the heavy odor of ozone as sirens wailed in the distance.

"I thought you said we'd beat the storm?" Matthew said.

"We would have, but you decided to stop for the stupid barbeque," she answered defensively.

Their argumentative banter was not an auspicious start to their life together, so she got her nerves under control, clamped her mouth shut, and they endured several miles of uneasy silence, punctuated only by thunder. They passed a fender-bender involving an old woman and a Hispanic gardener right at the turnoff to Matthew's road.

"Should we stop and help them?" she asked.

Matthew eyed the wreck, rolled down his window, and called out to the gardener, who apparently understood no English. The man held up a cell phone, indicating he'd dialed 911, then waved them away.

"Looks like he's got it under control," Matthew muttered.

They eased around the shattered glass as Matthew's habitually open expression screwed up with tension.

"Hey, I'm sorry." She touched his arm.

"Me, too."

They wound down the long lane leading to Matthew's home. At one point, they dipped into a flash-flooded valley, and the old truck almost stalled out. Not a good omen. When they finally reached his driveway, Matthew's dog Ursie was there to greet them. The valiant old Doberman charged towards them in a panic, whining, cringing, and cowering. Like many rescue dogs, she was terrified by thunderstorms.

"Damn it, Matthew, why'd you leave her outside? You promised you wouldn't do that anymore."

"I didn't leave her out." He gathered Ursie's wet head into his big hands and comforted her.

"Then how did she get out?"

"How the hell should I know?"

Thing was, Matthew almost never swore or used profanity of any kind, so at the moment he was very angry, likely at her. Should she apologize again, or put her inner bitch away once and for all? As they reached the back door, the lake out front was a churning sea of fog and whitecaps. Matthew found his house key, but before he could insert it in the lock, the door swung open of its own volition.

"That's funny. I'm sure I locked it." He reached inside for the light and hit the switch, but nothing happened. "Good lord, the power's out. What next?"

She grabbed hold of his waist and trailed him into the dark house. Ursie lagged behind whimpering, her ears pinned back. "What's her problem, Matthew?"

The muscles in his jaw tensed and his dark eyes glittered. "Stay right here, Diana, while I check it out."

"Did someone break in?"

"Don't move, you promise?"

She nodded and latched onto Ursie's collar to keep her from following, but then a growl rumbled from deep in Ursie's throat as Matthew disappeared into the dark kitchen. And for the first time, Diana felt truly afraid.

"Shh… be quiet, Ursie," she begged, but the dog wasn't listening.

The growl became downright menacing as Ursie struggled to break loose. Diana planted both feet, but the huge animal dragged her towards the living room. Suddenly, Ursie ducked backwards out of her collar and lunged towards the bedrooms. Toenails clattered on the hardwood hallway floor until Ursie reached the carpeted master bedroom and charged inside. Diana heard a high-pitched scream and furious barking. Then the barking abruptly stopped. Ursie yowled in pain just before Diana heard a loud thud, like a body falling to the floor.

She tried to call to Matthew, but fear sealed her throat. At the same time, her feet stumbled forward through the dark and she toppled a floor lamp in her rush towards the bedroom. When she got there, she almost tripped over the dog sprawled out near the entrance.

Her eyes stung from a nasty, sharp smell in the air, and then she spotted a dark figure lounging on Matthew's bed. The person was backlit by the picture window, a panorama of flashing lightning, and while the face appeared only in silhouette, she sensed the intruder was young and female.

"What did you do to Ursie?" Diana coughed through her aching throat as the stranger sat upright.

"Hey, it was self-defense. That dog came at me!" Although the intruder was coughing, too, her voice was deep, with a southern accent smooth as warm honey.

Diana groped closer through the dark. Adrenaline flooded her veins and fueled her fury as Ursie lifted her head, whimpered, and swiped at her eyes with her paws. At least she wasn't dead.

"It's only pepper spray." The woman laughed as she swung her boots off the bed.

Diana wanted to strangle her with her two bare hands, but as she approached, she saw slim, muscular forearms, covered with tattoos. "Who the hell are you?" she choked.

A bolt of lightning illuminated the woman's hand as she lifted it towards Diana. "More important, who the hell are you?" the stranger demanded.

Then Diana saw the small pistol, aimed directly at her heart.

TWO

A direct hit…

Diana's hand flew involuntarily to her chest, as if her fingers could stop a speeding bullet. She had been on the receiving end of a bullet before and did not want to repeat the experience. Blood drained from her head, depriving her brain of oxygen, and her knees started to buckle. Refusing to faint, she gaped at the black ceiling, hoping for what, divine intervention? Instead she saw a jumping beam of light dancing in the rafters like a deranged Tinker Bell.

"Drop the gun!" Matthew roared as the beam focused on the shiny silver barrel in the intruder's hand. "Do it now!"

Diana felt his body move in close behind her. She smelled his fear.

"Or what?" The woman giggled. "You'll beat me to death with that flashlight?"

"Drop it!" Matthew's left arm encircled Diana's waist, preventing her from sinking. He guided her around behind him, becoming her human shield.

The intruder's laugh was deep and throaty. "Jesus, Trout, it's only a starter pistol…" She tossed the weapon onto the carpet. "Don't you recognize it?"

Matthew's breathing was heavy and irregular as he aimed his light on the discarded gun, which now looked like a harmless toy. Ursie whined and crawled up to sniff the thing as Diana's knees decided to support her, after all.

Nonetheless, Matthew eased her down onto his desk chair and beamed his light at their unwanted guest. The woman's face was young and pretty, except for the dark streams of mascara trickling from her weeping eyes. Diana stared at the shiny silver stud embedded in her left nostril.

The stranger opened her palms in a gesture of peace. "Sorry about the pepper spray, Trout. Can we start over?"

Ursie, at least, was willing to accept the olive branch as she continued crawling on her elbows until she reached the girl on the bed. Then she actually licked the intruder's hand. Traitor!

"Who is she, Matthew?" Diana gasped.

But Matthew was staring like a zombie. He had seemingly lost the powers of speech and balance as he leaned against the wall for support. "How'd you get in?" he croaked at last.

"Would you believe I still have my key?" the girl answered.

What in God's name was happening? Suddenly Diana was the extra in someone else's drama. Her eyes burned, her throat ached, and she absolutely refused to draw another breath of this noxious air until someone supplied some answers. She got up from the chair and headed for the hall.

"I don't know about you..." she called over her shoulder. "But I'm outta here."

Diana felt her way along the walls, then groping the tops of Matthew's couch and easy chairs, she eventually made it to the back door and gulped the fresh, rain-soaked atmosphere.

Her lungs expanded while her mind raced with the possibilities—all of them disturbing.

The thunder had stopped, so eventually Ursie felt brave enough to join her, and they both stepped out onto the covered porch. The incessant rain was a solid gray sheet hanging all around them. Diana located a tissue in her purse, which miraculously still hung on her shoulder, and held it out in the rain. She took the wet tissue and carefully wiped Ursie's eyes. After all, the dog had taken a direct hit of pepper spray. She wet a second tissue and daubed at Ursie's dripping nose. By the time they stepped back into the kitchen, where she planned to offer Ursie her water bowl, the others joined them.

The strange girl acted like she owned the place.

"Hey, Trout, do you still keep the kerosene lanterns under the sink?"

Matthew appeared to be in shock as he shined the flashlight on the lower cabinets. Next the girl rummaged on hands and knees, extracted the lanterns, and then knew just where to look for Matthew's stash of matches in the jar on the fridge. Soon the room became visible in the warm, eerie glow.

"That's better." The girl dusted off her tight black shorts, rubbed her hands together. Her eyes narrowed as she frowned at Diana. "So, who the hell are you?"

In Diana's opinion, Matthew should speak up about then. Since their arrival, she'd been attacked with pepper spray, threatened at gunpoint, and still hadn't heard anything remotely resembling an apology.

Her temper simmered. Obviously this intruder had an intimate knowledge of Matthew's house, so clearly she had lived here with Matthew. Were they together before Diana's time, or since they'd known one another? Certainly the girl had resurfaced at a highly inopportune moment for Matthew, on the very day Diana intended to move in with him.

When the girl laid a possessive hand on his arm, then planted a loving kiss on his cheek, Diana's temper boiled over. She snatched Matthew's free arm and literally dragged him into the pantry. Once they were out of earshot, she balled her fist and delivered a punch to his chest. When he remained comatose, she hit him again.

"You should be ashamed, Matthew. That girl's young enough to be your daughter!"

He hung his head. When he finally lifted it again, his eyes were strangely unfocussed. "That's because she *is* my daughter, Diana."

He gently took her hand and led her back to the kitchen, where the girl now seemed embarrassed. She must have overheard Diana's stage whisper.

"Meet Ginny Troutman." Matthew's voice was hoarse with emotion. "I haven't seen hide nor hair of her in six long years."

THREE

Prodigal child...

The three of them remained frozen in suspended emotion, unable to proceed as fallen twigs skidded across the roof and rain gushed from a downspout just outside the door. They gaped at one another until Ursie plodded across the kitchen linoleum and lapped from her water bowl to clear the pepper spray from her throat.

"You're Matthew's daughter?" Diana tried to recall the story of this prodigal child.

Finally, Matthew took Diana's elbow and urged her forward. "This is my friend, Diana Rittenhouse," he said, regaining his voice.

"So you guys are *friends*?" The girl's tone was sly and suggestive. Her eyes, a shade darker than Matthew's, sparked with mischief under her thick shag of punk-cut black hair. "I'd love to chat, but first, I left something very important in my car."

Before they could respond, Ginny Troutman sprinted onto the back porch.

"I didn't see a car. Where'd you park?" Matthew called after her.

"At the launching site down near the beach," she hollered over her shoulder before the rain swallowed her.

"Why'd she park there?" Diana stupidly asked.

Matthew collapsed into his favorite chair. "She sneaked in to check the place out before making a commitment. Wasn't sure she'd be welcome."

"But she's your daughter. Why wouldn't she be welcome in her own home?"

He gave her a dark look, propped his elbows on the table, and buried his face in the fulcrum of his hands. "This can't be happening."

Diana agreed. This couldn't be happening. But it was. She slid into the chair opposite Matthew and tried to compose herself. The wobbly glow from the kerosene lamp made her seasick as it undulated across the Formica surfaces. Over the years, they had avoided talking about their children—his, and hers. They had both confessed their inadequacies as parents and shared some of the guilt they felt, but only up to a point. When it came to Matthew's sense of having failed Ginny, or to Diana's conviction that she had somehow abandoned Mandy and Robby, that point of retreat came fast. It hurt too much to look squarely at the truth of their dysfunctional families, and while it could be argued that they weren't to blame for their children's alienation, the end result remained the same. They had both screwed up.

"When did she get here?" Diana wondered aloud.

Matthew took a deep breath, rubbed his eyes. "I 'spect she arrived just before we did. Her hair and arms are still wet. She didn't have time to dry herself off."

Diana pictured Ginny prowling cat-like through the house, leaving wet paw prints with her boots and rummaging through the linen closet for a towel. Home invasion. Six years missing in action was a long time, yet the intruder had a blood claim. Diana had none.

Little bits of Ginny's story resurfaced in Diana's memory. She recalled Matthew telling her that Ginny ran away from home two years after her mother died. Matthew's wife, Lynn, had lost her battle with cancer when she was only forty-two, when Ginny was a vulnerable sixteen-year old. Then when Matthew suffered despondency and depression, Ginny rebelled. She fell in with the wrong gang of kids, used drugs and alcohol, and barely managed to graduate from high school. To hear Matthew tell it, he drove her away. He said he hadn't been there for Ginny, and had never forgiven himself.

She reached across the chasm between them and squeezed his fingers. "Look, you tried to find her," she reminded him. "You even hired that private investigator, right?"

"Yeah, Ginny called me from somewhere in Texas, said she'd married a rough neck who worked on an oil rig in the Gulf, but the detective couldn't find her."

Diana heard desperation in his voice, all the scar tissue peeled away. "Don't blame yourself," she pleaded.

His eyes hardened. "Let it be, Diana. You can't make this better."

Maybe not, but wasn't she entitled to try? Weren't she and Matthew best friends, lovers, and soulmates? That's what they'd said last night. "Why did she come home now?" she asked him.

"God only knows."

"Is she in some sort of trouble?"

Matthew sighed and pinched the bridge of his nose, a sure sign that he was fending off one of his migraines. "Ginny is always in trouble."

"But she's here now, so the two of you can work it out."

When Matthew brought his fist down on the tabletop, Diana nearly jumped out of her skin. When she crawled back inside, she was more than a little angry. "Hey, don't take it out on me."

"This isn't about you, Diana."

"No, it's about us." Before she could expand her argument, the screen door slammed and a damp gust of air blew through the kitchen, almost extinguishing the lantern flame.

Ginny was back, and she was not alone.

At first Diana thought the figure by her side was Ursie, because it barely came to Ginny's waist. But then she realized it was walking upright, holding Ginny's hand. At the same moment, the electricity blinked once and the power was restored, flooding the kitchen with bright, incandescent light. Absurdly, Diana believed the sudden illumination was a dramatic trick. Some heavenly stagehand had pulled all the right levers for ultimate impact.

Matthew and she saw the enchanting child at precisely the same moment. A little girl, maybe six years old, with enormous blue eyes, a milky complexion dotted with summer freckles, and short, curly, flaming red hair. Diana heard the sharp intake of Matthew's breath as Ginny guided the child towards them.

"This is my daughter, Melissa Troutman." Ginny grinned as she passed the girl to Matthew. "Trout, meet your granddaughter."

As Matthew silently gathered the shy child into his bear-like arms, Diana heard the jerky hum of the refrigerator as its motor powered up to speed. She heard Ursie panting above the air conditioner vent, which had begun to blow, and finally, Matthew exhaled.

"Are you really my grandpa?" The child jutted out her plump lower lip and her sleepy eyes conveyed her suspicion.

"Of course, he's your grandpa. Remember what I told you on the trip?" Ginny coached.

Diana was completely at a loss. Matthew had never told her he had a grandchild, because Diana was quite sure this was the first he'd heard of it. She could only imagine his shock, and in her opinion, Ginny had been damn insensitive to break the news that way. But Diana had no quarrel with the child. She reached across the table and patted her hand.

"Melissa's a pretty name." Diana smiled.

"Everyone calls me Lissa," the child informed her. "Are you my grandma? Mommy didn't tell me about you."

"No, Lissa, I'm not your grandma."

Ginny guffawed, then slid her long body into the chair beside Diana. She smelled of rain, sweat, and musky perfume. She urged Lissa into the fourth chair beside Matthew, so that now they were a table of strangers masquerading as a family.

Ginny pinned Diana with those eyes so eerily like Matthew's. "I've been gone a long time, so I'm out of the loop. Are you guys married?"

Diana shook her head.

"Okay…." Ginny turned to Matthew. "I was hoping Lissa and I could hang out here a couple of days, get to know you again?"

Matthew cast Diana a look of pure panic. "Sure, why not?" he answered slowly.

"Do you live here, Diana?" Ginny asked.

Diana thought about her suitcase, her cosmetics bag, and her cappuccino machine all enjoying a soaking in the bed of Matthew's truck.

"Absolutely not," she told Ginny.

FOUR

Tough enough…

Lucky for Diana, the Troutmans had agreed last night that due to the raging storm, it was only polite to invite her to spend the night. Matthew had been angry, upset, and torn with conflicting allegiances as he split their cold barbeque four ways. When Diana magnanimously refused her portion and excused herself, complaining of a headache, he had trailed her into the guest bedroom to apologize and reassure her that their plan to live together wasn't dead, only on hold.

Diana knew he hoped she would sneak into his room and share his bed once the others were asleep, but she couldn't do it. No hanky panky, no argument, no drama, no way. She had banished him to his newfound family and abandoned herself to a sleepless night and a growling stomach.

Also lucky for her, life looked more hopeful the next morning. By the time she had showered, towel-dried her short, prematurely white hair, and slipped into her slacks and one of Matthew's cuddly flannel shirts, she felt less like a forty-seven year old fifth wheel and more like her audaciously curious self.

She found Ginny and Lissa seated at the sun-drenched dining room table. They were overlooking the fresh lake rolling under a clear blue sky. As Matthew rattled pots and pans in the kitchen, Diana smelled brewing coffee and sizzling bacon. She figured he was making eggs, grits, and homemade biscuits.

"Lord, I'm hungry!" she told the girls.

"Me, too!" Lissa piped up. When she smiled, Diana saw an endearing gap between her two front teeth, which she hadn't noticed last night.

"Trout always does the cooking," Ginny explained, as if Diana didn't already know this. "Even when Mama was alive, he always made breakfast."

"Really?" Best not let Ginny know how intimately Diana appreciated Matthew's early AM culinary skills. "I'll go give him a hand…" she said as she drifted automatically towards the kitchen.

"Don't go in there, Diana," Ginny warned, stopping her in her tracks. "He hates it when you get in his way."

Diana turned around, crossed the room and sat down beside them. Maybe Matthew didn't appreciate his daughter bugging him at the stove, but he'd never objected to Diana hugging him. "Did you gals sleep well?"

"I did!" Lissa bounced up and down. Grandpa gave me Mommy's old teddy bear to sleep with."

"I can't believe Daddy saved that old bear," Ginny said, letting her guard down.

In the short time Diana had known her, she'd discovered Ginny usually called Matthew "Trout." But now she'd made an emotional slip-up and called him "Daddy." She wasn't as tough as she pretended. In fact, newly showered and dressed in an oversized Hard Rock Café T-shirt, Ginny looked barely old enough to be Lissa's mother. Without mascara streaming down her eyes, Ginny appeared guardedly innocent. The silver nose stud still threw Diana, though.

"How old are you, Lissa?" Diana asked.

The child held up five fingers. "But I'll be six tomorrow. Grandpa says he'll take me fishing for my birthday."

Taking kids fishing was Matthew's specialty. "You'll love it," Diana told her.

"Trout taught me everything about fishing," Ginny bragged. "I was the elementary school bass champion. I was famous."

"I won't put any nasty old worms on the hook." Lissa wrinkled her nose. "But I'm famous, too. Did you know Mommy named me for Melissa Etheridge, the rock star?"

"No kidding?" As Ginny explained why she had named Lissa after Etheridge, she also revealed her dream to play guitar in a band. Diana had heard something about this from Matthew a long time ago. When Diana had discovered Matthew's secret talent for painting watercolor landscapes, he'd said his absent daughter had a passion for music. He'd also said both their ambitions were as useful as a paddle in the desert.

"So you brought Lissa home to meet Matthew as a special birthday present?"

Ginny shook her head and began shredding her paper napkin. "Nope, that's just a coincidence. I came here because my girlfriend's getting married."

Just then Matthew arrived with a tray of coffee and orange juice. "Darn it, Ginny, I thought you came home to see me."

Ginny avoided his eyes. Clearly she wasn't about to give him any satisfaction. Eventually Matthew left, then returned with the food. He put out plates for everyone.

"Okay, so you came home to attend one of your old girlfriend's wedding. Who's getting' hitched?" he scowled. "Anyone I know?"

"Nope." Ginny loaded Lissa's plate, then her own.

Ginny's behavior was confusing. Maybe Ginny wasn't as tough as Diana had assumed last night, but she was tough enough to insult her dad. Clearly Matthew was hurt not to be the focus of their visit, and Ginny wasn't about to open up about her girlfriend. Maybe this girlfriend was one of those bad kids Ginny used to hang with after Matthew's wife died? But Diana was too hungry to speculate without fuel in her tank, so she gobbled two helpings of breakfast, including three homemade biscuits slathered with Matthew's special marmalade.

Ginny and Lissa ate well, too. Only Matthew picked at his food, which was most unusual.

"Are you okay?" Diana asked him.

His heavy brows were knit in a frown as he watched his daughter. He ignored Diana's question and decided to bite right into the meat of the issue. He turned his dark eyes on Ginny. "By the way, where is Lissa's daddy?"

Ginny froze, set down a forkful of egg. Her smooth face wrinkled, her expression sagged, and suddenly she seemed much older than her twenty-four years. "Charley Harkin is long gone, so don't ask me again."

Matthew glanced at Diana. "Seems like a reasonable question, don't you think, Diana? Ginny shows up at my door after six long years with a kid in tow. Person might wonder what happened to the husband...?"

"My daddy was an oil man in Galveston, Texas," Lissa proudly interrupted. "I was born there, but then Daddy lost his job when I was only two. Hurricane Katrina came and washed everything away."

Diana thought Lissa's explanation sounded more rehearsed than spontaneous. "So Charley Harkin worked on an oil rig?"

But Matthew demanded a straight answer. "Are you saying your husband is dead?"

"Not dead, just gone," Ginny snapped. "And he's not my husband. We were divorced soon after the hurricane."

"But Charley's still my daddy." Lissa crossed her skinny little arms in defiance.

Matthew sadly shook his head. He tried to capture Ginny's hand, but she pulled away.

"Leave me alone, Trout. I don't want to talk about this. Not now, not ever."

"Suit yourself." He collected the empty plates and stomped towards the kitchen.

For a few heartbeats, Diana was stunned silent. A flock of Canada geese flew honking across the lake and landed on the front lawn. Both Lissa and Ursie took notice.

"Can I go outside with the dog?" the child squealed.

"Yeah, sure, but don't get wet." Ginny laughed, breaking the tension. Then she smiled at Diana. "That's what Trout always told me, *don't get wet*. He's a pain in the ass, you know?"

Diana held up both hands in a gesture of peace. "Please don't put me in the middle, but yes, sometimes Matthew's a little stubborn."

"Not half as stubborn as his daughter." Ginny pushed away from the table and stretched out on the couch. "It's weird to be back, you know?"

Diana paused to watch Lissa and Ursie scamper down the yard. The geese squawked in protest as girl and dog approached. At first the birds fast-walked towards the shallow water, but as the attack advanced, they reluctantly spread their wings and took off.

"Yes, I can imagine it's strange to be home after all those years." Diana rose from the table and sat across from Ginny in Matthew's recliner. "So you've been living in Galveston the whole time?"

Ginny snorted derisively. "No way. Soon as I dumped the old man, I took Lissa and we moved to Las Vegas."

"You've had a hard life." In Diana's experience, a little heart-felt commiseration yielded a wealth of information. Sure enough, after Diana offered a few grunts of sympathy, Ginny began to open up.

"My husband was an old fart," she said without ceremony.

"Was Charley that much older than you?"

"I was eighteen, he was thirty-eight when we got married. By now the old geezer's forty-four, if he's still kickin'."

Diana could point out that she was three years older than Ginny's "geezer" ex, but she decided it wasn't the right time for sensitivity training. Instead she listened to Ginny describe Charley as a redneck who'd already been married twice before they met. He was a heavy drinker, and so was Ginny until she got pregnant and gave up alcohol. Reading between the lines, Diana gathered Charley was rough, if not downright abusive.

"I'm divorced, too," Diana confided. "I left my husband one fine day when he used his fists instead of angry words." She had confessed this fact to very few people. Even Matthew didn't know. But somehow, Diana wanted Ginny to trust her, and it worked. Because while Matthew washed dishes, while the women watched Lissa and Ursie tossing stones off the end of the dock, Ginny told more of her story.

"So you moved to Las Vegas hoping to hook up with a band, but ended up waiting tables?" Diana prompted.

"Classic, isn't it?" Ginny responded wryly. "Most everything I've done turned out wrong, except for giving birth to Lissa. She is my life."

Diana understood. Too bad Ginny hadn't swallowed her pride and come home sooner. She went by her maiden name, Troutman, instead of her married name, so Ginny must still love her father at some level. Hopefully it wasn't too late for them to mend their differences.

"So you're planning to stay in North Carolina?"

"God, no!" Ginny sat bolt upright on the couch. "I lease a terrific high rise apartment near the casino where I work. I'm a croupier now, so I make good money, you know? I earn more in one week than I could make all year in this shit hole."

Okay, Diana got it, but why was Ginny so angry? "So you only came home to attend your girlfriend's wedding?"

"What else?"

But Ginny wouldn't look Diana in the eye. The girl was lying, but before Diana could dig deeper, Matthew entered the room with a dishcloth in his hand.

"Aren't you gals done gabbing?" Matthew hurled the dishcloth at his daughter and moved out to the front porch. "Hey, did you know Lissa's playing in the lake?"

Both Ginny and Diana rushed outside to join him.

"Lissa, get your butt up here!" Ginny yelled.

The child and Ursie were leaping through the waves near the shore. Lissa was still tossing pebbles, while Urise dove to snatch them up before they touched bottom. When the girl and the dog reached the porch, Ursie shook, splattering everyone, and Lissa's pajamas dripped on the deck.

"Didn't I tell you not to get wet?" Ginny snapped the dishcloth at her daughter's bottom.

"C'mon, Ginny, you know it's impossible to stay dry at the lake. Especially when you're a kid." Matthew intervened.

Ginny grunted, then turned to Matthew. "If you think it's okay for Lissa to play in the water against my direct orders, then you can wash the sand off her feet and put her jammies in the dryer."

"Why can't you do it?"

"Because I'm driving Diana home," Ginny countered unexpectedly. "And we're taking your truck."

"Why?" Matthew gasped, questioning Diana with his eyes.

Diana was shocked. She and Ginny had discussed no such plans, but clearly Ginny wanted her out of the house—the sooner the better—just when Diana thought they were getting along so famously. Okay, so be it. She'd already decided moving in now was a mistake. But Ginny sure as hell owed her an explanation.

"Yes, Ginny, why are we both leaving?"

Matthew's daughter fidgeted. She fixed Diana with her dark eyes, silently begging her to play along. "You have work to do at the office, remember? And we're taking Trout's truck because my car's packed to the gills with junk, not enough room for two adults. And because you live in Davidson…"

"So what if she lives in Davidson?" Matthew interrupted.

"So, my girlfriend who's getting married lives nearby, and I want to deliver my wedding gift to her house. Then I'll buy Lissa's birthday cake on the way home."

Diana gaped. Clearly Ginny Troutman was not only a quick thinker, but also a take-charge kind of girl.

"But what about Lissa?" Matthew asked.

Ginny rolled her eyes. "Give me a break, Trout. You raised me all those years, so you know how to entertain a little girl. Take her fishing a day early, for god sake…. ready to go, Diana?"

Since she could find no legitimate excuse to stay, since Matthew wasn't about to stop her, Diana grabbed her purse. Ginny grabbed hers. She led Diana to the back door and easily located the truck keys hidden on a hook behind the breadbox.

"Bye, Mommy." Lissa shyly took hold of Matthew's hand.

"Bye, Punkin. Be a good girl and do what Pop-Pop says."

As Ginny dragged Diana outside, Matthew and Diana kissed each other goodbye with their eyes.

FIVE

An interesting twist…

Before leaving, Diana trailed Ginny down to Matthew's boathouse where Ginny's forest green Subaru wagon was parked. The vehicle was filthy with road dust and streaked by the recent downpour, but when she opened the rear hatch to remove a large wrapped wedding present, Diana noticed the auto was an expensive late model with all the bells and whistles.

"Nice ride," she commented. "Those casino tips must be good."

Ginny shrugged and slammed the hatch so hard the Nevada license plate rattled. "Let's keep moving, Diana, or I'll miss my girlfriend."

"You're really going to her house?"

"Yeah, where else?"

Ginny gave Diana a look that implied she was clueless, but hey, why should Diana know the agenda? Clearly Ginny had been in touch with the bride-to-be and was familiar with her schedule. It wasn't Diana's business anyway, was it?

"I'll drive." Ginny said when they reached Matthew's old truck. She hurriedly tucked her present in the boot behind the driver's seat, then hopped inside. "Let's get moving, Diana."

Diana scrambled into the passenger seat as Ginny cranked the engine. Gravel flew up from under the rear tires as Ginny peeled backwards out of the driveway. "I gather we're in a big hurry?"

"Fasten your seatbelt, Diana."

When Diana glanced back at the house, she saw Matthew framed in the doorway, arms folded across his chest in parental disapproval.

Ginny chuckled. "He hates the way I drive. Daddy didn't have the patience to teach me, so I went to driving school to learn."

Her words took Diana back to her own kids' driver's training. Their daddy had no patience, either, so the lessons were Diana's responsibility. Oddly, her son, Robby, was cautious, timid, and respectful behind the wheel, while her teenaged Mandy was determined to drive Diana crazy, no pun intended. Diana sometimes believed her hair started turning white during that ordeal.

Ginny turned east onto River Highway and gasped in disbelief. "Jeez, I don't recognize anything. When I used to travel this road, there was nothing but fields, woods, and Daddy's store. Now it looks like every other commercial street in America."

They sped past shopping centers and strip malls, auto stores and fast food joints. Even two years ago, these so-called amenities did not exist. Today they had Best Buy, Target, Super Wal-Mart, and countless other chain stores replicating like cancer cells as far as the eye could see. The effect must have been downright disorienting to Ginny.

"Your father hates the growth," Diana muttered.

"So do I," Ginny said. "These developers took something fresh and beautiful, then fucked it beyond recognition."

Ginny's vulgarity startled her, but the sentiment was not surprising. Most longtime natives abhorred and resented the fact that their culture had been homogenized. With the massive influx of northerners, indeed new citizens from all over the country, this little corner of the North Carolina Piedmont now looked, smelled, and tasted like pretty much everywhere else.

"I've only lived here a few years," Diana told the girl. "But even I hardly recognize the place."

"Well, you're part of the problem, Diana. Realtors encourage development, right? All this progress improves your bottom line, right?"

Diana swallowed the sharp retort at the tip of her tongue because Ginny was right... and wrong. True, until this recent economic downturn in the housing market, Diana's business had been booming. On the other hand, she was once a country girl, long ago in Pennsylvania, and her emotional response to the rape of this virgin land was very much like Ginny's.

"How come you moved here anyway, Diana?"

Diana supposed she could admit she'd come here to start a new life, and left to escape an old one, but her motives were too complex and private to explain. Instead she told the girl, "Slow up, we're coming to a speed trap. There's always a state trooper hiding in that pull-off."

Ginny nodded and eased up on the accelerator, dropping to forty-five miles-per-hour just in time to avoid arrest by the cop who was indeed lurking.

"Hey, thanks, Diana. You don't wanna know how many speeding tickets I've gotten." She pulled onto Interstate 77 at exit 36 and headed south towards Charlotte. She sped up to seventy, but kept watching both sides of the highway, taking in the changes and muttering obscenities under her breath. "Maybe I shouldn't have come home."

"Thomas Wolfe wrote *you can never go home again,*" Diana said. "Maybe he was right."

Ginny fingered the silver stud in her nose and studied Diana from the corner of her eye. "I sure came home at the wrong time for you, didn't I, Diana?"

Diana blinked. "What do you mean?"

Ginny cocked her black punk cut head towards Diana's suitcases in the truck bed. "That's your shit back there, isn't it?"

No comment.

"Look, it's plain as flies on a cow's tail. You were fixin' to shack up with Trout, weren't you?"

No comment.

"You guys are sleeping together. I can tell by the way you look at one another."

"Mind your own business, Ginny." Heat crawled up Diana's neck.

Ginny's deep, guttural laugh sounded so much like Matthew's. She laid five black polished fingernails on Diana's arm. "Don't get me wrong, I think sex is great. I haven't seen my old man this happy since my mom died. I'm just sorry I screwed it up for you two."

Much as Diana appreciated the vote of confidence, she was embarrassed speechless.

"Sorry my timing was off," Ginny continued. "If we hadn't shown up at exactly the wrong moment, you'd be living with Trout right now, done deal."

Diana gulped down the last remnants of her pride. "Don't worry about it."

"I'm serious, Diana. After I drop the gift off, we'll head back to the lake, you'll move in with Trout, and Lissa and me will get lost. We'll move into a motel... or something."

"No way. Not happening. Of course, you must stay with your father. Matthew and I will revisit our situation at some later date."

Ginny howls. "*Revisit?* Gimme a break, woman. You know you're hot for him right now, and you're ready to make this commitment. If it works for you, then Lissa and me will stay in the house with you guys."

Diana glanced pointedly at her watch. "Listen, we're wasting time with all this silliness. We better hurry to catch your girlfriend."

"Now you want me to speed up?" Ginny playfully tapped the accelerator.

No, I want you to shut up. "You're as bad as your father. He loves to tease me, too. I mean, what about this friend of yours who's getting married? You two must be very close, for you to drive all the way from Las Vegas…?"

"Okay, I get it. We're changing the subject." Ginny abruptly removed her hand from Diana's arm, gripped the wheel, and stared straight ahead. "No, as a matter of fact, we're not close at all. Lori Fowler is a selfish little princess who figures the sun rises and sets on her precious ass."

Whoa, what was that about? "I don't get it. I assumed you and the bride were best friends?"

"Not hardly." Ginny startled when the Davidson exit came up suddenly. She veered to the right and pulled off the interstate seconds before a barreling semi crawled up their rear end. "Jesus, where the hell are we? What are all those condos doing here, and that Hilton Hotel? This exit used to be a hill covered in wildflowers."

Diana grabbed the armrest and hung on as Ginny skidded into the first of two new traffic circles. "I live in one of those new condos on the lakeside, and my office is right over there. Want to drop me off?"

"Too late, you're comin' with me." Ginny squinted skyward at the new private school to their left. "This little town has delusions of grandeur," she said.

"So why did you come to Lori's wedding?"

Diana's young companion's face darkened. "I came to give the groom a really hard time. Used to date the dude."

Now this was an interesting twist. Obviously Matthew's daughter had some issues with her ex-boyfriend's marriage. "What's the guy's name?"

Ginny expelled a bored sigh, dug into her purse, and retrieved a pack of gum. After punching out two pieces from their blister foils, she offered one to Diana.

"No thanks."

Ginny tucked the gum back in her purse and extracted a compact. She flipped it open to inspect her face, wiped sleep from the corner of one eye, and then rubbed her lips together. "His name is Trevor. We went all through school together."

"So you've kept in touch?"

Ginny turned right on Main Street and they navigated through all three blocks of the little town, with old-fashioned storefronts on the right—Including a village store and a soda shop—and on the left, a community green and library. The chimes from the Davidson College clock tower told Diana it was 11 AM.

"At least this hasn't changed." Ginny smirked. "Heaven forbid that downtown Davidson should move into the Twenty-First Century."

Ginny was a hard gal to please. She hated progress, but scorned retro. "Where exactly does Lori Fowler live?"

"Map Quest puts her in some new development called Highland Gardens. Do you know where that is, Diana?"

"You bet, turn left right now." They moved up Concord road, passed the campus at a sedate twenty miles per hour. They made another left on Shepherd's Road and crossed back into Iredell County. Highland Gardens was built on one of several large farms that had been annexed by the town of Davidson. The farmers had considered it an illegal "land grab," but the new residents loved having a toney Davidson address. The whole scandal had resulted in murder and mayhem, so Diana remembered it well.

"I know Highland Gardens by heart, so I'll guide you to Lori's front door," Diana said. Indeed the new neighborhood was a cash cow for Realtors, and before the recession, Diana had made a decent living selling those upscale, single-family homes.

She directed Ginny to an address across from the golf course, with a scenic view of the pond. "Why don't you pull into her drive and park behind that Jeep?" Diana suggested.

Suddenly Ginny's face blanched dead white, in ghostly contrast to her purple lipstick and Goth eyeliner. Her long fingers trembled on the steering wheel.

"What's wrong?" Diana asked.

"Just nervous, that's all. I haven't seen Lori for a million years. It's weird, you know?"

Why in God's name was Ginny lying again? Diana could tell the girl had recognized the car, so why not admit it? At closer inspection, the Jeep was a classic, circa 1980, or thereabouts, with an army camouflage paint job, tan canvas soft-top, and a spare tire mounted on the rear door. The vehicle seemed a strange choice for a young woman like Lori.

For having been in such a tearing hurry, Ginny now seemed reluctant to proceed, but she took a deep breath, cradled the wedding present in her arms, and timidly exited the truck. Diana's curiosity shifted into overdrive as Ginny approached the grand, faux Tudor entry and rang the bell. Her instincts told her the Jeep had once belonged to a teenage boy, now matured to bridegroom age. A boy named Trevor—Ginny's ex. As her mind played with that delicious fantasy of two sweethearts coming face to face after all those years, in such a decidedly awkward circumstance, she noted with disappointment that no one seemed to be home.

As Ginny paced the brick porch, frantically masticating her gum, Diana scolded herself for anticipating such a showdown solely for her personal entertainment. Next, Ginny shrugged and pointed towards the back, indicating she intended to try the rear entrance. Diana nodded and gave her a thumbs up as she disappeared down a shrub walkway leading along the left side of the house.

In the meantime, a trio of pre-teen boys on skateboards appeared in the street behind Diana. The tallest one was showing off, likely for her benefit, and in the process managed to wipeout, crashing into the bed of Matthew's truck.

"Watch out!" she hollered, sounding crotchety and maternal.

"I didn't hurt this old truck, lady!" The kid sassed back as he replaced a blue Duke ball cap backwards on his curly blond head.

"Shouldn't you be in school?" Now she sounded even more like someone's uptight mama.

The kid offered an exaggerated sigh. "It's Saturday, lady."

"Yeah, you're right." *Earth to Diana!* What planet was she living on?

"But, hey, I'm sorry," the boy called as he mounted his board and skated away. His two mates rolled off with him, all snickering at her expense.

After all, this was a classy neighborhood, and the local juvies knew better than to bad-mouth a white-haired woman, even if she was sitting in a dated pickup truck in this conclave of BMW's, Jags, and Lexus's. Diana shifted self-consciously on the seat. How long should it take to deliver a wedding present? She checked her watch and realized Ginny had been gone only five minutes.

She listened to an angry mockingbird chattering from the dense branches of a nearby holly bush, and moments later, a white Siamese cat darted out from under that bush. Was it nesting season for mockingbirds? And what the heck was a cat like that doing outdoors? She had only seen them lounging on sofas or fancy pillows, never loose in the wild. She smelled the nostalgic odor of freshly cut grass and heard the hum of a jet plane overhead, but as she prepared to check her watch again, she saw Ginny rushing towards her. This time she was running down a path leading from the right side of the house. Now she was red- faced, panting hard, still clutching the gift to her bosom as she strong-armed the driver's door.

"What happened?" Diana gasped.

"Nothing. Lori wasn't home."

As Ginny stowed the gift in the boot, Diana expected to see the girl's lying nose growing like Pinocchio's. But instead of confronting her, Diana said in a neutral voice. "Too bad."

"Bummer." Ginny agreed. "I must've just missed her."

The needle on Diana's bullshit detector swung into the red zone as Ginny continued to gulp air. Her eyes, one shade darker than Matthew's, literally spun with her lies. "So you couldn't deliver your gift?"

"Course not. Couldn't leave it on the back porch."

Had Ginny and Lori had a knockdown, drag-out fight? Or juicier yet, maybe Ginny had walked in on the bride and groom doing the dirty. Diana suspected that if Ginny still harbored tender feelings for Trevor, then witnessing them having sex could ignite the short fuse, which she strongly suspected Ginny possessed.

"C'mon, tell me…" she urged.

"Back off, Diana!" She pounded the innocent dashboard with one balled fist. "Did anyone ever tell you you're one helluva busybody?"

So she'd been told. More than once.

Ginny treated her to a long, hard stare. "On second thought, Diana, maybe this *living together* business isn't such a good idea, after all."

Diana felt her hands clenching and unclenching in her lap as Ginny fired up the engine, peeled backwards out the driveway, sped down the street, and left the three skateboarders gaping in admiration. "My sentiments exactly, Ginny. Bad idea."

"So Lissa and me will move into a motel."

"Absolutely not," Diana answered in her most stern, bitchy mama voice. "Please take me to my condo and help me unload."

SIX

Liz McCorkle...

Liz crossed the speed bump and slowed down to a sedate ten miles per hour as she drove into Diana's condo complex. The joint was jumpin', as one would expect the first Saturday in May, with winter-weary boaters streaming from their apartments clad in shorts and tees, halters and flip- flops. They carried coolers filled with beer and hoagies, beach bags with sunscreen and romance novels. Looking forward to a day on Lake Norman.

"Lucky for them," Liz grumbled to Amazing Grace, who was stretched out across the front seat panting, her long head on Liz's lap, drooling on her knees. "Bet you'd love to go boating, wouldn't you, girl? Or maybe a nice swim off the dock?"

But the greyhound was indifferent as she rolled dewy brown eyes at Liz. After spending the best years of her life on the racetrack, Gracie was retired and not inclined towards swimming, or any exercise for that matter. Except an occasional sprint after the squirrels in Danny's back yard.

"Okay, never mind." Liz stroked the dog's smooth, buttery tan shoulder, then tilted the air conditioner vent towards her face. She lifted her hand and brushed long strands of bright red hair off her moist forehead. "God, it's hot."

When she slowed to a crawl and began looking for a free parking space near Diana's building, someone rapped hard on the rear of her Honda. Liz spun around to see the smirking face of a former client, his blunt nose peeling with sunburn, and he was grinning like a Cheshire. He loped up to the driver's side, so Liz stopped moving when he signaled her to power down her window.

"Hey, Corkie, what's happening?" He held up a beer grasped in his right fist, gave her a thumbs up with his left. "Business or pleasure?"

She stared at the fuzzy blond hair poking through the net of a black muscle tank shirt stretched tight over his bulging belly and recalled selling him a first floor unit here in Davidson Landing. But she couldn't remember his name.

"Business," she answered quickly and forced a smile.

"Too bad." His beady eyes strayed into the vee of her sundress.

"No rest for the weary." She sighed. "Gotta go…"

"That your dog?"

"Not exactly." Gracie's long skinny tail was beating a tattoo against the seat, and Liz wished she had an attack dog instead of this friendly wuss. A burglar could be raping her, and Gracie would either lick him to death or hide under the bed.

"Then whose dog is it?"

Long story. Liz and her longtime lover, Danny Cappelli, were keeping Gracie for Diana, but Danny had fallen in love with the animal. She sensed a major custody battle looming, should Diana ever try to repossess her pet.

"She belongs to my *boyfriend*," Liz answered pointedly.

The jerk frowned. "So where's the *boyfriend* today? You guys should be out playing, right?"

45

"Wrong." Liz powered up the window. "Sorry, I really have to work." Before he could protest, she inched her car forward, almost crushing his bare toes. He jumped aside, and she saw him waggling his fingers in her side mirror as she escaped.

"Creep." Liz glanced at Gracie. "How come you didn't bite him?"

Liz was tired of men who hit on her without the slightest provocation, and clients were the worst. Sometimes she longed for complete anonymity, but her Honda was what Diana called "a traveling billboard." Liz had paid a graphic artist to enlarge two photos of herself and laminate them to the sides of her car. Underneath the photos was her name, Liz "Corkie" McCorkle, and her motto, "You're in good hands."

Great advertising. The downside was that guys like the parking lot Romeo spotted Liz wherever she went. No privacy. But you'd think after working together for five years, Diana would appreciate the upside. After all, Liz attracted attention and got most of the listings. Although Diana closed most of the sales. They were a good team.

"What do you think, Gracie? Isn't your mommy Diana a conservative old poop?"

No comment.

In fact, Liz's only mission here today was to fetch Gracie's food, which she and Danny had forgotten when they picked her up. This shared custody shit was getting to be a drag, but Diana had left for some mysterious getaway, leaving Liz to baby-sit the greyhound, hold down the office, and complete a mound of paperwork.

But Diana was Liz's best friend, no doubt about it. Made no difference she was twenty years older than Liz. Sometimes

Diana was uptight, old-fashioned, and way square when it came to drugs, sex, and rock n' roll—but she was a straight shooter. She had supported Liz, mentored Liz, and picked her up each time she fell. So, yeah, she loved Diana. And if this mysterious weekend involved Diana and Matthew Troutman, she was all for it. If it meant Diana had finally said yes to the man—which Liz strongly suspected—then her sacrifice was well worth it.

Now, if she could ever find a damned parking slot, she'd use the key Diana had supplied, collect the dog food, and get on with her life. Her emotional thermostat soared into the red zone as she circled twice, furious because some ignorant fool had occupied Diana's clearly marked space.

Okay, she'd pull up behind the bastard and block him in. After all, she'd only need a couple of minutes to do her errand. So she choked off a smooth love song playing on the radio, cracked the windows, and twisted off the ignition.

She took a deep breath, got her temper under control. "You stay in the car, Gracie. I'll be right back…"

When she glanced a second time at the offending vehicle, Liz suddenly recognized the beat up red and white pickup. Jesus, it was Trout's truck! Good lord, had Diana and Trout had a fight? Fucked up the weekend? Or simply decided to stay home instead of opting for a romantic getaway?

Then she saw Diana's suitcase sitting outside the entrance to her condo, and beside it on the flagstone patio, was Diana's beloved cappuccino machine. What was that about?

At the same moment, before she could jump from the Honda to investigate, a woman's head lifted from beside Trout's truck. The tough-looking girl had black, punk-cut hair, purple lipstick, dark eyeliner, and a silver stud in her nose. Liz noticed the Hard Rock Café tee as the stranger reached a long

47

arm into the bed of the truck and lifted out Diana's cosmetic case. So what the hell? Was she stealing Diana's stuff?

Liz was frozen in fascination as the girl tromped up the three steps to Diana's door, then angrily dropped the case onto the flagstone. Was it Liz's imagination, or had the door opened from the inside? Diana? The exchange between them was not friendly. When Diana invited her inside, the girl refused to go. Liz remained immoveable, as though a giant hand was pinning her down. Gracie pulled upright, rested her jaw on the dash and whined.

Seconds later, Goth Girl stomped back towards the truck, a thundercloud on her shoulder, lightning in her eyes. She noticed Liz's Honda, and placed her hands on her hips.

"You plannin' on movin' anytime soon?" she hollered.

Something about the woman was familiar, like a well-known lyric just out of reach. She felt like calling out a name she couldn't quite remember. In the meantime, the stranger shifted foot to foot, communicating her bad attitude across the lot, inspiring Liz to start her engine as Gracie began to growl.

She backed out of the way as quickly as possible. The obnoxious creature fired up Trout's Ford and flew backwards, nearly grazing the Honda's hood. Liz kept backing while the stranger shifted into first gear and drove away.

The last thing Liz saw was Goth Girl's hand come out the window. She extended her middle finger and punched the sky.

SEVEN

Billy...

Billy was hungry and thirsty. He checked his official souvenir watch from the winter Olympics with a picture of Shaun White flying above the half pipe. It was almost lunchtime. Mom should be home from her tennis by now, and she'd promised to bring pizza rolls and chips. But when he tucked his skateboard under his arm and peered into their garage, he saw Mom's SUV had not returned.

Bummer. He should've boarded into town with the guys, bought a burger at the Soda Shop. But Billy had no cash. Miss Lori was the next best bet. She always kept Moon Pies and root beer for her boyfriend, and always shared them with Billy if the boyfriend wasn't around.

Besides, Lori was hot. He glided down the sidewalk, then carried his deck to the top of the hill. Placed his board, pushed off. All his friends agreed Lori was way sexy, with her long, soft brown hair and big boobs. He towed the concrete, picked up speed, did a couple kick flips. Billy remembered how Lori's compact little butt moved inside her shorts—those long brown legs

He planted both feet and held out his arms, like a soaring bird, and wondered if Lori and the dude she was planning to marry fucked each time he came over—which was every night. Sometimes he came during the day, since Lori had no job. Mom claimed Lori's dead parents had left her the big house on River Falls Road, plus a ton of money.

Billy crouched low, felt the pavement vibrate under his wheels, the wind in his hair, and pretended he was Tony Hawk, the huckster. He almost crashed when he jumped the curb, but corrected in time, skidded to a stop, dismounted.

Maybe Lori had watched his awesome ride from behind that curtain at her living room window. He'd seen her peeking out from there before, waiting for her dude to come. He glanced at the driveway, but her lover's army Jeep was gone. The coast was clear.

He pulled off his blue Duke cap, ran fingers through his curls, then put the cap back on his head. Lori's boyfriend, Trev, was chill, but he was kinda scary. Everyone knew he'd done three deployments in Iraq. The guys said he was a killer with a screw loose, but Billy didn't buy it. All the same, he got lost when Trev told him to.

Thing was, Lori was always in a good mood after screwing her boyfriend, always gave Billy something to eat or drink, sometimes hugged him. So he squared his shoulders, took a deep breath of the stinky, fresh-cut grass smell, and trudged up the lawn to her house.

Now all he needed was the right excuse and found it rolling around in the flowerbed. Kiki, Lori's big fat Siamese cat was loose. Her long white fur was stained grass green and mud brown. Lori would be pissed with Kiki, but grateful to Billy for catching her. Because Kiki was never ever allowed outside.

She was surprisingly light when he scooped her up, but she growled deep in her throat and nipped his chin. So he held her at arm's length, away from his face, and ran around to the back door. He figured Lori was in the kitchen, because the tough girl who'd been here a half hour ago, the one carrying the wedding present, the one who came with the grouchy, white-haired lady who didn't even know today was Saturday—that girl had gone round back.

But now everyone was gone. Billy jammed Kiki under his arm and knocked hard, but the door swung open to his touch. Weird. Billy hesitated, then shoved the door with his left sneaker.

"You home, Miss Lori?"

Nothing. He dropped Kiki inside. The cat crouched low and scuttled across the linoleum to her food bowl. Billy tried again.

"Hey, Miss Lori, it's Billy Martin. I found Kiki out in the bushes…"

The house was dead silent. He heard the low hum of the refrigerator and smelled the nasty stench of the cat box. He listened for the sound of water pulsing in the shower. This had happened once before. Lori came running downstairs with her hair dripping wet, with bare feet and pink toenails. She had a towel wrapped around her waist, but her big boobs hung out like vanilla ice cream cones topped with juicy red cherries. She'd screamed to find him there, and Billy had screamed, too.

But today—nothing. He moved cautiously inside as the small hairs on the back of his neck prickled. The kitchen was too cold. The air conditioning was running, but the windows were wide open. Not right.

Bottled water on the table and two coffee cups on the counter, with little brown pools at the bottom of each glass. Billy knew Lori kept the Moon Pies in the breadbox. He could almost taste the puffy chocolaty crusts and the marshmallow filling as he inched forward.

51

Then Kiki's tail stood erect and waved back and forth in the air as she tiptoed around the counter. Billy followed. Kiki stopped, meowed, sniffed at the bare feet lying loose on the floor. Each foot had five pink toenails. Billy froze.

The feet were connected to two long, tan legs, which were connected to the curly triangle of Lori's crotch. Billy stared at the lady lying on the floor. The white terrycloth bathrobe was twisted around her body and had fallen open in front. Her long, soft brown hair floated around her face like a halo. Her startled blue eyes gazed at the ceiling. Her red lips were parted in a silent scream. And a shiny carving knife grew from between her vanilla breasts,

Kiki's paws turned red in the pool of blood.

EIGHT

Some girl talk...

Diana was badly shaken by her confrontation with Ginny. She shouldn't have been so nosey, shouldn't have asked what had happened at the bride-to-be's house, or was it possible that Ginny's angry reaction had nothing to do with Diana? Whatever. She'd definitely gotten off on the wrong foot with Matthew's daughter and wished she could start the ill-fated weekend all over again.

She closed her eyes, counted to ten, then stepped out onto the flagstone porch to retrieve her cosmetic case and cappuccino machine. As she bent down, something caught her attention out in the parking lot. First she saw Matthew's truck bouncing across the speed bumps, next she saw a familiar Honda, with the silly photos of Liz McCorkle laminated to its doors.

She groaned when Liz drove into her slot and parked, because all she wanted to do was hide, to hole up and lick her wounds, but clearly that was not to be. When Liz opened the passenger door, Amazing Grace leaped out, panting and straining at the end of her leash. And although Diana loved her greyhound, she wasn't in the mood for company—human or canine.

As they approached, she noticed that Liz's face was almost as red as her hair, and by the angry set of her jaw, she knew her young partner was in a snit. But why? Diana forced a smile and braced herself as Liz let go of the leash and Gracie bounded up the steps. The dog jumped, planted her dainty paws on Diana's chest, and covered her face with long, flicky kisses. Okay, at least someone was in good spirits.

"Hi, Liz, I didn't expect to see you today."

Suddenly Liz was in her face. "Oh yeah? So what are you doing here at your condo? I thought you'd be long gone for that getaway weekend."

"Well I…"

"And who the hell was that rude woman driving Trout's truck?"

"Well, hello to you, too." Diana interrupted. "Want to come inside, or do we keep shouting at one another out here on the porch?"

Gracie made the decision for them. She rushed past and made a beeline for Diana's sunroom, where she knew she'd encounter Perry, Diana's foul-mouthed parrot. Moments later they heard good-natured barking, then inevitably, Perry's furious response.

"Damn dog, damn dog, damn dog!"

More barking. At least Gracie was having fun.

Both women had to laugh. Perry had been taught his salty vocabulary by his original owner, an equally profane old man who'd been Diana's client back in Pennsylvania. When the man died, he left Perry to Diana in his will, and the bird had been a source of endless embarrassment ever since.

"Will Gracie ever stop tormenting that bird?" Liz giggled.

"Nope. She thinks it's her mission in life to worry Perry to death. Joke is, Perry will likely outlive us all."

Diana picked up her cappuccino machine. Liz retrieved the cosmetic case with her left hand and looped her right through Diana's arm. "Okay, let's call a truce and start over, girlfriend."

So they moved inside, leaving the big, bad, inhospitable world behind. While Liz gulped in the cool air conditioning, Diana hurried to the sunroom and covered Perry's cage. She latched onto Gracie's collar and dragged her protesting all the way to the kitchen.

"C'mon, Liz, let's find something to drink."

Once Liz had joined them, Diana put up a baby gate to separate her warring pets. She filled Gracie's aluminum bowl with cold water and tossed her a dog biscuit. "Okay now, everybody chill."

Liz placed her hands on her hips and struck a pose. "Now you know you have some explaining to do, Diana. But before you do, what drink did you have in mind?"

"Iced tea?"

Liz glanced at her watch. "Eleven forty-five. Early, I know, but how 'bout a beer? I just encountered a former client in your parking lot. Jerk offered me a Bud, and I've been thirsty ever since."

Diana frowned. "Don't you have some paperwork to complete? We have a closing on Monday."

"As I recall, you dumped all that shit on me because you just had to get away, but here you are. I figure we can drink now, enjoy some girl talk, then split the work load later. Am I right?"

When Diana's plans with Matthew fell through, she had hoped to sneak home and wallow in self-pity, but now Liz was here, and God knew Diana needed a drink. She did a mental inventory of her refrigerator.

"Sorry, no beer. Want some wine?"

"Sold."

She felt Liz's curious eyes boring into her back as she took out two long-stemmed glasses and a chilled bottle of white zinfandel. Matthew didn't drink, but Diana had been planning to include this bottle along with her next load of possessions when, after their first week of successful cohabitation, she moved in with Matthew for their pre-marital test drive. Too bad.

"Is it shady on your patio yet?" Liz asked. "It'd be fun to get shit-faced while we watch the boats, if it's not too hot."

"It'll be hard to get mellow on this one bottle. But I do have a box of stale Saltines available to soak up the alcohol." Diana had pretty much used up all her food and snacks in anticipation of the move. "But yes, the patio is shady now."

"Bring the booze, skip the crackers."

Liz stepped over the baby gate and walked into the living room to gape at Diana's extensive art collection. The eclectic paintings were treasures from her former life, as were the oriental carpet and a ceiling-high antique case full of books. Liz didn't get it. She thought Diana's obsessions with art, books, and even classical music were crazy. Diana didn't mind.

Because as Diana watched Liz stare, she realized what she wanted from her young partner wasn't someone to share her aesthetics, but a friend to lend support, someone she could trust, an advocate to pull Diana out of her shell. That was Liz.

Gracie was determined to join them, so she asked Liz to open the glass doors to the patio while Diana removed the gate, and the greyhound galloped through the shoot to the great outdoors. A three-foot high brick wall surrounded the patio, so

Gracie was obliged to settle in with the girls, which suited her just fine. When the humans plopped down onto lounges, the dog slithered into the shade of the umbrella table and stretched out on the cool tiles.

"I came here because I forgot the dog food," Liz began. "Remind me to take it when I leave, or will Gracie be staying with you?"

Good question. At the moment Diana literally didn't know if she was coming—or going. Ever since she'd rescued Gracie last year, Fate had conspired to pull them apart. First the condo's home owners' association had voted to exclude large dogs, although Diana's pet was grudgingly given a pass since she had arrived before the ban. Next Perry and Gracie had decided they hated one another. So Diana fervently hoped Gracie would like Matthew's Ursie once they met, making her life a whole lot simpler.

"Well?" Liz persisted. "You know Danny will be heartbroken if I come home without her."

Diana sighed. "Okay, why don't you take her for now?" She sensed Liz's scrutiny, saw the girl watching through narrowed green eyes, and figured she was in for a grilling. Sure enough, Liz tore into her as soon as Diana finished pouring their wine.

"Truth time, Diana. What's up with you? It's about Trout, isn't it? Did you guys have a fight?"

"Of course not." Diana gazed at the lake, where power boats and water skiers zigged and zagged between the white triangles of bobbing sailboats barely holding their own in the choppy wake.

Liz took a long swallow of wine and cleared her throat. "Okay, then why was that girl unloading your stuff from Trout's truck?"

Diana heard children shouting and laughing down at the community swimming pool. She could almost smell the creamy sunscreen lotion warming their pink shoulders.

Liz leaned forward in her lounge. "Oh my God, you were planning to move in with him, weren't you, Diana?"

Diana nodded slowly. She wished somehow life could be as simple as it used to be when she was a young mother like the ones at poolside, when the most challenging decision was whether to feed her kids a nourishing tuna casserole for dinner, or the burgers and fries they preferred. The junk food guaranteed their good behavior for that evening, so too often she had taken the easy way out.

"Jesus, this is huge!" Liz was thrilled. "Do you know how long I've been praying for you and Trout to hook up? How many times did I beg you to give him a chance? You know he loves you, he's good for you, he's the rock-solid man you need, girl, so what the hell happened?"

Diana paused only a moment, squinted at a small private plane doing circles up in the clouds, then spilled the truth as she knew it. "His daughter happened."

Liz choked on her wine, wiped her mouth with the back of her hand. She stood up, placed her empty glass on the table, and began to pace. Diana could almost hear the wheels grinding in her head as Liz tried to shift out of neutral

Finally Liz clicked into gear. "I *knew* I recognized that girl in Trout's truck. She was his kid, General Ginny. We met on the hockey field a million years ago."

"You know her? But you grew up in Charlotte, and Ginny's from Mooresville."

"Yeah, but when I was ten, my folks started sending me up to Lake Norman for summer camp. It was only two weeks each year, but they were the worst weeks of my life. Mostly because of General Ginny."

Diana couldn't believe it. "How come you never mentioned Ginny before, all the time I've been dating Matthew...?"

Liz sank back down on the lounge and poured them each more wine. "Well, she was long gone, wasn't she? And I could tell she was a sore subject with Trout, so why bring it up? Truth is, I totally forgot about her until today, or maybe I put her out of my mind."

"But why did you call her General Ginny?"

As the sun passed high noon and began drifting down the afternoon side of the sky, as they finished the bottle, Liz explained how young Ginny had been the hockey field bully— fastest on her feet and first to trip the other girls. Diana tried to defend Ginny, saying perhaps the girl was acting out because her mother was dying of cancer, but Liz disagreed.

"Maybe she was insecure, but I'd say she was just plain mean. The boys loved her, though, and Ginny had a different date every night of the week. Everyone was jealous."

"Were you jealous?"

Liz licked the rim of her empty glass. "You bet your sweet ass I was jealous. Back then I was an ugly little red mop with freckles. Guys didn't give me the time of day."

Gracie practiced snapping at flies unlucky enough to land near her paws, while Liz and Diana swapped what little they knew about Matthew's wayward child. Eventually, after hearing about Ginny's daughter, Melissa, and the hard life they had both endured, Liz's attitude softened and she conceded that maybe the time had come to put her childhood prejudices behind.

"But why did Ginny come home after all these years?" Liz wondered.

Diana told her about Ginny's plans to attend the wedding of her ex-boyfriend, Trevor. "Was he in your summer camp, too?"

"Nope, I never knew any boy named Trevor. Who's he marrying?"

"A woman named Lori Fowler. She lives in Highland Gardens."

Suddenly Liz got pale and her mouth turned down at the corners. "Jeez, I don't believe it."

"Don't tell me you know Lori, too?"

Liz shook her head. "No, but my boyfriend Danny thinks she's sexy as all get out. She hired him to paint the interior of her house last summer, and I swear the man was half in love with her."

"So you're jealous of *both* Ginny and Lori?" Diana couldn't resist planting that barb, because as much as Liz professed to have put her childhood insecurities behind, when it came to Danny Cappelli, Liz was possessive as a queen bee guarding her honey.

But Liz didn't rise to Diana's bait. "In fact, Diana, Danny was invited to Lori's wedding, and instead of trying to get me invited, like he should have, he had the nerve to ask me to buy Lori's present."

"So, did you?"

"Sure, I delivered it to the church yesterday, per the bride's wishes."

"Hmm, that's funny." Diana explained how she and Ginny had attempted to take Ginny's gift to Lori's home that very morning.

"Well, maybe Ginny didn't know any better."

"Maybe not."

The wine must have gone straight to Diana's head, for suddenly she felt a little dizzy. "Hey, I need some food in my stomach. How 'bout I call out for a pizza?"

"You buying?"

"Absolutely." She'd carried her cell phone out to the patio, hoping that Matthew would call and restore her pathetic world to the more hopeful place it had been twenty-four short hours ago. But just as she prepared to speed dial for her favorite white pizza with spinach, mushrooms, and green peppers, the phone rang of its own accord. She glanced at caller ID, and Matthew's name popped up.

"Speak of the devil…" she murmured and picked up. "Hi, sweetie…"

As Diana listened to what Matthew had to say, her ragged emotions got squeezed through a myriad of wringers. At the same time, she wondered how on God's earth she could explain it all to Liz. Her face must have given her away.

"What?" Liz demanded when she hung up. "Please don't tell me our pizza date is off?"

"Will you take a rain check?"

Gracie caught a fly between her teeth.

Liz rolled her eyes. "Sure, and I bet you expect me to do all the office shit on my own."

"Would you mind, Liz?"

"But why?"

"It seems Ginny forgot to buy her daughter a birthday cake.

NINE

Matthew…

"Now what, Grandpa?"

Good question. Matthew didn't know if he was coming or going. Because ever since Diana left with Ginny that morning, shattering their plans to live together, since his long lost daughter showed up with her almost-six-years- old surprise package, he'd had no idea what his future would hold. And since sweet little Lissa had attached herself like his miniature shadow, Matthew hadn't had one free minute to contemplate, let alone resolve, any of those issues.

"Where are you taking our fish?" Lissa demanded.

She wore a purple swimsuit and pink flip-flops. Her amazing red hair was frizzy and tangled from multiple dips in the lake, and in spite of the many coatings of sunscreen he had slathered all over her, Lissa's nose and shoulders were pink and dotted with new freckles.

"I have to clean the fish now," Matthew told her. "You run up to the house and take a shower while I do it."

Her strong pony legs pumped hard to keep up as they walked through the yard to the cleaning table.

"But the fish has been swimming in the lake. Isn't he clean already?" the child persisted.

Matthew sighed. The three-pound bass swung dead on the chain between them. He hated this part. In fact, when he'd taken Lissa out on the promised fishing expedition, he'd hoped they'd catch nothing. He despised killing fish. Enjoyed eating them, though.

"Look, Lissa. Cleaning means I have to cut the fish up. I have to peel off its skin and slice it open. It's not pretty."

Matthew felt her big blue eyes questioning him as she chewed her lower lip. Point was, Lissa was a city girl from Las Vegas. Unlike Matthew's daughter, Ginny, Lissa wasn't accustomed to the raw, blood n' guts of country life.

"But the fish is dead, right?" she said.

"Yep."

"Then he won't care if you cut him up, right?"

"Right."

"Then why can't I watch? Maybe I can help?"

Like mother, like daughter. Matthew was squeamish about dissecting any of God's creatures, but as a child, Ginny had been fascinated by the process. She was the kind of kid who loved eviscerating frogs for her science projects and had eventually taken over the family fish cleaning responsibilities. Thankfully, Ginny had never gotten into guns or hunting.

"Okay, you can watch." Matthew conceded. "But if you don't like it, you can leave."

"Cool."

So they stood side by side at the rustic wooden table as the sun slid closer to the lake, staining the water on the far shore golden. Matthew sliced and diced, despising every moment, while Lissa watched spellbound. She was especially enchanted by the cutting off of the head and tail. She poked at the glassy eyes with a stick while Matthew worried.

He worried about Ginny, who had been strange and withdrawn ever since she returned without Lissa's birthday

64

cake. Ginny had refused to come fishing with them, and while he and Lissa were out in the boat, Ginny had restlessly paced the dock. She kept fiddling with her cell phone, attempting to call God only knew who.

While he and Lissa had drowned worms, Ginny did a series of vigorous laps from dock to dock, but the exercise didn't calm her incessant pacing, or her obsessive phone calling. She tossed tennis balls for Ursie, but remained utterly unable to relax. Her perpetual, nervous energy reminded Matthew of Ginny's behavior during her difficult teenage years, and he hoped his daughter's current problems were not quite as profound.

Finally, when he and Lissa had arrived triumphant at the dock with their prize-wining catch, Ginny barely acknowledged their arrival. She'd waved them away and made another phone call.

What kind of mother ignored her child's first fish, or forgot to buy her child's birthday cake? As he pondered these unanswerable questions, Ursie nosed up to the cleaning table and sniffed the fish offal. The dog backed away, a look of disgust on her long black face.

"How come Ursie won't eat it?" Lissa asked.

"Maybe she'll like the fish better once I roll it in my famous pepper batter and fry it up on the griddle?"

"Yum, that sounds good. My mama can't cook."

"That a fact?"

"Can you cook, Grandpa?"

"You betcha." He winked, then rolled the bass fillets into one of the sheets of aluminum foil he kept in the tackle box. He shoveled the fish guts into a plastic bag for the garbage, then turned the hose on the table and washed it down.

65

"Now what, Grandpa?"

"Now you take that shower."

"What are you gonna do?"

"Well, I'll take a shower, too. We don't want to smell like stinky old fish, do we?"

Lissa wrinkled her nose and shook her head. She folded her little hand into his as they moved towards the house, Ursie trotting behind. The child's fingers fluttered like butterfly wings inside his big paw, triggering powerful memories. Once Ginny had held his hand like that. Her small bare feet had padded in his footsteps as they trudged through the same grass, avoided stepping on bees hiding in the clover, back when Daddy could make everything right and keep everyone safe. In those days, Matthew's wife, Lynn, would be waiting in the kitchen to pan fry their fish. But then the cancer stole it all away, proving Daddy could not protect anything at all.

Matthew and Lissa paused at the dock, where Ginny was still pacing with the cell phone glued to her right hand.

"Hey, Ginny," Matthew hollered. "You best get ready for dinner now."

"Yeah, hurry up, Mama. Grandpa's cooking our fish."

For one brief moment, Matthew's eyes locked with his daughter's, and time warped them both backwards through the years. *Les temps perdues*—times lost. He sensed a softening in Ginny's wary glance and wondered if she remembered any sweetness from her childhood. Or had the betrayal of her mother's death dissolved any residual tenderness? Those days were like a fragile effervescence that had washed ashore across harsh sands, then got sucked back out into a sea of bitter brine, all iridescence forgotten.

Lord, Matthew, get a grip. He squeezed Lissa's hand. Lissa was not Ginny. This child was nothing like her mother, who had just lifted her hand to shade her face from the sun, and then Matthew had seen the softness in her eyes harden.

"Y'all eat without me. I'm not hungry," Ginny yelled.

"C'mon, Mama, it'll taste awesome!"

"Lissa's right," Matthew shouted. "I'm fixin' your homecoming dinner, so take one last swim and get your stubborn butt on up here!"

"Up yours, old man!" With that, Ginny Troutman carefully placed her phone on a deck chair, stuck out her tongue, held her nose, and jumped in the lake.

Lissa giggled nervously.

"Don't worry, Grandpa. Mama will come."

"I reckon so."

The odd sensation of déjà vu followed Matthew into the guest bedroom, where Ginny and Lissa were staying. As he rummaged through the child's suitcase, helping her choose a new outfit to wear once she was clean—bright red shorts and a blue polka dot blouse, panties with tiny green turtles printed on the cotton—he remembered similar fashion statements from Ginny's childhood. He brushed the sand off Lissa's feet, gave her a fresh washcloth, new bar of soap, big fluffy towel, and got her started in the shower.

Eventually he moved into the master suite, stripped off his filthy clothes, and buried them in the hamper. He laid out clean khakis and a soft blue shirt on the king-sized bed, where he should be sleeping with Diana, and his heart ached with regret. At the same time, he vowed to put the past behind and concentrate on the future.

After all, Diana was not Lynn. She was nothing like his lost wife. Where Lynn had been soft and compliant, Diana was spunky and independent. Less sugar, more spice. And Matthew loved them both.

He stepped into the pulsing shower and willed the hot water to wash away the pastel years. It seemed he always thought of Lynn in pale, muted tones—the gentle rose, fern green, and violet hues of a tinted sepia photograph. While Diana was vivid color and sharp definition, less comfort, more challenge.

Diana was the passionate surprise of Matthew's middle age, and he never saw her coming. She was the clear, cold north to his clouded, sultry south. Sun to his moon. And in the years he had courted her, she'd proved to be a skittish, proud, untamable filly. So that now, just when they were both ready to share the same corral—Diana would never wear a bridle and bit—Matthew's past had intervened and sent her galloping back to her own pasture.

He laughed out loud at the silly metaphor. One thing Matthew knew about himself: he was a sentimental romantic, prone to overblown rhetoric, at least in the secret passages of his mind. Diana was the sensible one, the down-to-earth realist, and more than once she'd brought him back to terra firma with a huge thud. He fully expected her to do so today, to arrive with the birthday cake she'd promised to buy and help put his world back in perspective. He needed Diana. Needed her badly.

Because yesterday when his past intervened, it hadn't come clad in benign watercolor hues, but rather clothed in the violent darks of a hurricane. And while he couldn't begin to fathom the trouble Ginny brought with her, he sensed the winds of change were powerful enough to blow his life apart.

TEN

The shopping cure…

Diana eased her white Crown Victoria, nicknamed Queen Vic, into a parking place outside the Super Target on River Highway. The shopping center was still crowded late Saturday afternoon, but in general, the flow of consumers was homeward bound to cookouts, twilight boat rides, or whatever other activities normal people enjoyed during a glorious weekend at the lake.

She took a long gulp of the Starbucks coffee she'd picked up at the corner and hoped the caffeine would jolt her system and override the sluggish effects from all that wine she'd drunk with Liz. On the other hand, how much more jumpy did she want to be? Ever since the panicky phone call from Matthew, her nerves had been on high alert. How could Ginny have forgotten to buy her daughter a birthday cake? Hadn't the cake purchase, along with the delivery of the wedding gift, been the whole purpose of their outing together that morning? What kind of bubble-headed mom would screw up her daughter's birthday?

Or maybe Ginny's bubble-headedness was the natural result of many recent conflicts. First she'd encountered Diana, a strange woman she'd never met, about to move in with her dad. Diana had first-hand experience with that strong, possessive bond that sometimes developed between daughters and their daddies. In the aftermath of Diana's contentious divorce, her own daughter, Mandy, had sided with Robert, Diana's abusive ex, and no reasonable argument or emotional appeal could convince Mandy to see Diana's point of view.

Ginny had been a vulnerable sixteen-year-old when she lost her mom, so the girl might have seen Matthew's anguish and felt a maternal, or even wifely need to protect and comfort him. So maybe the horrible argument between Ginny and Diana was rooted in jealousy. God knew their contentious parting had left Diana badly shaken, so she was dreading her imminent reunion with Ginny.

She took another swallow of coffee and a deep breath. Yet according to Matthew, Ginny had been a rebellious, bitter child after her mother's death. She hadn't loved him too much. Instead, she'd hated him enough to run away six years ago and never look back. She'd broken his heart and left him drowning in guilt. He blamed himself for wallowing in an all-consuming grief that had excluded Ginny and driven her away.

Bullshit. Diana finished the last drop of coffee, crumpled the paper cup, and jammed it into the car's side pocket. She hated psychobabble and second-guessing. All day she'd been trying to excuse Ginny's rude behavior—first to Liz, now to herself. Fact was, she didn't have one clue what made Ginny tick.

Most likely there was a simple explanation. Maybe the girl was exhausted after her long trip from Nevada. Maybe she was frustrated because she'd been unable to deliver Lori's gift. Or maybe she was just plain pissed because her ex-boyfriend was marrying someone else.

Diana didn't know the answers, but she did care. Because Ginny's unexpected arrival affected her future, too.

Suddenly Ginny was the monkey wrench in Diana's works. How long would she stay? Where was Diana expected to spend the night? Was she destined to bounce back and forth between Matthew's house on the lake and her condo in Davidson forever? She was now only three miles from Matthew's, and with each passing mile, her emotions got stretched thinner, like a rubber band at the breaking point.

She left Queen Vic's air-conditioned interior and stepped out onto the steaming blacktop, telling herself that she should be thankful for this shopping center, so convenient in an emergency. Only two years ago it had been a pristine pine forest, and while her inner conservationist hated the development, her outer pragmatist gave silent thanks. She yanked a shopping cart from its cage and wheeled it into the store.

Okay, first stop the bakery. She'd been agonizing during the drive about what kind of cake to buy a child she barely knew. In the end, she took what was available: chocolate with strawberry icing, and asked the woman behind the counter to write "Happy Birthday, Melissa" on top. As an afterthought, she ordered a musical theme to be added to the cake, including a little candy guitar.

"Can you get it ready while I shop?" Diana asked.

"No problem, ma'am."

As she moved away from the bakery, Diana feared the worst. If Ginny forgot Lissa's cake, had she also forgotten to buy the girl some presents? Certainly Matthew hadn't had an opportunity to get his granddaughter a gift, and Diana wanted to give Lissa a little something, too, so she decided to visit the toy department.

"So what do you choose for a six-year-old girl?" she asked the white-haired woman stocking shelves with plush stuffed animals.

"That depends…what does she like?"

Diana drew a blank. "I have no idea."

"Is she a little princess, or a tomboy?"

"I honestly don't know."

She realized she was pathetically ill equipped to make a decision. She'd been out of the loop so long, she didn't know what modern kids preferred. The elderly clerk did her best. She showed Diana boxes of plastic fairy dolls and a brightly colored polyethylene shell called a *bilibo* that Lissa could sit on, rock in, or use for a doll cradle, but Diana couldn't relate.

She turned to the saleswoman. "I've decided to choose something on my own. Something old-fashioned, you know?"

"Suit yourself. Is this child your granddaughter?"

Diana was taken aback. "Not yet…"

The old gal gave her a knowing look. "I see. Well, I hope you don't buy the wrong gift."

"I think I'll manage." But inwardly Diana was clueless.

She dug deep and came up with the classic options— rainy day toys/sunny day toys. Any kid needed both. Matthew was a closeted watercolor landscape painter, and his work was quite good. He kept this talent under wraps, but Diana figured some children's art supplies were in order. She chose plain pads and coloring books, crayons, poster paints, and a variety of brushes. Now on those drizzly lake days, Grandpa could entertain Lissa in his studio.

Diana wanted to give the girl a sunny day gift, so she selected a colorful inner tube float, a nest of sand baskets and digging tools, and a straw hat decorated with a band of sunflowers. Perfect.

But was it too much? By the time she retrieved the cake, took out her credit card, and the checkout boy totaled it all up, Diana wondered: *Am I trying to buy this family with gifts?* Nonsense. She added six birthday balloons and some candles before calling it quits.

By the time she loaded her purchases into her trunk, except for the cake, which she carefully placed on the front seat, her nerves were no longer stretched like a rubber band. The shimmering heat had retreated, making it much easier to breathe. And the parking lot was nearly empty, meaning the traffic had cleared, making the final voyage to Matthew's a five-minute straight shot.

She could do this. Like her mama Vivian always said when tempers flared and life seemed too difficult: "Take the shopping cure, darlin', and you'll feel just fine."

ELEVEN

No secrets 'round here…

Diana's mood plummeted when she pulled into Matthew's driveway and saw his face framed in the kitchen window. He was standing at the sink watching for her, and even at that distance, with the dramatic sunset burning behind the house, she saw the uncharacteristic slump of his powerful shoulders.

She braced herself as the screen door slammed and Matthew, followed by Ursie, burst from the house and loped towards her car. Before she could exit, he opened her door.

"Boy, am I glad to see you, Diana."

"What's wrong?"

He helped her out, gathered her into his arms, and suddenly he was kissing her. She felt the smooth, cool skin of his freshly shaved cheeks and his warm, welcoming lips. He smelled of aftershave and soap and was wearing her favorite blue shirt, so soft in her arms. She wished the embrace would never end, but too soon he eased away and searched her eyes.

"I've missed you so much," he said.

"Yeah, I missed you, too, but what's happening?"

Matthew shifted foot to foot. "I'm not sure, but Ginny's acting strange. She's moody and withdrawn, but she won't talk about it."

"Have you asked her?"

74

"Not exactly. I've tried to include her, but she wouldn't even come fishing with us. She's not herself."

"Look, Matthew, she's been gone six years. Do you even know who she is anymore?"

He paused, glanced at the sun as it dropped below the horizon and out of sight. "Maybe I don't know her at all." He walked around the hood of the car and spotted the special package on the front seat. "Good, I see you got the cake."

"Yes, but is the coast clear to take it inside now? I don't want the birthday girl to see all her stuff before tomorrow."

"What stuff? Is there more?"

Diana blushed as she led him around to the trunk. She opened it and captured the strings to the six balloons before they escaped. "Maybe I got carried away?"

Matthew laughed and began rummaging through the shopping bags. When he discovered the art supplies, his dark eyes betrayed his emotions. "Good choice, Diana, how can I ever thank you?"

She reached up with her free hand and pulled his head down to deliver a deep, probing kiss all her own. He tasted both salty and sweet, so she figured he'd been cooking up something special in the kitchen, and all her anxieties began slipping away until Matthew abruptly disengaged, leaving her breathless.

"What?" she gasped. At the same time, she felt something tugging at the knee of her slacks. She glanced down, expecting to find Ursie, but instead discovered Lissa standing there. The child was grinning so wide Diana found herself staring at the endearing gap between her two front teeth.

"Are those balloons for me, Miss Diana?"

Diana was flustered and looked to Matthew for support. "Oh, oh, it looks like we've been caught out. Is it okay if Lissa gets her balloons one day early?"

In the meantime, Matthew quickly grabbed the shopping bags and held them behind his back, but Lissa wouldn't be fooled.

"What are you hiding, Grandpa?"

"None of your business, girl." He hefted the packages higher, out of reach, as Lissa began scanning Queen Vic's interior for more surprises. She stood on tiptoes and checked the front seat.

"My birthday cake!"

Diana and Matthew groaned in unison.

"No secrets 'round here." Matthew tromped around and opened the passenger door, just as Ursie lunged for the cake.

Diana collared the dog in the nick of time and handed Lissa the balloons. "You hold these tight, or else Ursie will eat your cake."

"Okay, Miss Diana."

Poor Matthew held the cake aloft in his right hand, the surprise packages in his left, then led the procession to the house. Diana realized that holding Ursie back was much like controlling a big black jumping bean, but somehow they all made it into the kitchen without incident. Matthew slid the cake atop the refrigerator and stowed the shopping bags out of reach in the utility cabinet, while Lissa carefully secured the balloon strings to the framework of a table lamp. Once the helium orbs were safely bobbing out of harm's way, Matthew snatched the child under her armpits and swung her in the air.

"Shame on you, Punkin. Didn't I tell you to stay put and tend to the fish?"

"Yes, Grandpa," Lissa squealed. "But I saw you two kissing!"

Diana flushed with embarrassment, but suddenly realized she had more pressing challenges. She rushed to the stove, located a potholder, and eased the cast iron skillet off the burner. The room smelled delicious, like deep-fried hushpuppies and battered bass, which had just begun to smoke.

"Close call..." She turned a disparaging eye on the two at horseplay. "Never leave a stove unattended. Lucky you didn't burn the house down."

But Matthew and Lissa seemed unrepentant. He quit swinging the girl and put her down, butt first, on the linoleum. "No harm done," he chuckled.

Lissa popped up and captured Diana's hand. "I saw you kissing Grandpa. Is he your boyfriend?"

Diana sighed. She had two choices: continue in the role of sourpuss Grandma, or let it all go. She chose the latter, planted a big kiss on Lissa's curly red head. "Yes, Lissa, your grandpa is definitely my boyfriend, and he acts more like a little boy every single day."

Lissa let go of Diana's hand and spun in delight. "Diana loves Grandpa, Diana loves Grandpa..." she chanted as she twirled.

Finally Matthew stopped the whirling dervish. "Enough of that. Where's your mama?"

Lissa stood still and considered. "She's in our room getting dressed."

"That's good, Lissa. Now I want you to go fetch her. Tell her dinner is served." He gave the girl a little swat on the rump, and the child took off in the direction of the bedrooms. Once she was gone, Diana and Matthew heaved a sigh of relief.

"So, are you all right?" Diana began.

"Sure, how 'bout you?"

"I'm hanging in." As their eyes locked in understanding, both wondering what had become of their future together, Diana longed for that celebratory bottle of wine she had wasted with Liz.

"I still want you to move in with me, Diana," Matthew abruptly stated. "I want you to stay here tonight and never leave."

She sank onto the nearest chair. "But you know, Matthew…"

He crossed his arms. "I mean it now, so please don't argue. Anything else is nonsense."

"What about Ginny and Lissa?"

"Plenty of room for everyone. Way I see it, Ginny can like it, or lump it."

"*Lump it?*" Diana had to giggle, but Matthew was dead serious. She knew this by the aggressive set of his jaw and the tiny muscle twitching at the corner of his eye.

"Yeah, like it, or lump it," he repeated.

Diana slowly got to her feet and moved to the stove. She hoped Matthew didn't notice her hands trembling as she shifted the griddle back on the burner and picked up a spatula. "I'll make you a deal," she said at last. "If we all survive dinner without a crisis, I'll think about it."

"That's all I can ask." He slipped his arms around her waist and nuzzled the tender skin at the back of her neck. "In the meantime, this is still my kitchen, so please move aside and let me cook. Otherwise no one will eat tonight."

TWELVE

Headed for trouble...

Ginny and Lissa appeared while Diana was setting the table, and although she was still nervous about encountering Matthew's daughter again, she sensed Ginny was even more apprehensive.

"Lissa, please go help Pop-Pop get up the food," Ginny said.

"How come you call him Pop-Pop, Mommy?"

Ginny shrugged. "That's what I called my grandpa when he was alive."

"That's stupid." Lissa looked to Diana for affirmation.

"No, it's not stupid," Diana told the child. "I called my grandma Nana."

"That's stupid, too," Lissa stated with less conviction. "But I'm still calling him Grandpa."

Ginny did an eye roll. "Suit yourself, squirt, but if you don't get in there and help him, you'll be sorry."

Lissa took off for the kitchen, and Ginny offered Diana a shy, grateful smile. "Thanks for backing me up. Lissa can be a pain."

"No problem." Diana noticed Ginny looked entirely different after a day at the lake. She was scrubbed and wholesome, and without the mascara and makeup she seemed much younger. Her freshly-washed black hair was less punk, more Peter Pan, and her skin was tanned a healthy bronze. Her oversized yellow T-shirt and raggedy cutoff jeans made her seem like an innocent teenager, but the nose stud and the bottle of rum in her hand spoiled that illusion.

Ginny caught Diana staring at the bottle. "I suppose you're like Trout. Don't approve of my drinking?"

"No, I was hoping you'd share." Diana smiled at the startled young woman. "I know Matthew doesn't keep tonic in the house, but maybe we could dig up a couple of Cokes?"

"All right!" Ginny high-fived her. "And look, Diana, I'm sorry I behaved like an asshole this morning."

Now it was Diana's turn to do a double-take. "Forget it, Ginny. We got off on the wrong foot, so let's start fresh."

"You got it."

So as the lake outside the dining room window darkened from sunset crimson to twilight blue, everyone enjoyed the sumptuous meal Matthew had prepared. Diana savored her rum n' Coke, so did Ginny, and Matthew uttered not one word of objection. Diana had known all along that Matthew's dislike of alcohol was not a moral issue, but rather he had never developed a taste for it. Ginny had experienced a father bitterly opposed to his daughter's underage drinking, but far as adults were concerned, Matthew's philosophy was *live and let live.*

"Can I tell you how we caught the fish, Miss Diana?"

As Lissa told the story they'd heard three times already, Diana listened contentedly and decided that all the Troutmans had benefited from their lake day together. Matthew and Ginny were brown, Lissa was pink, and whatever conflicts they'd experienced during the day seemed to have washed away with the waves. By the time they finished eating slices of birthday cake, Lissa was yawning and ready for bed.

"C'mon, Punkin, I'll tuck you in," Ginny said.

"She's a cute kid." Matthew bragged after his daughter and granddaughter left the room.

"Ginny or Lissa?"

"Both." Matthew conceded. "Want some coffee?"

"Oh, yes, it's exactly what I need," Diana answered gratefully.

Soon all three adults were seated together on the sofa, Diana in the middle. They balanced coffee cups on their laps and watched the local TV news. As Diana grew drowsy, she realized they had made it through dinner without a crisis, so now she was obliged to consider Matthew's proposal that she should spend the night and never leave again. Whew. Maybe it was the calming effect of the liquor, but she had almost convinced herself that she could move in with Matthew and they'd all live together in harmony.

But then a breaking news story flashed across the television screen and captured her attention. Suddenly Diana was wide-awake. She snapped fully awake as a uniformed Davidson policeman strung yellow crime scene tape around the perimeter of someone's front yard. The flowerbeds, bushes, and faux Tudor brick home were immediately familiar, as was the young boy with curly blond hair and a blue Duke cap. The boy looked scared as he pointed towards the back of the house, then gestured wildly to a plainclothes cop who was writing in a notebook.

Diana felt Ginny stiffen at her side.

A pretty African American news anchor from Channel 3 was covering the story. Her dark, expressive eyes were wide and her hand gripped the mic:

The sleepy college town of Davidson rarely sees a murder, so the violent stabbing of a young woman from the exclusive suburb of Highland Gardens has the village stunned in disbelief...

Diana gasped. "Look at that house, Ginny. Isn't that your friend's place?"

Ginny latched onto Diana's elbow and squeezed hard. "Can't be..." She stared at Diana, attempting to convey a pleading message with her eyes.

The newswoman continued: *The body of Lori Fowler, twenty-four years old, was discovered by a neighborhood boy around noon...*

The cameraman panned to a close-up of the kid in the cap, and Diana's stomach churned as she realized this was the same boy who had skateboarded into Matthew's truck. "Oh my God, Ginny, your friend Lori was murdered!"

"No way!" Ginny vigorously shook her head, her body trembled.

"Who's Lori Fowler?" Matthew sat forward on the couch as the broadcast continued:

Ironically, Miss Fowler was to be married next weekend, making this horrible death by stabbing doubly tragic. Local police are gathering evidence, but so far no suspect has been identified. Authorities are appealing to the public to come forward with any information pertinent to the case.

"Did you hear that, Ginny?" Diana could hardly catch her breath. "We have to call the police."

"No, I can't watch this!" Ginny sprang to her feet and turned off the television.

Matthew gaped at his daughter. "Lord, don't tell me that's the house where you two took the wedding gift this morning?"

Diana nodded. She felt stunned, disoriented. Ginny was pacing like a caged animal, and her frenetic motion made Diana seasick. "We went there, but no one was home. Right, Ginny?"

But Ginny could not answer. She made an odd, garbled noise deep in her throat, which might have been a sob, since her eyes were brimming with tears. "Look, I gotta go…" Ginny almost choked on the words. She snatched her purse and pulled out her car keys.

"You can't drive, girl," Matthew protested. "You've had too much to drink."

"Not nearly enough," Ginny mumbled as she moved out the door.

"But where are you going?" Diana was right behind her.

"You can't leave now. Tomorrow is Lissa's birthday!" Matthew shouted as he charged the door.

"Don't worry, I'll be back." Ginny broke into a run. Seconds later, they heard her car start, and soon the red eyes of her taillights disappeared down the country road.

"What just happened?" Matthew's voice reflected his rage.

"I think she's in shock," Diana said.

He pulled Diana back into the house, closed and locked the door. "But where will Ginny go? She doesn't know anybody 'round here anymore."

Don't be too sure, Diana thought to herself as she visualized the classic Jeep she'd seen parked in the dead woman's drive. She had imagined the Jeep belonged to Trevor, Ginny's ex-boyfriend, the groom who had just lost his bride.

"I hope she's not headed for trouble," Matthew said.
"But what can we do about it?"
Matthew drew her into his arms. "Absolutely nothing."

THIRTEEN

Ginny...

Ginny didn't need her GPS to find Trevor's house. She could get there blindfolded, or in the middle of the night, like now. The moon was a white fingernail clipping hung above the black ridgeline of pines. It cast silver ripples on the lake when she crossed Perth Road Bridge and drove north towards Troutman.

She wiped away unwanted tears with the back of her hand and realized she looked a mess. She had always imagined this moment quite differently. Her reunion with Trev, after six long, tumultuous years, was supposed to blow him away. Ginny had fantasized each detail, seen herself wearing something hot and sexy, and visualized his admiration when he saw her expensive new ride, her fully-loaded forest green Subaru wagon. She knew he'd be impressed by her glamorous job in the Las Vegas casino, and he'd marvel at how well she had learned to play the guitar.

But her dream was not to be. Instead, she was a total wreck, physically and mentally. Dressed in an ancient T-shirt and raggedy cutoffs, with no makeup and red-rimmed eyes, she looked every inch the stressed-out mother of a soon-to-be six-year-old. Her Subaru was filthy with road dust, and any hope she'd had of presenting herself as the eat-your-heart-out ex-girlfriend, who'd arrived for his wedding just in time to make him understand how much he'd missed, how badly he'd screwed up by not choosing her—that hope was dead. Dead as Trevor's bride-to-be.

As she drove through the sleeping suburbs and dark fields alive with cricket song, she visualized the bloody horror of Lori Fowler stabbed to death. The vision brought fresh tears of panic, and she could only imagine how devastated Trev must be feeling. She wished she had her baggie of little white chill pills, wished she'd drunk more rum instead of sharing with Diana Rittenhouse, the unexpected woman who had recently come into her father's life. She wished she could start over at age sixteen, and wished she'd never come home.

But mostly she wished she could erase the awful image of Lori's death.

She hyperventilated as she slowed down to look for Dula Road. Clearly she was suffering from emotional overload, so she took a deep breath and willed herself to put the ugly present aside and think only of the older, sweeter days.

Back then, horny young Ginny would tell her daddy she was going out with girlfriends, but instead she'd borrow the truck and sneak up to Trev's place. Trev had worshiped her then, or at least he'd been awed by the fact that her great grandpa Troutman had founded the little town where Trev grew up.

That small status made her special, as did the fact that her mom had died of cancer. Trev's parents had been killed in a car crash when he was eighteen, the year he graduated from high school. So he was an only child, an orphan, and she was an only child and practically an orphan, so that made them soulmates. They'd found comfort in their mutual tragedies and comfort in one another's arms.

Ginny slowed up when she saw the crooked old landmark oak looming in the pale moonlight. She made a sharp right onto Dula, and was part way down the rutted dirt road when she slammed on the brakes to avoid hitting a rabbit blinded by her headlights. It scampered off to the side, where three newborn bunnies waited, and Ginny cursed the mating season and all creatures born of simple instinct. Animals got to live lives already programmed into their genes, ignorant of the complex human world where Ginny dwelled. Lucky them—no worries, no hard decisions.

At least Trev had achieved a measure of animal freedom. He was old enough to live on his own after his folks died, so he inhabited the family's two-storied frame farmhouse and did as he pleased. Ginny remembered how a summer breeze would blow the lace curtains at the bedroom window as they lay naked and sweaty on the sheets. How good it felt to fuck like rabbits, until they could no longer lift their heavy heads, or legs and arms, and how her belly quivered and sighed when the lovemaking was done.

If Ginny was famous because she was a Troutman, then Trev was infamous because he was a Dula. Like many others in that part of North Carolina, he claimed the Civil War murderer, Tom Dooley, as a direct ancestor. But Trev and Ginny were true outlaws. They had lived free—screwing, eating, drinking liquor, and smoking pot until their young bodies were satiated.

She turned into Trev's driveway and began the long ascent to his house, through the cornfields and cow pastures where Trev's tall, lanky body had turned bronze in summer. His thick, curly black hair and laughing blue eyes still danced through her dreams.

Ginny's heart was pounding double-time as she looked for signs of life at the farm. She'd been trying to call him all day, but he'd never answered the phone. God, where was he?

She pulled all the way up to the back door, then turned off the engine and killed the lights. She powered down her windows, and the chilled air from the car's interior got sucked out into the humid night. She listened to insects buzzing in the overgrown yard and watched several moths commit suicide inside the porch lamp. Otherwise, everything was silent. The house was dark, no sign of Trev's Jeep

No need to call his name, pound on his door, or lay on the horn. Because she knew he was gone. She also knew he was in trouble.

Another image of Lori's body pounded behind her eyes. Had she come here because she wanted Trev, or had she come to warn him? She'd never tell anyone about seeing the Jeep in Lori's drive, but Diana would almost certainly spill her guts to the cops. Either way, Ginny's trip was futile, so there was only one thing left to do… She propped her head on the steering wheel, lowered her head and cried.

FOURTEEN

The wee hours…

Matthew washed dishes and Diana dried. By the time they'd put all the leftovers away, let Ursie out for the last piddle of the night, and checked on Lissa, who was sleeping with one arm flung over her head like a little princess, Diana was exhausted. Mostly by Matthew's relentless barrage of questions.

He was both angry and worried about Ginny. Diana understood. As a mother of two, she remembered being most furious with her kids at precisely those moments when she was most frightened for them. Matthew wanted to know the nature of Ginny's relationship with the dead girl, Lori Fowler, so eventually Diana broke down and told him he should be more concerned about her relationship to Lori's fiancé, Trevor, who had once been Ginny's boyfriend.

"Trevor Dula?" Matthew shook his head. "That boy was nothin' but trouble. Kid ran wild after his parents' death."

"You're kidding." Diana interrupted. "Trevor's last name is *Dula*? As in Tom Dula who got hanged?"

But Matthew ignored her. "I'm afraid that young man was responsible for leading Ginny astray."

Astray? Such a quaint word, and Diana wondered if it included drugs, sex, rock n' roll, or all the above? "Were they lovers?" she bluntly asked him.

"Absolutely not. Ginny was too young for that stuff," Matthew said.

Wanna bet? She strongly suspected that like most fathers, Matthew was in deep denial regarding his daughter's sexuality.

"You think Trevor had something to do with the murder?" He frowned.

"How should I know?" She folded her dishtowel and moved towards the master bedroom. "But since he was planning to marry Lori next week, I'd guess he wanted to kiss her, not kill her."

"I see your point." Matthew turned off the lights, locked the door, and followed her. "So who was Ginny trying to call all day? Who'd she go to see?"

"I don't know, Matthew." But she had her suspicions. She was also disturbed by that Jeep they'd seen in the dead girl's driveway and felt she should inform the police.

She showered, then stepped out onto the deck overlooking the lake, where the moon was a white sliver suspended above the far shore. And she realized, with a tiny twinge of regret, that she had always visualized this moment quite differently. She had fantasized each detail, seen herself in a sexy new nightgown. Maybe she and Matthew would have shared this romantic moment on the deck, and then he would have carried her across the threshold to the bed, where they'd have begun the rest of their lives together.

But that dream was not to be. When she returned to the room, Matthew was already tucked in, pretending to read a mystery novel. He smiled at her from above his reading glasses.

"Ready for bed, honey?"

She dropped her robe, he switched off the bed light, and moments later she was in his arms. She closed her eyes and let out an involuntary sigh as Matthew cupped her breasts. She loved the rough texture of his workingman's hands as they gently caressed her. He lingered in the velvety softness between her thighs, igniting a primal longing locked deep inside, a desire that had begun the day they met, an enduring passion that never failed to lift her up and out of herself each time they made love.

His mouth traveled down into her secret canyon, while her hands explored the hallowed valleys between his shoulders and the muscles in his back. Finally, she pulled his head up to meet her lips for an urgent, probing kiss. She tasted her future in his mouth.

When they finally came together, her body was alive with need. And when he entered her wet, sacred stream, she cried out in joy. And as she floated into a deep, untroubled sleep, she dreamed she was Matthew's private river.

FIFTEEN

Ginny...

Ginny pulled herself together, backed out the driveway, and for old time's sake, decided to follow Dula Road to its dead end. These hundred-plus acres were what was left of the family's farm. Before they died, Trev's parents harvested corn and kept milk cows, while Trev's uncle Maynard opened a construction company at his end of this lane.

She noticed a new stretch of high chain link fence growing from the scrub brush on both sides of the road, marking the perimeters of Dula Construction. Stacks of new lumber, piles of rock, and cubes of concrete block lay sleeping beyond the fence, illuminated by the eerie yellow glow of security lampposts. And at the end of the street, Maynard's basic brick ranch house had lights burning in every window.

Ginny slowed to a crawl. Once upon a time, Maynard had been a good friend to her and Trev. Although he was Trev's uncle, he was only fifteen years older and seemed more like an eccentric big brother. Many a night he had fed the orphaned Trev bowls of chili, and he'd never judged Trev and Ginny for screwing around and raising hell.

At the same time, Ginny had always been a little spooked by Maynard's loose lifestyle and strange gray eyes that always seemed to linger too long where they shouldn't. But now Trev was in trouble, and maybe he was hanging out at his uncle's place, so she made a quick decision. If Maynard was up and about at that ungodly hour, then he could receive company.

Without thinking too hard, she drove into his parking area, went up the short sidewalk bordered by neat flowerbeds, and rang the doorbell. Almost immediately the aluminum screen door, decorated with the scrolled letter "D", swung open. But instead of Maynard, Ginny was greeted by an angry woman about her same age.

"What do you want?" The woman was a tough blonde, with thick hair pulled back in a sloppy ponytail.

"Is Maynard home?" Ginny was so surprised she could hardly speak. Never, not once in the whole year she and Trev had dated, had she known Maynard to entertain a lady friend— as if this person could be called a lady.

"Whatever the hell you're selling, we ain't buying. You know what time it is?"

"Is he home?" Ginny stared into the hard green eyes, enhanced by smeared mascara and flaking eye shadow.

"Who wants to know?" The woman crossed her arms under an ample bosom spilling from a skin-tight orange tank top. Her buff biceps indicated she either worked out a lot, or she was a female wrestler.

"I'm Ginny Troutman, a friend of Trevor's. Who are you?"

The blonde's harsh laugh implied years of cigarette smoking. "I am Mrs. Paula Dula, Maynard's wife."

No way. Ginny's jaw dropped so far open it took a conscious act of will to haul it shut. "Okay, can I speak to Maynard, then?"

While Paula considered her options, the preferred one seeming to be sending Ginny packing, a large shadow appeared behind her and threw the door wide open. Before Ginny knew what was happening, a tall man pulled her inside and hugged her hard.

He held her at arm's length for inspection. "Good lord, it's lil' Jailbait, and she's all growed up. Look at you, girl. Ain't you a sight for sore eyes?"

Ginny caught her breath and smiled. Maynard had changed, too. His hair was now long and silver gray, pulled Hippie-style into a ponytail like his wife's. He had a beard, moustache, and his body had thinned out so that his jeans and black T-shirt hung loose on his rangy frame.

"Good to see you, Maynard."

"Likewise." He turned to his wife. "Ginny here used to be Trevor's main squeeze."

"Her and everyone else." Paula snorted derisively.

"So come on in and make yourself to home. I haven't seen you in a coon's age."

He dragged Ginny through a cluttered living room dominated by a huge flat screen TV and countless roaming cats. The space smelled like cigarette smoke and dirty kitty litter. They went directly into the kitchen, dodging the nasty ribbons of hanging flypaper Ginny recalled from her teenage years, and then sat right down at the round, pink Formica table. Paula followed like an angry storm cloud.

"Bring us some beers, Paula," Maynard commanded.

She clearly resented the order, but Maynard's wife opened the refrigerator door and pulled out three bottlenecks. She plunked them down on the table. "Do you require a glass, Ginny?" she sweetly asked.

"Guess not."

"Well that's good, because all the dishes are dirty." Paula pulled up a chair and sat so possessively close to Maynard their shoulders brushed. "What do you want?" she said.

Maynard elbowed his wife. "Be nice, Paula."

Ginny took one long drink, and then another. She looked straight into Maynard's strange gray eyes. "I'm worried about Trev. You know his fiancée, Lori Fowler, was murdered this morning."

The kitchen got so quiet Ginny heard the cats shuffling around in the living room and water dripping at the sink.

Finally Maynard shook his head. "Horrible thing. We heard it on the evening news, and I gotta tell you, Ginny, my nephew really loved that gal. After all his tomcattin' around, I do believe Trevor had found him the right mate."

Maynard's words wounded Ginny in a deep and secret place. She already knew Trev had moved on, but it was painful to hear the word "love," a word Trev had once reserved for her. "I've been trying to call him all day to see if he's all right," she said. "He's not here, is he?"

"Nope, haven't seen him since yesterday morning," Maynard said.

"What's it to you?" Paula interrupted. "Every young girl in the county's had her fling with Trevor, but they aren't beatin' down our door in the middle of the night."

Ginny glared at the woman and wondered if Paula had been one of the many girls who had shared Trev's bed. From the level of hostility, she figured something was going on.

"We're worried, too." Maynard gave Paula a stern look. "I know Trevor must be real upset. I just hope he ain't done nothin' stupid."

"Like what?" Ginny asked.

95

"Like none of your business," Paula snapped. "I'm the one upset, because Lori was my cousin, you know? After Maynard and me got married, I introduced the two of them. Worst mistake I ever made."

"Lori was your *cousin*?" She couldn't believe it. "Then I'm sorry for your loss."

"Yeah, well…" Paula took a long gulp of beer. "We weren't close, you know? Still, it's shitty what happened to her. No one deserves to die that way."

"Amen to that." Maynard sadly shook his head. He got up and brought more beers.

As they sat drinking, it occurred to Ginny that Paula did not fit the profile of a grieving cousin. Indeed, the woman seemed mad at the world as she explained how she and Trev had been in the same graduating class at Statesville High. Her cousin, Lori, had been two years younger, same age as Ginny, so Trev hadn't met Lori until Paula introduced them.

Ginny's head began to spin as the alcohol saturated her bloodstream. She'd never known any of those kids because she had graduated from Mooresville High. She'd only met Trev by accident when he stopped into Trout's store one fine day to buy a soda and smokes. The rest was history.

"So is Trev hiding out somewhere?" Ginny asked.

"Why should he be?" Paula said. "He didn't do nothing wrong."

Paula staggered as she walked to the counter to fetch a framed photograph. Evidently the beers were affecting everyone present. She placed the photo in Ginny's hands, and Ginny saw her beloved Trev staring back at her. But this man was shaved nearly bald and wore camouflage army fatigues. He held an evil-looking automatic weapon in his strong hands, and his blue eyes were cold and dead.

"He's changed," Ginny murmured.

"He's a hero." Paula bragged. "After two tours in Iraq and one in Afghanistan, of course he's fuckin' changed."

"Mind your mouth, Paula." Maynard sighed.

"Just sayin'…" Paula slurred. "Trevor's a war hero. He's never done nothing wrong."

Ginny's eyes blurred as she placed the picture of the stranger back on the table. What in God's name was she doing here where she didn't belong? They opened more beers. She tried to concentrate on the conversation, but was mesmerized by the rhythm of Paula's red fingernail casually twisting the gray hairs on Maynard's arm.

She listened to the couple's many grievances. Maynard, now forty years old, was having trouble getting Paula pregnant, and Paula desperately wanted a child. Maynard complained how the economy had landed his construction company in the crapper, how his business was down the toilet, and how could a man justify starting a family when he didn't have a pot to pee in?

It all made Ginny so ill she feared she might throw up. She stared as Maynard fiddled with the turquoise-laden silver cross hung round his neck.

"Look, you guys, I'm wasted," she told them. "Do you mind if I crash on your couch?"

In the end, she fell into a deep, drunken sleep with two felines on her chest, kneading her old yellow T-shirt.

SIXTEEN

A rude intrusion…

"Where's Mommy?"

Diana felt little fingers playing with the neck of her nightgown as she swam to consciousness. She remembered awakening in the deep of night, being swept from her private river onto a shore of worry as she listened for Lissa to wake up and find out her mother was gone. She had listened into the wee hours for Ginny's car to return, but it never did.

She lifted her heavy lids and found herself looking into two enormous blue eyes. She heard the shower running in the master bath, ran her hand along the sheet beside her, and discovered that Matthew was missing. Good, at least his granddaughter hadn't caught them in bed together.

"Happy birthday, Lissa." Diana touched the tip of the child's nose. It was pink with sunburn and beginning to peel.

"Guess what? I'm six years old!" Lissa's smile included that amazing gap between her two front teeth, but then the smile drooped. "When I woke up, I couldn't find Mommy."

"I know, honey, but she'll be back soon."

"But where did she go?"

Diana knew she needed some very strong coffee to answer that question, or even to come up with a proper lie. "Maybe she went shopping for the birthday girl?"

"Goody! Presents for me?"

Diana wanted to bite her tongue. Now she had created unreasonable expectations. More likely Ginny would come dragging home empty-handed, and Lissa would be crushed. Diana's anger at Ginny rekindled with a vengeance. She recalled the distressing news broadcast about the murder, followed by Ginny's abrupt departure, and all the turmoil of the past two days came crashing back like a runaway train.

It was Sunday morning. Was it possible that only two days ago, Friday afternoon, Matthew and she had visited Whippoorwill Village? That day they had planned to quietly move in together, but instead Ursie had been attacked with pepper spray, Diana had been threatened with a starter pistol, and Ginny and Lissa had burst unexpectedly into their lives. Diana had drunk wine with Liz and rum with Ginny, she'd been ping-ponged in and out of Matthew's future, and most upsetting—she had somehow drifted into close proximity of a brutal murder. At the moment, she felt like the damsel tied to the railroad track, and that runaway train was heading her way.

"Can I snuggle in bed with you, Miss Diana?"

Oh, wouldn't that be lovely? To cuddle up with this sweet child, just like she'd nested with her own daughter, Mandy, and together they could sink into oblivion. But instead, Diana swung her legs out of bed and discovered she was deliciously stiff from lovemaking, but that was okay.

"We'll snuggle some other time, Lissa. But right now we'd better get dressed and go to the kitchen. Your grandpa will be out soon, and I bet he'll make you some special birthday pancakes."

"Yummy, I love pancakes!"

At least that prediction came true, but it had been a no-brainer. Matthew always made pancakes on the Sabbath, his holy communion in lieu of church. Today he added bacon, eggs, apple juice for Lissa, and blessedly strong coffee for the adults.

The day was clear, windless, and sunny, so they set the table on the patio and lit candles on Lissa's pancakes.

"Shouldn't we wait for Mommy?" Lissa's eyes darted back and forth between the candles and the road, likely hoping to see Ginny's green Subaru drive up any minute.

"Go on and blow 'em out," Matthew coached. "We'll do it again when your mommy gets here."

"Don't forget to make a wish," Diana said.

Lissa screwed up her eyes and blew hard, snuffing out six little flames. "Can I say what I wished for?"

"Nope, it's bad luck," Matthew cautioned. "If you tell, then maybe the wish won't come true."

"But don't I get another wish when we light the candles with Mommy?"

Matthew glanced at Diana, and Diana nodded.

"Yes, Lissa, you'll get a brand new wish," he told her.

"Okay, then I can tell you…" The child jumped up, spread her arms wide and twirled. Her gesture encompassed the lake, sky, trees—everything in her immediate universe. "I never want to go back to Nevada. I want to stay here forever."

Diana and Matthew gaped at one another. Clearly Lissa's pronouncement had rendered him speechless, while Diana's maternal instincts kicked into overdrive.

"That's a wonderful wish," Diana said. "But you'll have to ask your mommy about that."

"I will. I'll ask her. But I know she'll say yes."

Matthew pulled Lissa back to her seat. "No more talking, young lady. I want you to eat your breakfast, because

Grandpa turns into a mean old black bear when children let their food get cold."

"It's true, he does," Diana confirmed.

So they all ate quickly and with gusto. Diana kept her eye on the road. The plan was to give Lissa the gifts Matthew had stashed in the utility closet right after breakfast, with or without Ginny.

The wind picked up, and while Lissa helped them carry the paper plates inside, Ursie pricked her ears and shifted her attention from the table scraps to a cloud of dust swirling down the road. Animals were always the first to know, but eventually all three humans heard the crunch of gravel under tires.

"Mommy's here!"

Lissa and Ursie took off towards the rear of the house. By the time Matthew and Diana got the breakfast trash safely deposited in the kitchen and charged out the back door, Ginny's Subaru was already parked beside Diana's Queen Vic, and Ginny was hauling something big and shiny out of its hatchback.

Matthew's neighbors lived out of sight down the road, but Diana bet they heard the high-pitched squeal of delight when a bright pink bicycle came to rest in the Troutman's driveway.

"Mommy, you bought me a bike!" Lissa screamed. "I've been wanting it forever, it's awesome!"

Everybody clapped and made a fuss. Diana offered up a little prayer of thanks that Ginny had come through for Lissa. She had expected the worst of Matthew's daughter, but was thrilled to be proven wrong.

"It's really beautiful." Diana stroked the padded saddle seat and rang the chrome bell. The bike was retro, almost like the one she'd grown up with, pedal brakes and all.

"Very cool." Matthew adjusted the training wheels. "These will help you learn to ride like a pro."

"Thanks, Mommy. Can I ride it now?"

"Sure, take a spin down the road, but be careful."

Lissa was off in a flash, giggling and wobbling, with Ursie trotting alongside, her ears pinned back as she watched the spinning spokes and considered biting the tires.

"Lookin' good!" Matthew hollered. He wrapped a loving arm around Ginny's waist. "Lissa's a quick-study, just like her mama. Remember your first bike, Ginny?"

But Ginny was busy watching Lissa's jerky progress, breathlessly awaiting the first spill, the first skinned knees.

"She'll be all right," Diana assured her. "The bike was a perfect choice, Ginny."

Ginny smiled and lifted her bloodshot eyes. "Thanks. I bought it at Wal-Mart. It was the only place open Sunday morning."

Ginny's dark hair was tangled and her clothes were way past wrinkled. She stank of sweat, stale beer, and second-hand smoke. "Are you okay, Ginny? We were worried," Diana said.

"Yeah, where were you?" Matthew demanded. "You should have called."

Ginny snorted and faced Diana. "Now you know why I left home. Trout treats *me* like the six-year-old."

Diana refused to be caught in the middle of a father/daughter squabble. "I'll fix you some breakfast, then we can give Lissa the gifts from Matthew and me."

Ginny lifted a suspicious eyebrow. "When did you find time for shopping, Diana?" She trudged wearily towards the house. "Look, all I want is a nap, but I guess I could eat some leftover birthday cake."

Before Matthew could launch into a tirade about Ginny's unorthodox eating habits, they were distracted by a dust cloud and the sound of a car approaching much too fast.

"Shit, I hope Lissa's not riding in the middle of the road." Ginny's tired eyes stretched wide open with fear.

"She'll get outta the way," Matthew said without conviction.

Diana wondered who was coming. Matthew lived at the end of a dead-end street, so the only people who ventured this far usually had business with Matthew. Before she could speculate further, a black and white Davidson police car skidded to a halt, scattering gravel at their feet. She was astonished when a familiar cop in plain clothes climbed out and approached. To say the least, it was not a welcome intrusion.

"Hello, Mr. Troutman, remember me?" The officer tipped an imaginary hat. "My name is Peter Sokolsky. It's *Lieutenant* Sokolsky now." He extended his hand, which Matthew reluctantly shook.

"Did you see a little girl riding her bike?" Matthew growled. "You were driving way too fast for this neighborhood."

Sokolsky shrugged. "Yeah, I saw her and the dog up near the corner."

The bright sunlight glinted off the patrol car, so that Diana had to lift her hand and shield her eyes for a better look. Sure enough, she remembered this character Sokolsky from several years ago, when she'd had a break-in at her condo. He was a small, wiry little man with nervous gray eyes set in a pale face. He had wolf-like features and a Napoleonic complex, but as far as she knew, he was a good cop. They had struck up an uneasy friendship back then because Sokolsky hailed from Camden, New Jersey, right across the river from Diana's native Philly, but that was where the common ground ended.

Ginny blanched white at Diana's side.

"What can we do for you, Lieutenant?" Matthew asked as the officer drew near.

Sokolsky stood too close to Diana and Ginny. Diana noticed the man still favored baggy trousers and colorful Hawaiian shirts—rather flashy attire for conservative little Davidson.

"I have no business with you, Mr. Troutman." Sokolsky stared at both women. "But I want a word with you, Mrs. Rittenhouse, and with this woman I presume is Trout's daughter?"

"Yes, Ginny's my daughter. What do you want?"

"Do you own an old red and white Ford pickup, license plate says *Trout '58*?"

"I do," Matthew answered coldly.

Diana saw the warning tick behind Matthew's left eye and knew his temper was about to boil over.

"But you didn't use it yesterday morning, did you, sir? These two women drove it, didn't they?"

"Yes, we did." Diana broke in. "Ginny did the driving, I was the passenger."

"And you delivered a wedding present to Lori Fowler, is that correct?"

Diana felt Ginny's body trembling. She reached out to give the girl's hand a reassuring squeeze, then held on tight.

"Yeah, we went there." Ginny's voice shook. "But no one was home."

Sokolsky inched so close, Diana could smell lifesavers on his breath. "Did you go inside and search the house, Miss Troutman?"

"Of course not. I rang the doorbells front and back, but no one answered, so Diana and I took the gift and left."

"Dead women don't answer doorbells. Are you sure you didn't go inside Lori Fowler's house?" Sokolsky whispered in a low, menacing voice.

"I told you, no!" Ginny shouted.

"We have a witness, Miss Troutman, so you should level with me."

Matthew anchored a heavy hand on Sokolsky's shoulder. "You heard the lady, Lieutenant, so back off."

At that moment, Lissa arrived on her bike. She was flushed with excitement, with Ursie in tow. The dog was barking like a maniac. She looked up at the cop. "Are you coming to my birthday party?"

Sokolsky ignored the child. "I intend to question you both, Mrs. Rittenhouse, Miss Troutman, so please get into the patrol car. I'll take you to the station in Davidson."

"But it's my daughter's birthday!" Ginny cried.

"Ask your questions here and now, Lieutenant." Matthew said firmly. "No one's going with you to Davidson."

Diana's mind raced as she remembered the fateful day she'd taken Ginny to Highland Gardens. She recalled driving up Shepherd's Road and passing into Iredell County. Sokolsky was a Davidson policeman. He had jurisdiction in Mecklenberg, not Iredell.

"Why are you here, Lieutenant?" she challenged him. "Considering where the murder took place, shouldn't the investigation go to the Iredell County Sheriff?"

Doubt rippled across Sokolsky's face as he checked the watch on his skinny arm. "It's complicated. Lori Fowler died at a Davidson address, and the rest doesn't concern you," he snapped.

But Diana could tell she'd hit a nerve. She knew Sokolsky was insanely ambitious and not above blurring a fuzzy boundary or two. In fact, she'd seen this pissing contest before when a murder occurred on a bridge over Lake Norman—Davidson on one side, Mooresville on the other—and Sokolsky had duked it out for jurisdiction back then.

Nevertheless, today he was the law, and they'd have to put up with it. A large cloud floated across the sun, and Diana felt its chill as she screwed up her courage and whispered into Sokolsky's ear. "Please don't do this. You don't want the child to see you taking us away in a squad car."

"But I need to question you separately." He frowned.

"No problem." Matthew captured Sokolsky's arm and led him decisively towards the lake. "You can sit on the patio and enjoy this beautiful day. Chat with one lady, and then the other."

"Well, I am pressed for time, so it might be more efficient to do it your way."

"And you can eat some of my birthday cake," Lissa said.

Diana peeked at Ginny as the men moved ahead. The young woman's hand was cold and clammy, her eyes expanded in panic. 'Are you okay with this?" she whispered once the men were out of earshot.

"Not really. What should we do?"

Sokolsky spun around. "No more talking, ladies." He crooked his little finger at Diana. "You first, Mrs. Rittenhouse."

"Just tell the truth," Diana warned as she let go of Ginny's hand and moved through the lawn to her interrogation.

SEVENTEEN

Wish come true…

Sokolsky spent about fifteen minutes with Diana, mostly asking questions about the Jeep Diana freely admitted she'd seen in Lori's drive. *Did Diana know who owned the Jeep?* Of course not. *Did Diana go into the house with Ginny?*

"Is that a trick question?" Diana finally lost patience with the man. "I already told you I stayed in the truck the whole time, and I never saw Ginny go into that house."

"Maybe not, but you couldn't see what happened once Miss Troutman went around back, could you?"

"I stayed in the car," Diana repeated.

Sokolsky smiled. "Yes, I already knew that. As I said, we have a witness, and he verifies your story."

Obviously Sokolsky's witness was the blond kid with the skateboard, the one who had crashed into Matthew's truck, the one on TV. That being the case, Diana knew for a fact the boy had stayed out front the whole time, so he couldn't have seen what happened in back, either. If he'd said anything different, he was lying.

"Very good, Mrs. Rittenhouse." Peter Sokolsky smirked. "You passed the exam with flying colors, now I hope your friend Miss Troutman scores half as well."

Bastard.

Diana and Matthew watched Ginny's interview from behind the glass sliders in the living room, as Diana fumed with indignation. She prayed Ginny wasn't doing anything stupid, like lying to a police officer. Diana hated to admit it, but she feared Ginny was lying to everyone. Or at least she was withholding the truth. She was certain Ginny knew who owned that Jeep, but was afraid to implicate him. And she strongly suspected Ginny had entered Lori's house. But her stressed imagination refused to consider the unthinkable.

That worst-case scenario was impossible, because Ginny was Matthew's daughter, the recipient of a genetic code that precluded violence of any kind. Matthew abhorred harming any of God's creatures, let alone a human being, and Ginny had his blood.

Diana believed this at her core, but would the authorities? Judging from the girl's body language during the interview, Sokolsky was giving Ginny a very hard time. As the sun continued to duck in and out of the clouds and whitecaps churned on the lake, Ginny waved her arms, then retreated into her shell. Her complexion shifted from pale to flushed, then back again.

Sokolsky was equally erratic—scowling then smiling, nodding then shaking his head—until Diana no longer knew what to think. No doubt the cop was cross-referencing their stories, and she hoped Ginny would say nothing contradictory. She was dying to know how Ginny had fared, but the only way to find out was to get her alone somehow once Sokolsky left. So Diana began scheming to do just that.

During the ordeal, Matthew avoided watching too closely. Instead, he tossed a tennis ball back and forth to Lissa, with Ursie playing man in the middle.

"Ursie didn't like that cop," he said. "Did you hear her growl? She never does that."

"Yes, I heard." But Diana was more interested in the fact that Ginny's interview was over.

Lissa noticed, too. "Can the man have some cake now?"

"No!" Diana and Matthew said in unison.

"I can wrap it in a napkin and take it to him," the child generously offered.

"No, Lissa, the man is leaving now." Matthew snatched the tennis ball and tucked it in his pocket.

Sure enough, Sokolsky spotted them watching from behind the glass, waggled his fingers and smiled before loping around to his car. Moments later, he fired up the cruiser and left.

Ginny came inside, running nervous fingers through her tangled hair. "Bastard," she muttered.

"My sentiments exactly," Diana called out as Ginny headed for the bathroom. "How did you do?"

"I'm beat. I'm going to bed."

"No, Mommy! We have to light the candles on my birthday cake..." Lissa latched onto Ginny's leg. "Please?"

Ginny grunted something that sounded like assent, so moments later, they all moved to the kitchen. They set plates on the table and were about to light the candles when they noticed Ursie growling at the back door.

"Now what?" Ginny groaned.

"She's waiting for the big bad wolf to come back in his black and white cruiser," Diana said. "Ursie took an instant dislike to the good lieutenant."

"That's one smart dog," Ginny said.

"Is the big bad wolf coming here?" Lissa whispered nervously.

"Oh no, honey." Diana glanced around the corner to be sure everything was okay, and saw a chipmunk taunting Ursie from just outside the screen door. "It was only a joke, now light your candles."

"Don't forget to make a wish." Matthew located matches and did the honors.

Lissa blew hard, and for the second time that morning, six little flames were extinguished. After everyone finished eating, as Ginny prepared for her nap, Lissa shyly approached her mother. "Mommy, can we stay here with Grandpa and Miss Diana?"

Ginny exhaled. "Tell you what, Punkin, that wasn't the plan, but things change. The big bad wolf won't let me leave town…" She cast a meaningful glance at Diana. "So yeah, we can stay here for now."

Lissa took only a moment to process out the stuff about the big bad wolf before digesting the good news. Her little face expanded in a huge smile. "Awesome! My wish came true!"

EIGHTEEN

The presence of a stranger...

Diana was determined to get Ginny alone. She wanted to know, once and for all, exactly what Ginny had seen that day at Lori's house. But once Lissa blew out the candles, the Troutmans began to scatter. Lissa went to get her new bike, Matthew moved towards the storage shed in search of Ginny's old bike, intending to dust it off, add air to the tires, and accompany his granddaughter up the road. Ginny rushed towards the bedroom.

"Wait, Ginny, we need to talk."

"God, Diana, can't you see I'm wasted? I can't function one more minute without some sleep."

Diana clamped a restraining hand on Ginny's wrist. "Sorry, but I want the truth. I also want to know what you told Sokolsky."

Ginny stared out the back window to where Matthew and Lissa were starting out on their adventure. Lissa was hunched over her handlebars, riding gleeful circles around Matthew, who was wobbling and weaving on a rickety old bike much too small for him.

"Check it out..." Ginny said. "Trout looks like a circus bear on a tricycle."

Diana chuckled at Matthew's antics. The man was a good sport, she thought, as the odd couple disappeared up the road. But then she tightened her grip on Ginny. "Please don't change the subject. Did you go into Lori's house that day? The boy witness on the news claimed he found the back door open."

"Jesus, NO! How many times do I have to tell everybody?"

"Okay then, did you see your old boyfriend Trevor at the house?"

Ginny sighed and yanked her wrist free. "Of course not. Why would you ask such a stupid question?"

"It's obvious, isn't it? Did you tell Lieutenant Sokolsky about the Jeep?"

Again Ginny glanced out the window as Diana watched the girl's eyes for the telltale shifting that preceded a lie. Instead, she saw Ginny's eyes change from defiance, to surprise, and then finish with an emotion akin to shock.

"What is it?" Diana followed her glance.

"Speaking of that Jeep..."

Sure enough, the same classic Jeep they had seen in Lori Fowler's driveway was now pulling into Matthew's driveway. The two women huddled close together as it parked. The driver hesitated, extracted his long body from the vehicle, and then stood to his full, tall height in the flickering shade of the pecan tree.

"Is that Trevor?" Diana gaped at the handsome young man in a lightweight tan suit. He tugged at his collar, loosening his tie, then looked warily around the yard. He was like a stealthy hunter stalking prey, or perhaps by the look of uncertainty in his darting eyes, he felt more like the prey— prepared to bolt at the first sign of danger.

"What's he doing here?" Ginny seemed at the point of panic.

"I'd guess he's come to see you, Ginny."

Satisfied the coast was clear, the man took a deep breath and strode towards the house. Diana felt Ginny's cold, trembling fingers on her arm.

"What should I do, Diana?"

"Invite the man in."

"But he hasn't come here in years. Trout hates his guts."

Diana tried to steady the girl. "That was then, this is now. For heaven's sake, get a grip."

Trevor's first knock was timid, his second more bold. Diana practically dragged Ginny to the door. "Listen, you came all the way from Nevada to see him, and now he's here." She opened the door and offered what she hoped was a cordial smile. "Hello, I'm Diana Rittenhouse. Come on in."

He ducked slightly as he crossed the threshold, a habit often shared by tall men used to bumping their heads. He held out his hand. "Hello, I'm Trevor Dula."

"Pleased to meet you." She shook his hand and introduced herself. His skin was warm and moist as he shuffled nervously foot to foot, his soulful eyes never leaving Ginny's face.

"Trev, what are you doing here?" Ginny retreated several paces as Trevor moved into the kitchen.

"Better question is, what are *you* doing here? I never expected to see you again." He peeked at Diana as he tried to keep his emotions in check. He was unsure how much to reveal in the presence of a stranger. Then he focused back on Ginny. "Maynard and Paula said you came looking for me last night."

"I was worried." Suddenly Ginny took Trevor's hand. "God, I'm so sorry about what happened to Lori. I can't imagine…"

"Yes, I'm sorry, too," Diana said. "Her death was a horrible thing."

But Trevor held up one hand in a silent plea. He seemed to want them to stop with the condolences. And at this close range, Diana noticed the man's gorgeous eyes were rimmed with red as he brushed self-consciously at the lapels of his suit.

"Have you been to church?" Ginny was obviously at a loss for words.

Trevor's laugh was bitter. "Since when do I go to church? No, I've been across the street from the church, though, to the damned funeral parlor."

Both Diana and Ginny told him that they were sorry.

"Can I get you something to drink?" Diana felt his curiosity as she inched towards the refrigerator. Clearly Trevor hadn't anticipated finding an unknown woman in Matthew's home.

"No, ma'am, I can't stay."

"Diana is Dad's girlfriend." Ginny blurted it out. "She lives here now."

"No kidding?" Trevor's amazing eyes widened in surprise and a smile tugged at the corners of his expressive mouth. "I never expected Trout…"

"Never mind." Diana cut him off as her neck and face burned. She could have cheerfully murdered Ginny at that moment, because she hated being cast in the role of an on-site mistress. No matter how open-minded Trevor Dula might be, she still felt a wee bit guilty about living in sin. "Are you sure you don't want something to drink?"

"No thanks, really. I need to get home. But I do want to talk to Ginny."

Okay, Diana could take a hint. But before she could excuse herself and hide out in Matthew's bedroom, Ginny captured Trevor's arm and led him through the living room towards the door to the lake.

"We'll talk down on the dock, Diana," she said.

"Nice to meet you, Diana," Trevor called as they left.

Now what? Diana's heart raced as she watched them stroll out onto the pier. Was she simply embarrassed, or frightened by Trevor's sudden appearance in their lives? Something about the man was deeply disturbing, and it wasn't just the animal magnetism that made him sexually attractive. Was it the raw grief she'd seen in his eyes? Trevor's manner was gentle, his bearing almost apologetic as he arrived, and yet... She sensed something hard and cold beneath his polite surface, as though he had two personalities. She had been following the news since the murder and knew Trevor was a decorated war veteran, the recipient of a Purple Heart, a hero by any measure.

But hadn't his military background trained him to kill? Who knew what atrocities he'd seen or perpetrated while in Iraq and Afghanistan. Did he suffer from PTSD? What if the man on the dock with Ginny was a murderer?

Diana watched the couple's body language as they talked. God knew the pair had a lot of catching up to do, lots of blanks to fill in, so no wonder they were waving their arms and gesturing. Trevor ran his hands through his thick black hair. He pulled Ginny into his arms and held her.

Diana panicked. Should she call the police? Surely Matthew had seen Trevor's Jeep pass them on the road. She felt jittery and helpless. She felt like a voyeur. So that by the time Matthew and Lissa returned on their bikes, she was enormously relieved. Matthew spotted the Jeep instantly, and his expression changed from joy to anger as he sent Lissa inside and began stomping through the yard to the dock.

Trevor lifted his head, like a stallion scenting the breeze, sensing trouble. Ginny quickly pulled from his embrace, and Diana was grateful that at least the former lovers had not been kissing when Matthew saw them. She braced herself for a confrontation that never came. Instead, everyone smiled. Matthew shook Trevor's hand, and then all three began walking back through the grass to the parking area.

"Who's that man with Mommy?" Lissa asked.

"He's an old friend of your mother's."

"I want to meet him!"

Before she could stop her, Lissa dashed out the back door and hurled herself at Ginny just as the trio arrived at the Jeep. As Diana emerged, she realized the outward cordiality she'd witnessed down at the dock was an illusion, because the hostility in the air was palpable. Hopefully exuberant little Lissa would improve that atmosphere.

"Hi, Mommy. Does the man want to see me ride my new bike?"

The look on Trevor's face could only be described as shock when Lissa jumped away from Ginny and landed at his feet, hands on her hips, her gap-toothed grin wide and expectant.

"Who are you, honey?" he asked.

"Melissa Troutman. I'm six years old today."

Trevor blinked in confusion as he looked to Ginny. "I didn't know you were married."

Ginny rolled her eyes. "I'm not. It's a long story."

Diana held her breath. Obviously the short conversation on the dock had not filled in all the blanks.

"So, you wanna ride bikes with me?" The child was not to be deterred.

Trevor touched the child's hair and smiled. He glanced at Matthew standing disapprovingly, his arms crossed as he frowned.

"Not today, honey." Trevor quickly walked to his car and climbed inside. Moments later he was gone.

NINETEEN

Life cycles…

Trevor had asked Ginny to attend Lori's funeral, but when the Friday morning of the service arrived, rainy and cold for May, Ginny panicked and decided not to go. Diana had agreed to take her and was already dressed in her somber navy blue suit with matching pumps.

"You can't back out now, Ginny. Trevor's depending on you."

"Not really." She pouted. "You're the one with a morbid fixation on this murder, so you go without me."

Diana heard too much truth in Ginny's words. Somehow being at Lori Fowler's that fateful morning, knowing two of the principals involved, had peaked her curiosity. Matthew had often accused her of having a nose for trouble, or worse, sticking her nose in where it didn't belong, and this time he was right.

"Look, you still have time to get ready, Ginny, so I'll have a cup of coffee, then wait for you in the car."

As usual, Matthew had opted to stay behind and entertain Lissa. Today they planned to try out the new art supplies and paint watercolors together.

"Don't hold your breath, Diana. Ginny won't come. And by the way, why are *you* going?" Matthew had sneaked up behind her. He fixed her with his warm brown eyes and swallowed some coffee.

Diana thought fast. "I already promised Liz and Danny I'd be there. Danny was one of Lori's admirers. He had even been invited to Lori's wedding, so they are going."

"Whatever." Matthew shrugged, strode to the sink, rinsed out his cup. Conversation over.

As Diana walked to Queen Vic, the damp air smelled of pinesap and mist rose off the lake. The odd chill clung to her linen jacket, so once she settled in the car, she turned on the heat. She'd give Ginny ten minutes and prayed she would come, because so far the girl had not been remotely forthcoming about anything involving the murder. And while Ginny was proving to be as stubborn and tight-lipped as her father, Diana had hoped to coax out some information during the ride to the church.

She checked her watch, gave up, twisted the ignition, and was just backing out of the driveway when Ginny burst out the back door.

"Hey, wait up!"

Matthew's daughter had thrown together an outfit that was more than appropriate for the solemn occasion. Her long skirt, boots, and peasant shawl were all black—what Liz would call her "Goth Girl" look. Diana was especially thankful to see she had limited her makeup and removed the silver nose stud.

"Do I look okay?" She jerked the passenger door open and slid in next to Diana.

"You look fine. Let's go."

But clearly Ginny was not in the mood for conversation. As soon as they were on the road, she punched on the radio. It was preset to Diana's favorite classical music, but Ginny immediately switched to heavy metal.

"Not happening." Diana changed back to classical.

"Whatever." Ginny clammed up, and Diana realized they were in for a silent, blessedly short journey.

The heavy rain began about the time they crossed the Perth Road bridge. It sluiced in noisy waves across the water's surface, transforming their world to a blinding gray fog. Diana turned on her headlights and the defroster as the atmosphere inside the car became hot, moist, and oppressive.

"Too bad, today of all days," Diana said. "There's nothing more depressing than a burial in the rain."

"No burial," Ginny mumbled. "Trev said Lori would be cremated."

"Really?" Diana turned the wipers to high and hunched over the steering wheel so she could see.

"Yeah, they sent her body to the medical examiner in Raleigh for an autopsy. He cut her all up to determine cause of death. Maybe they figured it was better to carry her ashes home in a box, rather than bury the pieces."

The coffee in Diana's stomach roiled as she glanced at Ginny. Was the girl unbelievably insensitive, or simply horrified by these details? "So, what was the cause of death?"

"Duh. She was stabbed through the heart."

Diana decided she preferred it when they didn't talk. She made the turn onto Main Street in Troutman and started looking for the turnoff to the Lutheran church, where Matthew was a member. She and Matthew were nominal Christians at best, but she had attended services with him on Christmas Eve and had even met the young pastor.

At the turn, she noticed the funeral home was right across the street, just like Trevor had said. How convenient. Now if only there were a small community hospital nearby, where babies could be born, then folks from Trinity Lutheran could tend to all their life cycle needs, corporal and spiritual, in one easy block.

The church lot was full, so Diana was forced to select a space not far from the front door, a location usually reserved for the deceased's immediate family. She parked directly beside a Davidson police car and groaned inwardly. Surely the cops weren't required today, but who knew? She looked at the colorful array of bobbing umbrellas clustered at the entrance and found them incongruous and wrong somehow. Stupidly, she and Ginny had come without one.

"Let's make a run for it," she said.

"Sure, why not?"

By the time they pushed inside the crowded vestibule, Diana's short white hair and Ginny's black punk cut were wetly plastered to their cheeks. But they had no time for a visit to the ladies' room and a touch-up, because the organ had already begun to play.

"Where should we sit?" Diana wondered as they crept dripping into the chapel. It seemed the mourners had self-segregated, with friends and neighbors of Lori's on the left and the older church regulars on the right. Way up front on the right, Diana spotted Trevor Dula seated with two others. He seemed very much alone and ill at ease in spite of his companions. As usual, the church was packed from the back forward, forcing Diana and Ginny to move up front.

"Aw shit," Ginny muttered as they walked forward. "Everyone's staring at us."

"No, they're not," Diana assured her, but then she noticed Lieutenant Peter Sokolsky seated in the back row, and he was indeed watching them pass. Today he had put aside his baggy trousers and flashy Hawaiian shirt in favor of a conservative dark suit. His wolf-like eyes scanned the crowd.

She also noticed a young deputy from Iredell County standing in the back of the church. He seemed ill-at-ease, arms crossed and shifting from foot to foot as he surveyed the congregation.

Young Billy, the boy from Lori's neighborhood, was also in attendance. His curly blond hair was freshly cut and he sat ramrod straight, looking scared and uncertain. She also saw her partner Liz's red head, along with her boyfriend Danny's curly brown one, lifted above the crowd and was relieved to spot someone she knew. They noticed Diana at exactly the same moment, and Danny beckoned Diana and Ginny to come join them.

"Those are my friends Liz and Danny," she told Ginny. "Do you want to sit with them?"

Much to Diana's surprise, Ginny took her elbow and steered her forward. "No, let's sit near Trev, he needs our support."

They moved into a pew directly behind Ginny's old boyfriend and took a seat. When Ginny tapped Trevor on the shoulder, he turned around and offered a weak, grateful smile. If anything, Trevor's eyes looked worse today than they had last Sunday when he visited them at the lake. They were bloodshot, haunted, and somehow unconnected to his tragic, present reality. Although the man was stunningly handsome in his dark suit and patterned maroon tie, his curly black hair was rain-soaked and his spirit was elsewhere.

A tough-looking young blond woman sat close beside him, her thick hair pulled back in a ponytail. Her heavily made-up face had wilted in the rain and her hard green eyes stared at the altar, where a small wooden box was prominently displayed. The box sat on a table covered with a white silk holy cloth and was flanked by burning candles. Undoubtedly it contained Lori's ashes.

Ginny whispered into Diana's ear. "The woman is Paula Dula. She's Lori's cousin."

The man seated beside Paula was considerably older than his two companions. He had long, flowing silver hair, which matched his carefully trimmed beard and moustache. He was dressed in a neatly pressed black dress shirt, and in place of a tie, wore a silver crucifix encrusted with turquoise around his neck.

"The man is Maynard Dula. He's Paula's husband, and also Trev's uncle," Ginny whispered again.

Diana's mind wandered as the pastor delivered the eulogy. She figured the people with Trevor were the folks with whom Ginny had spent Saturday night. She also assumed that many of the attendees, mostly women, seated on the Lori side of the church were the do-gooders from the many charities Lori had worked with. According to the pastor, the deceased had not held a job, so she had devoted herself to fund-raising for various worthy causes. Had Lori been independently wealthy? Most likely, when one considered her expensive home in Highland Gardens. How had she hooked up with a war vet like Trevor? They seemed an unlikely pair.

As Diana's mind ran wild with hapless speculation, she mouthed the words when they stood for the closing hymn. They remained standing while the minister said a final prayer, telling the murdered girl to rest in peace. He picked up the wooden box and nodded, signaling Trevor and Paula to come forward. He placed the box into Trevor's hands.

As Lori Fowler's two loved ones carried her ashes down the aisle, the rest of the congregation watched their progress. Was it Diana's imagination, or was Paula Dula clinging too possessively to Trevor's arm? While his eyes were blurred by tears, Paula's eyes were adoringly fixed on her husband's nephew's face.

It was not Diana's imagination when Lieutenant Sokolsky slipped into the procession behind Trevor and followed him into the vestibule, out of sight. At the same time, Danny Cappelli, Liz's boyfriend, struggled out of his pew and rushed ahead of the other parishioners who had begun to file into the aisle.

"What's happening?" Ginny craned her neck to see what was causing the commotion in the vestibule. They heard voices raised in anger, and then Maynard Dula jumped from his seat and ran towards the voices. Suddenly everyone wanted to leave at once, pushing and shoving to be the first out, first to satisfy his curiosity.

Rain hammered the roof, and Diana was momentarily paralyzed by the unseemly stampede. Liz then appeared in the aisle and waved cheerily to Diana.

"Where was Danny going in such a hurry?" Diana demanded.

Liz winked. "Call of nature," she answered before being swept away in the tide of people.

By the time Diana and Ginny got out, Danny was just emerging from the men's restroom. Diana grabbed his sleeve. "What's going on?"

"I had to pee," he answered in typical Danny fashion.

"Look outside, Diana." Liz materialized at her side and pointed to where the Iredell County deputy was leading Trevor towards his squad car. It appeared Trevor's hands were cuffed in front of him as the deputy opened the rear door, placed a protective hand on Trevor's head, eased his prisoner into a seat, and closed the door.

At the same time, an irate Lieutenant Sokolsky stood at the sidelines fuming. Apparently he had lost the jurisdictional pissing contest.

In the meantime, Paula stood in the downpour clutching the little wooden box, while Maynard shook his fists and shouted obscenities at the top of his lungs. Ginny looked like she was about to faint, so Diana lowered her to a bench.

"Why is he taking Trev?" Ginny moaned.

"I was right here when it happened," Danny said importantly. "That deputy read the Miranda rights, then arrested the guy."

"But why?" Ginny said.

"For Lori Fowler's murder."

TWENTY

Trust, but verify…

Saturday morning the sun came out and the world was fresh-washed and new. At least that was the hopeful tone Diana tried to impose upon the family as they sat down to breakfast. The adults were glum and silent after a difficult evening and sleepless night. The story of Trevor's arrest dominated the local news, and whenever Ginny caught sight of the television, she paced, ranted, and bit her purple fingernails to the nub.

Matthew sought to avoid the topic altogether, yet it was clear he thought Trevor was guilty. Only Lissa remained oblivious. She ran outside to practice riding her bicycle, with Ursie in tow.

Finally Diana, having exhausted her supply of false good cheer, decided to escape the tension. "I'm going into town for groceries. Anyone want to come along?"

Both Matthew and Ginny shook their heads, so Diana hurriedly dressed, made a shopping list, and rushed out the door before anyone had second thoughts. She badly needed some downtime, a chance to sort out her own conflicted emotions. Not only regarding the murder, but also her role in the Troutman household. Had she made a terrible mistake by moving in during these volatile times? Matthew was distant and distracted, Ginny alternated between indifference and downright hostility, while Lissa was Lissa, the one bright beacon of joy in everyone's life.

She slid into Queen Vic and turned on the engine. Maybe she should skip the groceries and head home to Davidson? After all, her condo remained a little haven of peace and sanity, where she could regroup and rewind. But what about her parrot? No doubt he'd assault her with obscenities the moment she walked through the door. Her kind neighbor had been caring for Perry for over a week now, so it was high time Diana either moved back in, or relocated the bird to Matthew's.

And what about Liz? She'd be waiting to ambush Diana with real estate issues, and truth be told, Diana had forgotten all the details of their pending projects, and she was ashamed. Liz and she were supposed to be partners, but Liz was shouldering all the work. It wasn't fair.

But life wasn't fair. In the end, she didn't have the strength to deal with foul-mouthed parrots or real estate hassles, so for the moment, she'd buy groceries and go with the flow.

"Wait up, Diana!" Suddenly Ginny burst from the house. "Mind if I tag along?"

Diana's spirits sank to the soles of her sensible sandals as Ginny crawled into the passenger seat. Déjà vu. The same last minute decision had occurred yesterday morning, when Ginny decided to attend Lori's funeral. But today, instead of her all-black persona, Ginny wore a pretty yellow sundress and actually looked like a normal southern girl.

"Since when do you like grocery shopping?" Diana asked as they headed down the road. She paused to wave at Lissa riding her bike, with Ursie at her wheels.

"I hate grocery shopping, but that's not why I came along…"

Diana allowed the unfinished sentence to hang between them, almost afraid to ask. Obviously Ginny was agitated about something, but Diana drove all the way to the stop sign and had turned east on River Highway before she dared pursue it.

"Okay, what's up?"

"Everything's fucked up, Diana. The cops have it all wrong. Trev didn't kill Lori, and I can prove it!"

The girl was nearly hysterical. Her words caused Diana to swerve so badly, she decided to get off the road. Luckily, a public pullout was dead ahead, so she drove onto the gravel and stopped.

"Please help me, Diana," Ginny pleaded.

Diana took a deep breath. "Calm down. What are you trying to say?"

"Trev didn't do it!" She pounded the dashboard. "He told me what really happened, but the cops will never believe him."

Diana stared as the girl twisted her hands in her lap. She was in full meltdown. "Just start at the beginning. When did Trev tell you all this?"

"Remember last Sunday when he came to the lake? We went down to the dock together?"

"Sure, I remember."

"Well, I told him how we saw his Jeep at Lori's the day before..." Ginny began to cry. "And I told him how you and I ratted him out to Lieutenant Sokolsky. We told the cops, Diana, and that's why Trev's in jail."

Traffic roared by on River Highway and the sun beat down on the windshield. Diana switched on the ignition, powered up the windows, and turned on the air. "We only told the truth. What else could we do?"

"But it's *our fault,* don't you get it?" Ginny sobbed.

Diana pulled her wits together. "No, it's not our fault. That boy from the neighborhood saw Trevor's Jeep, too. I'm sure he'd seen it at Lori's many times, so the kid told Sokolsky first. Sokolsky was only testing us, to see if we'd lie."

"So it's not our fault?" Ginny daubed at her eyes with the hem of her skirt.

Diana dug into her purse, handed her a tissue. "That's not the point. Fact is, Trevor was there, so he's the prime suspect."

"Not true."

Diana hesitated while Ginny loudly blew her nose. "Do you mean Trevor wasn't there, or Trevor's not the prime suspect?"

"Both," Ginny insisted. "He never drove his Jeep that morning. Someone else must have borrowed it."

"Why should we believe that?"

"Because he has an alibi. He wasn't anywhere near Lori's the day she died."

Diana watched Ginny closely. Trevor had sold her a bill of goods, and she had bought it. "Okay, I'll bite. What's his alibi?"

For the first time that morning, Ginny smiled. "Trev's a veteran, and he has lots of friends at the VA hospital in Salisbury. Some guy named James is in their abuse program, and that morning James was having a birthday breakfast. Trev and his buddies were invited."

"You're saying Trevor was having breakfast at the VA hospital?" Diana blinked in disbelief. "If that's true, then all he has to do is tell the police, and he's a free man."

For a moment Ginny seemed at a loss. She stared out the window at a white fast food bag skidding across the lot. The wind picked it up and tossed it into the highway. "I hear what you're saying, Diana, and believe me, I get it. So why is Trev still in custody? Thing is, I believe Trev, but I don't really know him anymore. He's changed."

Diana read between the lines. Had Ginny seen what Diana had seen in Trevor's eyes? That behind his smile lived a hardened soldier who had witnessed too much horror? Clearly Ginny still cared for the boy she once knew, but did she trust the man?"

"So what can I do to help?" Diana asked.

"Take me to the Veteran's Hospital. Take me now."

TWENTY-ONE

The perfect alibi…

Naturally Diana agreed to take Ginny to Salisbury. The opportunity was like finding a big, ribbon-tied hatbox in her closet. She couldn't resist opening it, and hoped she'd find something beautiful inside, instead of the bloody, severed head she expected.

She couldn't understand, though, why Ginny had included her in this outing. She had her own car, was perfectly capable of making the journey alone, so why hitch a ride with Diana? Diana chose to think that ` their relationship was improving and that the girl needed to bond for moral support, but as they completed the fifty- minute trip, Ginny's true motive emerged.

"I haven't been here for years, so I don't know my way around. Do you know how to find the hospital, Diana?"

So much for bonding. "Yes, I do, we're almost there."

She entered the large campus of the W.G. Hefner VAMC from Brenner Avenue and drove directly to the medical care facility straight ahead. Ginny ran inside for directions, while Diana idled and admired the banks of azaleas in full bloom. Indeed, surrounded by a multitude of imposing brick buildings in the lush, park-like setting, she felt like she was visiting a lovely college campus rather than a facility dedicated to warriors damaged in ugly wars. When Ginny returned, they

132

moved to Building Four for Inpatient Mental Health and parked near the front door.

"I'm nervous," Ginny confessed. "Do you think they'll let us see him?"

"I guess so." But Diana was far from certain. They had arrived not knowing the visiting hours, or even whether patients like Trevor's friend were permitted visitors. Sure enough, they encountered problems at the reception desk.

"Hours for the rehab program are weekends and holidays, 9:30AM – 9:00PM," the young man told them.

So far, so good. Since this was Saturday morning, they had lucked out. The hours also confirmed that Trevor could well have visited last Saturday.

"What's the patient's ID number?"

Diana and Ginny looked at one another.

"His name is James," Ginny said. "I don't know his ID."

The young man frowned. "You must provide the code. Our clients in Substance Abuse have earned their privacy."

But Ginny was determined. She smoothed the bodice of her sundress and turned on the charm. "Please, sir, my brother was here last Saturday morning for James' birthday breakfast and forgot to give him a card."

"Can I see the card?" The man was smitten from the tip of his red head to the soles of his white nurse's shoes. He could not take his eyes off Ginny.

"C'mon, you said the guys deserve their privacy, so why should you get to see James' card?" Ginny batted her eyelashes. "By the way, were you working last Saturday during James' party?"

The man's eyes narrowed. "I was on vacation. So what?"

"Never mind." Ginny sighed.

The man glanced at Diana, who nodded reassuringly, like someone's upstanding mother. "Please tell James we're here, and I'm sure he'll want to see us."

But the guy was still fixated on Ginny. "What's your brother's name?"

"Trev Dula," Ginny lied.

That got his attention. "You shittin' me? Your brother's a certified hero, and he comes here all the time. Jeez, I can't believe they've arrested him for murder. You guys must be really upset..."

"Yes, we are," Diana said solemnly. "Now, may we see James?"

The man seemed shaken by Trevor's predicament and decided to cooperate. "Yeah, I heard some guys came around for his party last week, so yeah, I'll tell James. Can you wait a minute?"

He ushered them into a waiting area, and about ten minutes later, the receptionist returned and invited them into what appeared to be a recreation room. They saw a pool table, small library, large wide-screen TV with a lockbox on the remote, and a row of vending machines. An emaciated young man in pajamas sat alone in a wheelchair.

"What the...?" His sunken eyes darted back and forth in his handsome brown face and finally settled on Ginny. "You really Trev's sister?"

Ginny explained, while Diana's heart went out to the disabled vet. He had lost a foot in combat. His large dark hands trembled on his armrests, but he had a great smile. Once he understood the true nature of their visit, he welcomed them like long-lost friends.

"Can I buy anyone a soda?" Diana asked. She took orders, fed the machine a fistful of quarters, then passed out three cold drinks. She and Ginny settled on the sofa, and while Ginny explained Trevor's need for an alibi, Diana tried not to stare at the single slipper on James' remaining foot.

"How can I help?" James asked.

"Just tell us what happened that morning."

But before getting to the point, the young soldier needed to tell his story—how he suffered from PTSD, which had led to his abuse of alcohol and painkillers, which had led to his ruined liver. Although James seemed upbeat about his future, Diana realized again how much she hated war. This brave young warrior ignited her pacifist fire big-time.

"So it was cool the guys came 'round to celebrate my birthday," he finished.

"How many guys?" Ginny asked.

"Trev and four others. That's how come Trev drove his old station wagon, so they'd all fit in."

"Trevor owns a station wagon?" Diana said.

James laughed, winked at Ginny. "Oh yeah, but he hates drivin' it. Prefers his Willy's. We call it his macho machine, the chick magnet."

"Right, like Trevor needed a chick magnet when he was engaged to be married." Ginny said sourly.

Suddenly James got very serious. "You're right. Trev don't play around no more. Like, he really loved Lori. She was his life. That's why it's such a fuckin' joke they arrested him. Dumb-ass cops." He shot an apologetic look at Diana. "Pardon the language."

So in your opinion, Trevor did not kill Lori?" Diana wanted clarification.

135

"No way."

In the silence that followed, Diana noticed Ginny had gone a little green around the gills. Perhaps all the talk of Trevor's love for his lost Lori had upset her.

"So this is good news," Diana said. "When the police come here, and they will, you'll tell them Trevor spent the morning with you. The perfect alibi. End of story."

But James rolled his eyes at the ceiling and sighed deeply. "Not exactly. I'm afraid it didn't go down like that."

"What do you mean?" Ginny demanded.

"I can't alibi Trev." James was a picture of misery. "My party never happened 'cause I got sick. Convulsions. They had to take me out and stabilize me, so everyone left around 9:30."

Diana's hopes plummeted. "I'm so sorry, James. Do you think the guys went out for breakfast someplace when they left? Stands to reason. They were together, they were hungry…"

"Nope, 'fraid not." James cut her off. "I've heard from the others since. They told me Trev was really upset because I got sick. He dropped them off at the pancake house, then said he was going home. Alone."

"Shit," Ginny muttered.

Diana did the math. If Trev dropped the guys off, then returned home for his Jeep, he still had time to reach Lori's place in Davidson ahead of Diana and Ginny, and that would explain his Jeep in her driveway.

Shit! Diana kept that sentiment to herself.

TWENTY-ONE

Back to work…

Sunday passed without incident. They cooked hotdogs and hamburgers on the grill. Lissa played with her new beach toys, while Ginny sat in the shade of a willow oak tree strumming her guitar and staring out at the lake. She was actually a very talented musician. Matthew and Diana fell asleep before the end of a Disney movie they had rented, and no one discussed the futile trip to the VA hospital. By Monday morning, Diana decided it was high time to get off her butt and back to work.

"I'll pick up Perry when I'm in town," she told Matthew as she was leaving.

Matthew attempted a smile. "Great."

"Awesome! I can't wait to meet your parrot," Lissa squealed.

Liz was waiting to pounce the moment Diana entered their office. "It's about time you showed up to earn your keep. I was beginning to forget I had a partner."

"Sorry, you're right, Liz." Diana walked across the sea-green carpet that always reminded her of the Mediterranean on a sunny day. She dropped her purse on her blond butcher-block desk, which remained as clear of work as it had been when she deserted it a little over a week ago. It felt like she'd been gone a month. "What's happening?"

"Not much. I got a terrific lead this morning."

Diana glanced at Liz in surprise. No wonder she was in such a sassy mood. Her cheeks were pink with excitement, her green eyes sparkled. "So tell me about it."

"Not yet. First tell me about *you,* girlfriend. Seems like you and yours are at ground zero in that Lori Fowler murder. How are you and Trout handling the notoriety?"

Diana sighed as her eyes drifted around the little office condo she and Liz had purchased. Usually the casual tropical décor—cheerful pastel fabrics on comfortable wicker furniture, modern posters with Lake Norman themes—helped her relax. After all, they had designed the space to put potential clients in a vacation mood, but lately, with the market crash and a two-year dearth of business, she and Liz often panicked. They worried how they'd pay the mortgage, let alone buy groceries. They were adrift in a real estate dead zone.

"Please tell me some good news," Diana begged.

But Liz was hungry for juicy details. "C'mon, Diana, how is General Ginny holding up now that her old boyfriend's been arrested?"

Diana flopped onto the couch, pushed off her sandals, and told Liz about their visit to the VA hospital.

"Ah, so Trevor has no alibi, after all." Liz seemed delighted by the bad news.

Diana decided to clear the air. "Look, Liz, I understand you and Ginny had issues when you were kids at summer camp, but it's time to box up the past and put it away. Over the past week, I've gotten to know Ginny, and she's okay. She's had a hard life and she's doing the best she can. She's wonderful with

Lissa, and I really want her to reconcile with Matthew, so can you give the old animosity a rest? Please?"

Liz paused to consider. Her amazing green eyes shifted back and forth, scanning Diana's face for wiggle room. "Okay, you've got a deal. I lay off Ginny, if you dish some dirt about you and Trout. How do you like living together? How do y'all handle the bedroom issues with family in the house?"

Diana's face burned. She swung her legs off the couch and sat bolt upright. Even had she been inclined to answer Liz's impertinent questions—which she was not—she was so personally conflicted about the whole co-habitation situation she wouldn't know what to say.

"Well, I never signed on to be a Mama and a Grandma, that's for sure. I've been there, done that."

"I hear you. Do you think Ginny will stick around?"

"I really don't know." She did know Trevor's arrest had upset Ginny a great deal. The past two days she'd been drinking too much and seemed restless.

"But if Ginny decides to stay, how will it affect you and Trout?"

That question was even tougher. "Time will tell."

Liz crossed the room and sat down beside her. Her fingers brushed Diana's hand. "Okay, then, if Ginny and Lissa keep living with Trout, will you move out?"

Diana laughed and squeezed Liz's hand. "Not if I can help it. In fact, one of my missions today is to collect Perry and take him back with me. Lissa's dying to meet him."

"Oh yeah? Wait 'til your parrot starts teaching that little girl to cuss." Liz grinned. "Does that mean Danny and I get to keep Amazing Grace? You know Danny adores your dog."

"No, but nice try. By next week, if we're still together, I'll pick up Gracie and introduce her to my extended family."

Liz frowned. "I'm serious, Diana. We really want to keep Gracie."

"Sorry, but the answer is no. Now, will you please tell me about your big lead? I need some good news."

Liz skipped to the mini refrigerator and took out two diet sodas. She popped the caps and handed one to Diana. "You won't believe it. The call came in first thing this morning, so this commission is all mine."

"Oh, give me a break and start talking."

"My hot new client wants to buy that big monstrosity under construction up at Lakeview Estates."

"No way!" Diana had received that listing from a young couple in financial trouble. They had built a partial foundation and studs for a six- thousand square foot mini-mansion on three acres when the stock market crashed. The husband was suddenly an unemployed banker, and they were offering the property "as is" at the distressed sale price of just under two million.

"Am I not amazing?" Liz beamed. "And would you believe the client does not require a mortgage? It'll be a cash sale."

Diana was stunned. In the current financial crisis, such clients were manna from heaven. "Who is this guy? How did he find us?"

"First, it's not a *guy*, it's a *gal*." Liz gloated. "And second, I put my business card in her hot little hand at Lori Fowler's funeral last week. You know me, Diana—always networking."

"Please don't tell me you were doing business when they arrested Trevor Dula."

"Actually, I met this woman before all that shit hit."

"Who is she?"

Liz took a slow, seductive swallow of soda. "Would you believe the client is married to Trevor's uncle? She is Paula Dula. That name has a certain ring about it, don't you think?"

Diana was blown away. Her memory of Paula and her husband, Maynard, was still quite fresh. She saw them standing in the rain—Paula holding the wooden box with Lori's ashes, Maynard shaking his fists and shouting obscenities at Lieutenant Sokolsky.

"There must be some mistake…"

"No mistake." Liz insisted. "I'm meeting Mrs. Dula at the site this afternoon. She's already seen it from a distance. Seems her husband supplied some of the lumber. She says she'll bring her checkbook."

"But where would she get the money?" Ginny had told Diana that Maynard's construction company was on the verge of bankruptcy. "Ginny said they live in a dump."

"Maybe that's the whole point? Paula Dula doesn't want to live in a dump."

Diana could not wrap her mind around the entire bizarre event. "How does Maynard feel about buying such a property?"

"Beats me." Liz shrugged. "Near as I can tell, Mrs. Dula's buying it on her own. She didn't mention anything about bringing Hubby along."

Diana was in shock. "I don't get it. Isn't Paula Dula Lori Fowler's cousin?"

"Who the hell cares?" Liz lifted her soda can in a toast.

141

Diana toasted back. "May I come with you this afternoon, Liz? I have to see it to believe it."

But Liz shook her red curls. "Sorry, girlfriend, you have a shitload of paperwork to catch up with. So why don't you put in a couple hours floor time, then collect your parrot and go on home?"

TWENTY-TWO

Dinner with Mama…

A small notice in the local paper stated that Trevor Dula would be arraigned that coming Friday afternoon at the Iredell County Courthouse, and the news sent Ginny spiraling downward—more drinking, more cursing. Sometimes she and Perry seemed like soulmates, and Diana wasn't sure which influence was teaching little Lissa to use foul language. Either way, Matthew did not approve. He moved the parrot to the bedroom they shared, and warned his granddaughter to stay clear.

Then Wednesday night Lissa stepped into a fire ant hill, and the vicious little buggers stung her feet until she screamed in pain. Matthew went running for Club Soda, the sure-fire southern fire ant killer, and doused the mounds. Diana slathered Lissa's toes with allergy cream, while Ginny fed her ice cream, but nothing would comfort the stricken child.

When torrential rains arrived the next day, Diana decided everyone, especially Lissa, needed a change of pace, so she invited the child to accompany her to dinner with Diana's mother. Vivian lived at Shady Oaks Retirement Community in Statesville, and it was her habit to eat with Diana every Thursday night.

"You missed our date last week," Mama scolded as she led Diana and Lissa into the Oaks dining room.

"Sorry, it was a busy time."

"Yes, so you said."

Diana heard the disapproval in Mama's voice. They spoke on the phone most every day, so Diana had filled Viv in about Ginny, Lissa, and the family's unlucky proximity to the Lori Fowler murder. Mama highly approved of Matthew and had long been encouraging Diana to take their romance to the next level, but she'd never anticipated the ready-made family. She hated Diana's involvement with the sordid crime, that was a given, yet she was titillated by the idea of finally getting a great-granddaughter.

As they entered the airy dining room and moved towards Mama's table, Lissa took Mama's hand. The child had dressed all in pink for the occasion, from her dainty bow and lacey dress to her flip-flops.

"I got bit by fire ants." Lissa pointed at her feet.

Mama frowned. She was a stockings and patent leather pumps type matriarch. "Yes, I see your toes are covered with little bumps. They must be quite painful."

"They hurt like hell!" Lissa's high-pitched voice carried all through the room.

"Watch your language, young lady." Mama's stare was as cold as dry ice.

"Whoops, I'm sorry." Lissa smiled, then skipped to where a distinguished-looking white haired gentleman was laughing and beckoning them to join him.

"Who's he?" Diana was shocked to see a man at Mama's table. He was a distinct rarity in that sea of elderly women.

Mama was proud as a peacock with a brand new egg. "If you bothered to visit, you'd know that he is Lincoln Davis. We've been dining together for two weeks now."

"Sounds serious," Diana mumbled as the courtly fellow held out chairs for Vivian, Diana, and Lissa. "Is your name really *Lincoln Davis*?" she asked once they were seated.

Again the hearty laugh. "I'm afraid so. Mother was a Yankee and Father was a Reb, so they compromised with my name. Please call me Linc."

"So your parents were like my parents,' Diana said. "Mama's from right here in Statesville, but Daddy was a Pennsylvania farmer."

"Yes, I know. Your mother and I have much in common." The wink Linc tossed at Mama got her blushing to the roots of her white pageboy haircut.

Diana liked the man already. He made a fuss over Lissa and helped her choose a burger and fries from the always excellent menu. He ordered tilapia, while she and Mama opted for the sinful fried chicken. Traditional southern sides were always delicious at the Oaks. Linc's manner was convivial, his conversation humorous, and by the time they finished dessert, Diana was very happy she'd come.

"Take a look over there, Lissa." Linc pointed to the door where a beautiful golden retriever was greeting the residents as they left their tables. "That's Dory, our therapy dog. Wouldn't you like to meet her?"

"Can I, Diana?"

"Sure, go ahead."

The child was off in a pink blur of excitement, and suddenly the adults were alone. Typically, Mama's conversation would then turn to Diana's inadequacies and short- comings, but Linc diverted the topic to his many years of service as a local attorney.

Diana liked him even better. "What kind of law?"

He poured coffee for everyone. "Nothing sexy. Mostly contracts, wills, and trusts. In fact, I was old Loveless Fowler's lawyer, God rest his soul. Poor Love would flip in his grave if he knew one of his beloved nieces had been murdered."

"The uncle's name was *Loveless*?" Diana was aghast.

Linc nodded. "Old family name. Fowler always claimed he was doomed from birth to be a lonely bachelor. He owned the brick factory here in Statesville, and anyone can do that math. We live on red clay, red clay equals brick, and everyone in North Carolina wants a brick home. So Love was a multimillionaire, but the money never made him happy."

"I remember Loveless." Mama took a sip of coffee. "He was two grades ahead of me in school, and he was a queer duck even then."

"Never married, never had children, but Love's two brothers provided him with the nieces he adored," Linc said.

"What happened to his money?" Mama had a knack of getting to the juicy heart of any topic. "Were the brothers rich, too?"

Linc shook his amazing head of snowy hair. "Both brothers are dead now. Lori's daddy was a thrifty man, so he left Lori enough to buy her a fancy house in Davidson. Paula's daddy, however, blew his fortunes on gambling, drink, and fast women. Left Paula only a fistful of change. I hear she gave that money to her husband, Maynard Dula, to start his construction company."

"Maynard is Trevor's uncle, and Trevor was engaged to Lori. Seems like an awfully tight little circle," Diana commented.

"Our whole world is one very small town," Linc said.

Diana's mind scrolled back to Monday at the office, when Liz told her that Paula Dula was their new client. She was poised to buy a property worth nearly two million, and Diana explained the situation to her mother and Linc. "So where would Paula get that kind of money?"

Lincoln Davis put down his coffee cup and carefully daubed at his moustache with a linen napkin. Most residents had left the dining room, so the only sounds were the muted clatter of dishes being washed and the faraway chatter of the kitchen help. "That's an excellent question, Diana. I can only assume that Lori's untimely death has unlocked old Love's trust fund."

"Trust fund?" Diana and Vivian echoed in unison.

"Oh, yes." Linc's deep brown eyes were thoughtful. "Love set aside close to ten million for his nieces in a trust. As I recall, the money was to be divided equally between the girls provided certain odd conditions were met…"

At that moment Lissa burst into the room, shattering the stillness. She hopped up to the table and propped one tiny foot on her empty chair. "Lookee…" She wiggled her toes. "Dory the dog licked me, and now the ant bites don't hurt at all."

"That's good, dear," Mama said.

"Damn right!" Lissa grinned, exposing the gap between her two front teeth, as Mama recoiled in disgust.

"Sorry, Mama, she's going through a phase."

Linc laughed and stood up. He helped Vivian and Diana by easing out their chairs. "We all have bad habits…" He patted a box-like lump in his breast pocket. "Mine is smoking. I'm stepping out on the patio now to indulge. Care to join me, ladies?"

Diana checked her watch. "We need to get home."

Mama scowled. "You know how I feel about cigarettes, Lincoln."

But Diana's brain was still stuck on the Fowler nieces. She turned to Linc. "Do you recall what those odd conditions were that were placed on the Fowler Trust?"

Linc scratched his head. "I'm sorry, ma'am, but it was a long time ago. I don't remember one damn thing about it."

TWENTY-THREE

Arraignment...

Diana knew all along that Ginny would want to attend Trevor's arraignment, so when Friday afternoon rolled around, they went together. It seemed they had bonded over a murder investigation, of all things, but Diana was grateful for any opportunity to gain Ginny's trust. Besides, by now Diana was hooked on the mystery and wouldn't miss this next chapter for all the barbeque in Carolina.

They drove into Statesville. Diana turned onto East Water Street and approached the modern façade of the new Iredell County Courthouse. Deep shadows stretched across the parking lot and the sky was robin's egg blue, a perfect May afternoon. County workers fled the building in droves. They were eager to start the weekend, and it struck Diana that this was an odd time to hold an important arraignment. Surely the court officials would be grouchy and restless, even the judge, which might not bode well for poor Trevor.

They parked and entered the court against the flow, and because she'd been there before, Diana wasn't surprised by the tight security. They gave up their purses to be searched for weapons, then walked through the scanners. The process made Ginny excessively nervous.

"Do they think we're gonna shoot someone?"

"You never know…" Diana glanced at Ginny, who had taken special care dressing in a lightweight wheat pants suit. Her dark hair was freshly washed, her makeup minimal. She had offered a half apologetic explanation for her conservative attire, saying, "Maybe Trev will need a character witness?" But Diana suspected a simpler motive—that Ginny wanted to look drop dead gorgeous when she came face to face again with her ex-boyfriend.

Diana steered them towards the large courtroom where she'd once done jury duty, but instead they were turned away and sent to a smaller chamber, where most pre-trial hearings were held. As they drew near, Diana saw Lieutenant Sokolsky skulking off by himself. As he walked rapidly towards them, she noticed a service revolver strapped under his flapping Hawaiian shirt, plastic cuffs hung on his belt—a bizarre fashion statement.

"I've been looking for you," he said. "I called the house, but Mr. Troutman said you were coming here. Since this arraignment was also on my to-do list, I figured we'd hook up sooner or later."

"What now?" Ginny eyed the lieutenant with utter contempt. "This isn't even your jurisdiction."

"It'll wait until after." He treated them to his famous, wolf-like smirk.

They filed into the room behind a small group of fidgety young men dressed in suits and ties. Diana guessed they were Trevor's veteran buddies. She spotted Paula and Maynard Dula holding hands. They seemed tense as cats on a hot tin roof—during a lightning storm.

"Hi, guys." Ginny rushed right up to the couple.

"Hey there, Jailbait." Maynard gave Ginny a friendly hug. He looked much the same as he had at Lori's funeral—same black dress shirt, same gray hair—only today his mane was controlled in a tight ponytail.

"Hello again." Paula's hard green eyes gave Ginny the once-over, not liking what she saw. When Ginny introduced Diana, Diana wondered if Paula's cold appraisal of Ginny might not be pure jealousy. She still recalled the possessive way Paula had clung to Trevor's arm at the funeral.

"I know who you are." Paula eyed Diana with curiosity. "You are Liz McCorkle's partner, right?"

"Yes, we share a real estate office…" Diana was about to take it further, to ask Paula how she'd liked the property at Lakeview Estates, but then she saw a subtle, intense warning in the woman's eyes and the slight shake of her head. If what Liz suspected was true, that Paula had not yet shared her intention to purchase with her husband, then Diana had better let the subject drop.

"What's gonna happen at this hearing?" Ginny whispered as the bailiff began herding them deeper into the chamber.

Diana explained that the arraignment hearing was simply a formality, where the accused is advised of his rights, informed of the specific charges against him, and either released on his own recognizance or had his bail set. Sometimes, when a serious felony was alleged, the accused might be remanded to jail without bail.

"God, I hope they don't set the bail too high," Ginny said. "I don't think Trev has much money."

"Neither do I." Maynard obsessively fingered the silver crucifix hung round his neck. The man was in obvious misery.

"Don't worry, I'll post the bail." Paula haughtily shook her long blond hair. "I can afford it."

Diana was the only one not surprised by Paula's statement. Ginny's eyes blinked, and Maynard's mouth hung open as the bailiff shushed them to silence. He ushered the four of them into a row together. Paula scooted in first, with Maynard beside her, then Ginny and Diana. Trev's veteran buddies sat halfway back, while Sokolsky remained standing.

Next a guard brought Trevor Dula in from a holding cell. Diana had expected the prisoner to be clad in the traditional orange jumpsuit, or even the black and white stripes still used for county inmates, but instead, Trevor wore his funeral clothes. The guard released his handcuffs, and as Trevor sat at a simple table left of the judge's bench, a serious young man in a crisp suit and horn-rimmed glasses greeted him.

"Is that Trev's lawyer?" Ginny asked Maynard. "He looks familiar."

"Yeah, that's Mecklin Adams all growed up," Maynard said. "He and Trev went to school together."

"You're kidding? That's Geek?" Ginny giggled. "He tutored in my school. Guy's a real computer wiz. Does he still stutter?"

"Lord, I hope not."

"But we know he's as smart as Einstein, so maybe he'll get Trev off," Ginny said.

"Lord, I hope so."

As Diana listened to their banter, she watched Trevor's face. He was pale, withdrawn, still carrying his grief for Lori Fowler like a yoke around his neck. Ginny was right. No way had this man murdered his beloved fiancée.

"All rise!" the bailiff called out, and the judge entered the room.

His Honor wore shorts under his black robe and seemed exceedingly irritated. He glanced at Trevor, then pointed to a television monitor mounted on the wall. "Why is the defendant present? We usually do these hearings via video conference."

Trevor's lawyer inched nervously from behind his table. "Lieutenant Sokolsky from Davidson has been cooperating with Iredell. He requested that Mr. Dula be present in the courtroom today."

The judge was unimpressed. "And why the hell am *I* presiding? These Friday add-ons are supposed to be held in Mooresville."

Geek loosened his collar. "Again, Your Honor, Lieutenant Sokolsky requested the bail hearing be set in Statesville. I understand there's new evidence."

"Well, whoever's pulling the strings 'round here better have a damn good explanation…"

"That would be me, Your Honor." Lieutenant Sokolsky sprinted front and center. He beckoned to Geek. "Join me at the bench, Counselor?"

The annoyed judge crooked a finger at the two men, and they moved in close. Geek kept his head low, speaking in soft, measured tones, while Sokolsky gestured and waved his arms. Diana would have given her favorite hiking sandals to hear their conversation. The judge frowned, nodded, and shook his bald head. Finally, Diana and everyone else heard the judge say "oh shit" louder than a stage whisper.

"What's happening?" Ginny wondered.

At the same moment, Trevor glanced back at Ginny and their eyes locked in what Diana would describe as an intimate embrace. It all happened so fast, the spectators never had a chance to be seated.

The judge stood and raised his hand. "Listen, folks, it looks like this whole sorry mess was a false alarm. Case dismissed. Sergeant Major Dula, you are hereby cleared of all charges, you are free to go."

The audience froze in momentary disbelief, and then pandemonium broke loose. The veterans cheered and pumped their fists in victory. Ginny hugged Diana so hard her ribs ached. Maynard Dula, who still seemed in shock, turned to his wife, Paula, and wryly said he reckoned she could put away her checkbook now.

Trevor was stunned, but a tentative smile tugged at the corners of his mouth as he shook hands with his lawyer. Gradually they moved down the aisle to freedom.

"Way to go, Trev!" his buddies yelled.

Paula stumbled across three sets of legs to be the first to hug Trevor. Next Ginny trampled Diana's feet to be next in line. Ginny gave Trevor a big kiss on the cheek. Finally, Diana and Maynard offered their congratulations, and the relief in the room was palpable. No one wanted to condemn a war hero.

"I guess we'll never know if the lawyer still stutters," Diana muttered stupidly, but no one heard her.

At the same time, Lieutenant Sokolsky and the Iredell deputy came up behind them. The deputy planted a hand on Ginny's shoulder. "May I have a word, Ms. Troutman?"

"Later…" Ginny shrugged off his hand. "Can't you see we're celebrating? Maybe next time you dumb cops will get it right."

"Yeah, maybe we will," the deputy said. He yanked the set of cuffs off his belt, held Ginny's wrists together, and suddenly she was his prisoner.

"What the hell do you think you're doing?" Diana intervened.

Sokolsky stepped forward. "It's obvious, isn't it? He's arresting her for Lori Fowler's murder."

TWENTY-FOUR

About Ginny's character...

Tears blinded Diana as she tried to drive. The scene at the courthouse had been intolerable as the deputy read Ginny the Miranda Warning, then dragged her away as she cried to Diana for help. Trevor had lost his temper, calling the young officer every obscene name a Sergeant Major could conjure. Maynard and the lawyer tried to reason with the deputy, and only Paula stayed calm. Diana hadn't seen Paula offering to pull out her checkbook on Ginny's behalf.

She drove into Matthew's driveway, wiped her eyes with the back of her hand, took multiple deep breaths in an effort to compose herself, and wondered how in heaven's name she could explain all this to Matthew. Eventually, she opened the car door and stepped shakily onto the gravel. Only then did she notice the Iredell County Sheriff's car parked a discreet distance down their road. Maybe the explaining had already been done.

God help them all. Diana started up the walkway, entered the kitchen, then moved towards the muffled voices coming from the living room. Matthew was seated in his chair facing a big man on the couch. Matthew climbed to his feet, opened his arms, and gathered her into his embrace. She felt the heavy beating of his heart and the defeated slope of his shoulders as he held her tight.

"Oh, Matthew, I'm so sorry." Clearly he'd heard the news.

He returned her hug in a feeble attempt to comfort them both, then turned to their visitor. "Wayne was kind enough to come here and give me an update."

"Hello, Wayne." Sheriff Wayne Bearfoot was a longtime friend. Over the years, the physically imposing Cherokee lawman had supported them through some difficult situations and socialized with them in the good times. Today he was somber and unsmiling, and because he wore shorts and a casual shirt, Diana knew he was there unofficially, working off the clock.

"Where's Lissa?" Suddenly Diana was worried about the child.

Matthew nodded out to the lakefront, where Lissa was blissfully throwing tennis balls into the shallows. Then Ursie would gallantly retrieve them, gallop through the grass, and drop them at her feet.

"Does she know?"

"Of course not." Matthew was firm. "And for now, all she needs to know is that her mama's staying with some friends." He guided Diana to sit beside Bearfoot, then returned to his chair.

"I'm so sorry, Diana." Bearfoot's dark eyes were sad, his angular jaw and high cheekbones betrayed his tension. "I hate being the bearer of bad news, but Sokolsky gave me a heads-up. He knew we were friends, so he suggested a face-to-face."

"Sokolsky's a jerk," Diana muttered. "The man can't seem to get anything right."

Bearfoot stared at his large hands, weighing words before he spoke them. "I can't help but agree. I've never met your daughter, Trout, but considering the family she comes from, I can't imagine Ginny would be capable of such a crime."

"And I was with her that morning," Diana interrupted. "Ginny never entered Lori's house, never had time to stab that girl. I say again, Sokolsky's crazy."

The sheriff ran his long fingers through his raven black hair. "Sokolsky's ambitious, but he's not crazy. He jumped the gun with Trevor Dula, but he feels he's got enough to bring Ginny to trial."

Diana felt sick. She glanced at Matthew, who had aged ten years since she'd left that afternoon. His habitually tanned face was pale, his warm brown eyes glazed with pain. "Has everyone gone mad? Where's the evidence?" she demanded.

The men glanced at one another. Neither was willing to speak first, but at last, Matthew cleared his throat. "We have a problem, Diana. Ginny lied. She outright lied to you, to me, and to the cops. She did enter Lori Fowler's home that morning."

His words hit like a sucker punch to her gut, and suddenly she felt slightly dizzy. "But that's ridiculous. How do you know?"

"I'm afraid Ginny left fingerprints," Bearfoot said. "They found a bottled water on Lori's counter. Ginny had taken it from the refrigerator, twisted off the cap, and taken one sip. Her prints were on the fridge and the bottle."

Diana was unconvinced. "No, I don't believe it. How do they know they were Ginny's prints?"

Matthew broke in. "Yeah, how the hell could they tie those prints to Ginny? She's never been in any serious trouble."

Again Bearfoot hesitated, seemingly lost in watching little Lissa toss balls. While they waited for a response, Diana listened to the incessant ticking of Matthew's grandfather clock.

"Okay, here's the story, folks," Bearfoot said. "I don't love Sokolsky, either, but he is efficient. Before we took over the case, his crime team ran all the prints found in Lori's house through the National Database, and Ginny popped up with big red flags beside her name. Seems she got into trouble out in Las Vegas. While she was working in a casino, she stole some old lady's slot machine winnings, a bag worth close to six thousand dollars. Security caught Ginny hiding it in her locker. It was an ill-conceived theft, considering they have cameras all over those casinos. Long story short, Ginny was convicted on a felony theft charge and served some time. She has a criminal record."

Diana and Matthew were speechless, staring miserably at one another. "Did you know about this, Matthew?"

"Not until this moment."

Diana noticed a little vein throbbing beside Matthew's eye and realized his initial shock was being replaced by anger. As she considered Ginny's lies, Diana's dizzy sensation turned to frustration. "What was Ginny thinking? What happened to Lissa while she was in prison?"

Wayne Bearfoot lifted a file from the floor near his shoe and began to read. "Believe it, or not, I can actually answer that question. Like I told you, Sokolsky was thorough. At the time Ginny was arrested, she had divorced her husband, Charles Harkin, and had been employed at the casino only two months. She claimed she stole the money out of desperation to support her minor child. The file says Ginny showed extreme remorse, and oddly, Miss Washam, the old lady she stole from, took pity. Miss Washam owned a Bed and Breakfast in Vegas and

159

convinced the authorities to allow Melissa to live with her during Ginny's brief incarceration...

"Oh, and here's a footnote. After she was released, Ginny also stayed at Miss Washam's for several years, and they became good friends."

"That's a strange story," Diana said.

Matthew agreed. "Doesn't the fact that Miss Washam forgave Ginny and took her in make a difference? Doesn't it say something positive about Ginny's character?"

Bearfoot shook his head. "Not really. It says something positive about Miss Washam, but Ginny still did the crime. Ginny still left her prints at the scene of Lori Fowler's murder."

"And Ginny lied," Matthew added. He looked as grim and angry as Diana had ever seen him.

Diana understood. If Ginny had been nearby, she'd have cheerfully wrung her stupid neck. On the other hand, she refused to believe Matthew's daughter was a murderer. "But what about Trevor's Jeep in Lori's drive, and what was Ginny's motive?"

Bearfoot closed his file. "You're right about the Jeep, Diana, no one's got a handle on that yet. But the police psychiatrist interviewed Trevor backwards and forwards, and she believes he loved his fiancée and did not kill her. The military provided Trevor's history, and while he has some problems with PTSD, those shrinks still insist Trevor is not a psychopath capable of murder."

"Were any other suspicious fingerprints found in Lori's house?" Matthew asked.

"Nothing in the Database. Of course, Trevor's were everywhere, but since the guy practically lived there, that was to be expected. The knife itself had been wiped clean."

Bearfoot turned back to Diana. "And I promise you, our department still has Trevor under surveillance. Worse case scenario? Ginny and Trevor planned and executed the crime together, in which case it would be premeditated murder— subject to the death penalty. It would be better for Ginny to plead an old-fashioned crime of passion."

"Except she didn't do it." Matthew rose abruptly and left the room.

Diana knew Matthew had redirected his fury at Bearfoot. He wanted his old friend to presume Ginny innocent, but that was asking too much. Even Diana realized the case against Ginny was damning, and she suspected the cops had discovered some sort of a motive. But Diana didn't ask, didn't want any more bad news. Instead, she thanked Wayne for coming and requested the particulars: where had they taken Ginny, and what came next? Once he had answered all her questions, she walked him to his car.

"This is hard on Matthew, Wayne. I'm sure he doesn't blame you."

Matthew had refused to bid his friend goodbye. He had gone down to the lake, where he was now tossing balls with Lissa. Diana and Bearfoot watched them playing for a long, silent moment.

"What's Matthew going to do?" Bearfoot was at a loss.

Diana swallowed the lump in her throat. "Right now, I suspect he's trying to decide how to tell that little girl why her mommy's not coming home."

TWENTY-FIVE

The legend…

Lissa finally fell asleep, but not until Diana read her three chapters of *Alice Through the Looking Glass*. They had promised to rent the new movie "Alice in Wonderland" next time they visited the video store, but Diana had some doubts. The entire story—pot-smoking caterpillars, the evil red queen, the horrifying Jabberwockyt—these characters scared Diana, so what would they do to a six-year-old?

True to his word, Matthew had concocted a story for Lissa about Ginny staying with some old friends for a few days. They made sure she didn't see the evening news, which most certainly covered the arrest, and they basically let her eat too much ice cream. For the moment, Lissa was satisfied, but kids were smart. Eventually she'd question all the extra attention, sense something was wrong, and they'd have to share some version of the truth. At least that was Diana's assessment.

But Matthew was either in denial about his daughter's predicament, or unable to discuss it. Or maybe he feared his anger would explode if he let it out, causing collateral damage to both Diana and Lissa. Diana appreciated that he was a man of few words, who wanted to shield his loved ones from hurt, who was uncomfortable with emotional excess. So she wasn't surprised when he got restless listening to the details Bearfoot had laid out and commented only when Diana mentioned they might have to post bail.

"If it comes to it, I have money, Diana. I'll mortgage the damned house, if necessary."

Matthew was seldom profane, but when he was, Diana knew to steer clear. Their great experiment of living together was exactly two weeks old. Matthew had set aside that block of time as a vacation from his store, hired extra help, but was scheduled to return to work Monday morning. Looking back, the entire time had been the honeymoon from hell.

After showering and changing into her nightgown, Diana tiptoed into their bedroom and found Matthew pretending to read a mystery novel. But the book was still open to the same chapter he'd been reading on her first night there.

She crawled in beside him. "How are you doing?" She kissed his cheek. He grunted something welcoming, but did not put his book away. Okay, two could play that game. She reached into her bedside table and brought out the little paperback about Tom Dooley she'd bought two weeks ago at Whippoorwill Village.

Unsure she could concentrate, she started to read, and a half hour later, she felt like Alice—like she had fallen down a rabbit hole, backwards through time, to a place that mirrored her own recent life.

"Matthew, do you believe history repeats itself?"

Another grunt.

"No, seriously, listen to this…The Legend of Tom Dooley, or Dula, the historically correct name. Doesn't it seem weird that we now know Trevor Dula is an ancestor with the same initials? Tom was a Civil War hero—Trevor is an Iraq War hero."

"Please, Diana, I told you there are dozens of Dulas 'round here. Plenty of veterans, too."

"Yes, but Tom came home from the war and got engaged to Laura Foster—almost the same name as Lori Fowler, Trevor's fiancée. Then Tom's Laura was murdered, remember?"

"Sure, Tom killed her and got himself hanged."

"But did he do it? Everyone back then had doubts. There was also a woman named Ann Melton involved. She was Laura Foster's cousin, married to an older man, and she had an ongoing affair with Tom."

"Are you trying to compare this cousin to Lori's cousin, Paula? And I suppose the 'older husband' is supposed to Maynard?"

"Maybe I am comparing them, because the story is so much the same. I've always sensed that Paula was attracted to Trevor. Maybe they were sweethearts before the war, just like Ann Melton and Tom Dooley."

"That's a boatload of *maybes*." Matthew closed his book, and then his eyes

"But listen to this…" she persisted. "Ann actually confessed to stabbing Tom's Laura, and Laura had been pregnant with Tom's child."

"Please give me a break." Matthew yawned. "Lori Fowler wasn't pregnant, or else we'd have heard all about it on the news. And even if history were repeating itself, where does Ginny fit in?"

Diana paused. She was somewhat surprised that Matthew had even been listening to her Twenty-First Century conspiracy theory based on a Nineteenth-Century murder. She read on. "Okay, here it is. Another woman was involved with

Tom. Her name was Pauline, and she was another of Laura's cousins…"

"Stop right there." Matthew grabbed Diana's wrist. "Shouldn't this Pauline person be compared to Paula Dula? Their names are almost the same. By your reasoning, my Ginny should be the Ann Melton character. After all, Ginny loved Trevor before he went away to Iraq. Then she got herself married to a much older man—that Charley guy. Aren't you putting Ginny square in the shoes of that adulteress who confessed to the murder? You don't want to do that, do you, Diana?"

"Please hush up, Matthew, you're giving me a headache." She closed her book. His reasoning had put her off track, yet the Tom Dooley legend remained a compelling parallel. She'd go back to it in the morning.

Matthew turned towards her and ran his hand up under her gown. His finger lightly circled her bellybutton, then traveled up the center of her chest to her breasts. As he cupped each mound, then teased each nipple, she felt her anxiety melt away.

"Do you still have a headache?" he asked.

"Nope, all gone," she told him."

TWENTY-SIX

The dream…

After they made love, Diana fell into a deep sleep. But then the dream materialized in the early morning hours, and the ghost of Tom Dooley came to haunt her. She was transported to 1866 and that misty morning when Tom lured his fiancé away on horseback and into the mountains. Laura believed he intended to marry her and become a father to their unborn child. They galloped through foothills alive with rhododendrons and mountain laurel, but Tom was thinking of Ann and Pauline, the other two women in his life. He carried the pickax he had borrowed from a neighbor, and when he returned home, he came alone.

Tom refused to join the search party. Instead he ran off to Tennessee and changed his name. Finally, acting on a tip from Tom's married lover, Ann, the searchers climbed higher into the mountains. One of the horses scented blood in the weeds, and sure enough, they found Laura's corpse in a sad and shallow grave.

That fall, Tom was located and brought back to Wilkes County in chains. Both he and Ann were indicted for murder. Then two long years later, Tom alone was hanged for the crime, and the mystery of who may actually have committed the murder lingered through the centuries and into Diana's dream.

She awoke with a start, sweating and troubled. The room was too hot, and she was tangled up in the sheets. She couldn't get her bearings, felt she was suffocating in a lonely grave, and she feared for an unnamed baby—or child—as she listened to water cascading from a faraway waterfall above ground. She heard the child calling to her.

"Wake up, Diana!" Lissa was bouncing on her bed. Matthew had left her side. He was taking a shower one wall away, in the master bath. "Grandpa's going to work today. Will you stay and play with me?"

Diana reared up on her elbows and thought she heard birds singing in a highland forest, but it was only Perry chirping from inside his covered cage. The parrot wanted breakfast. He was eager to start a new day and teach Lissa some brand new curse words.

"Good morning, Lissa." Diana blinked the sleep away. "Sure, I'd love to play with you." Slowly Diana remembered the plan. Matthew intended to visit Ginny every day. First thing in the morning, he'd stop by the jail in Statesville, then return to Mooresville to work at his store. For the foreseeable future, their babysitting roles were reversed, so it fell to Diana to care for Lissa.

"What are we gonna do?" Lissa jumped off the bed and twirled. Her antics brought Ursie into the room. Perry squawked, Ursie barked, and then Diana threw on her robe and hustled the child and dog into the kitchen.

"Let's start with breakfast, okay?"

As Diana scrambled eggs and toasted bread, Lissa watched cartoons. Matthew rushed in, gave her a heartfelt kiss, accepted coffee to go, and then he was gone. Diana watched his shirttail flopping untucked from his jeans as he climbed into his truck.

Yet through all the confusion, she couldn't rid herself of the dream. She obsessed about Ann Melton, Tom's married lover, about Laura Foster's unborn child, and decided she needed to find out more about the present-day cousins, Lori and Paula. She must discover the terms of that trust fund set up by their eccentric uncle, Loveless Dula. By the time she called Lissa to the table, an idea had taken shape.

"Would you like to go out for an adventure today, Lissa?"

"What kind of adventure?"

"Maybe we can have lunch with my mother, Miss Vivian, and her friend, Mr. Linc. Do you remember them?"

"Yes, I like them, even though they're really old. Will that yellow dog come, too?"

Diana struggled to interpret Lissa's question. "Oh, you mean Dory the therapy dog? No, she has to stay at the building where my mother lives. I want us all to go out to a restaurant, then maybe ice cream after."

"What restaurant?"

Diana hesitated. It was risky asking a six-year-old to choose a lunch destination. Somehow she couldn't picture Mama and Linc agreeing to dine at McDonalds, even though Diana was paying. Still, she took the chance. "Where do *you* want to go?"

Lissa bit her lower lip and twisted a curl of red hair around her finger. "I want Mexican."

Diana did a double take. "Like Taco Bell?"

The child made a face. "No, Diana, I want to go to a really nice place with pretty tables, where they bring the food right to you."

Ah, so this child was accustomed to the finer things in life. Apparently Ginny had schooled her kid in international cuisine, and although Mooresville was not Vegas, Diana knew just the place. "That sounds good to me, Lissa, but I'll have to call my mother and make sure they can come."

"So what are you waiting for? Call them."

Diana told Lissa to wait, then moved to the privacy of the master bedroom to dial Mama. Her request was a long shot at best—that Lincoln Davis would still have a file on Loveless Dula after all these years. Plus, Vivian would be surprised and suspicious of Diana's motives in wanting to meet, let alone treat, at a nice restaurant. Hopefully Mama would be anxious to see her surrogate great granddaughter again, or perhaps be enchanted by the idea of a date with Linc. Diana figured nothing ventured, nothing gained.

She made the call.

TWENTY-SEVEN

Trust...

Diana was lucky. Mama had agreed to ask Linc for the huge favor, although she'd grumbled a bit, saying asking a lawyer to reveal a client's personal affairs was asking him to breach his professional ethics. Yet Mama promised to ask, and after a morning of phone tag, the couple agreed to meet Diana and Lissa not for lunch, but for dinner.

Diana was also lucky because unlike most residents of Shady Oaks, Linc owned his own car. It was just past six when his bottle green Buick drove up and parked in the handicap space outside Monty's Mexican Restaurant.

Diana and Lissa were waiting just inside the air-conditioned foyer. Diana watched her plucky mother whip a handicap license from her purse and hang it onto Linc's rearview mirror. And when the elderly couple stepped inside, Diana couldn't resist making a comment.

"Really, Mother, you're not handicapped. Talk about a breach of ethics, what gives you the right to keep on using that tag?"

Vivian smirked. "Gets us in the best spots, doesn't it? At my age, I think I'm entitled."

Mama had hip surgery many years ago, when the tag was first issued, and ever since, she'd been charming subsequent doctors into renewing it. Mama turned to Lissa. "How are you, young lady? Have you been waiting long?"

Lissa cocked her head. "Kinda like all day. We left a note for Grandpa that he'll have to cook his own supper."

"Well, it's too bad he couldn't join us." Vivian gave Diana a look of disapproval. "Luckily we have Linc here to escort us." In Mama's world, women worth their salt seldom ventured out without male companionship.

A smiling Latino in a crisp white shirt, black trousers and string tie, led them to a quiet corner booth far removed from the mariachi music being piped in near the bar. The charming restaurant had a colorful yellow and cobalt blue tiled floor, comfy dark wooden booths, and festive lanterns hung around the interior. Better than that, Diana knew they also had a menu to die for.

Even their group's resident connoisseur was impressed. "Nice place," Lissa pronounced. "I hope they make a good chicken quesadilla."

The adults laughed.

"I promise they do, but first let's order drinks," Diana suggested. Linc chose bourbon and branch, Mama white zinfandel, Lissa a cola, while Diana splurged on the killer lime Margarita with salt on the rim. She'd called for the balance on her credit card before they left, so she figured she could afford one big gesture before maxing out.

They enjoyed small talk during the meal. Diana and Mama pigged out on El Combo—which included one each of chalupa, chille relleno, enchilada, taco, burrito, plus rice and beans. Lissa got her chicken quesadilla, then fried ice cream for dessert, while Linc asked for Mole Poblamo, a house specialty of chicken breast cooked in a dark sauce made with dry

171

peppers, chocolate, and spices, served with beans, rice, and flour tortillas.

Needless to say, by the time they folded their napkins, everyone but Lissa was groaning like overstuffed Thanksgiving turkeys. Mama took an acid reducer tablet, then made a proposition to Lissa.

"Lord, I need to walk this off. Lissa, do you want to visit the pet store next door with me?"

"Oh, yes please!" The child jumped to her feet.

"Don't buy anything alive," Diana cautioned.

"Not even one goldfish?"

"Not today. Why don't you make a new nametag for Ursie? They have one of those machines there."

That suggestion met with approval, so Mama and Lissa left on a mission, leaving Diana and Linc facing one another across the table. The waiter cleared away the dishes, and they ordered coffee.

"Thanks for meeting me like this," Diana began.

"The pleasure is mine." Linc patted his tummy, then brought a small notebook from the breast pocket of his summer shirt. "Please understand, I would not be free to reveal this information without permission, which fortunately, has been granted."

"I understand. Thank you." Diana felt awkward, but she appreciated Linc's direct approach to her request for details regarding the Loveless Fowler Trust. Over dinner she'd come to like her mother's gentleman friend even more, both his easy humor and his dapper style. She hoped Mama considered him "a keeper."

"I keep all my old files on CD, you see, and they were in storage with my other possessions. I had to visit the storage facility to retrieve them, and then I had to consult with Paula Dula's current attorney to ascertain the status of that trust." Linc paused to sample the strong coffee.

Diana licked a few grains of salt from her Margarita glass, feeling more indebted than ever. "Who is her attorney?"

Linc chuckled. "Young fella named Mecklin Adams. Everyone calls him Geek. He is a contemporary of Paula Dula and her deceased cousin, Lori, so the two hired him after I retired, and naturally I gave him copies of my files."

"Yes, I've seen Geek in action. He represented Trevor Dula at his arraignment."

"That's true, and now Geek represents Ginny Troutman, would you believe? All these young folks know each other, and from what I hear, she asked her father to hire Geek just this morning. So you see, my young lawyer friend has more than one horse in this race."

Well, that was certainly a news flash. Diana gulped what was left of her Margarita. "Small world," she said.

"Indeed. Geek explained that after Lori's death two weeks ago, old Love's trust was automatically dispersed in its entirety to Paula Dula. So that information is now part of the public record, nothing secret about it."

Diana nodded. "So how rich is Paula?"

He glanced at the ceiling, where white fiesta lights twinkled against a midnight blue background. "Love's trust has accrued interest all these years, and Miss Paula has received upwards of ten million dollars."

Diana gasped. "No wonder she offered to post Trevor's bail. No wonder she can afford a mini-mansion at Lakeview Estates."

Linc shrugged. "You could have discovered what I just told you on your own, Diana, but you asked me for the *terms* of Love's trust. After reviewing the CD, I remembered how very odd those terms were..."

The attentive waiter topped off Linc's coffee, then faded away. Diana's brain raced with questions. Had Paula ever told her husband, Maynard, that she was a wealthy woman? "What if Lori had not been murdered?" she asked aloud as those questions took on a more sinister aspect.

"In that case, the girls would have split the fortune—provided Love's conditions had been met. As I told you before, Diana, Loveless was a lonely bachelor with no offspring, and he adored little kids. So in order to inherit, he insisted that both nieces must be married, and their goal was to have children."

Diana was stunned. She took her first sip of coffee and allowed the caffeine to jolt her system before responding. "Those terms are ridiculous. It's like the old man required his beloved nieces to mate and breed on demand. Was he living in the Dark Ages?"

Linc laughed. "I know. It's awful, isn't it? I thought at the time that Love was a tyrant. He treated those girls like prime racehorses. He insisted they find a stud, then drop little prize-winning foals."

"Nobody told him about women's lib." As Diana reviewed the facts, she noted that Paula had fulfilled part of the bargain. She had married Maynard, but according to Ginny, the couple had thus far been unable to have babies. Lori was about to marry Trevor, but as far as babies were concerned... "Linc, what would have happened if neither Paula nor Lori produced children?"

"Then, provided both were married, they'd split the money fifty/fifty."

"What if both were married, but only one had birthed offspring?"

"Then the niece with children would receive the lion's share, while the childless one would get only a pittance to supplement her social security."

"So it was all about babies. The man was diabolical." Diana's mind continued to race as Mama and Lissa returned. Lissa was holding a big box that contained a hell of a lot more than a dog tag.

Old Loveless' trust seemed like a recipe for murder—pitting the two cousins against one another in a high-stakes contest. Blackmail for babies. As Diana remembered the disturbing dream she'd had that morning, she considered Tom Dooley's Laura, pregnant with child—murdered. "My God, Linc, do you think Lori was pregnant when she was murdered?"

The proper gentleman blushed again. "My dear, I can help you with many things, but not that. Was Lori pregnant? I have no clue."

TWENTY-EIGHT

The direct approach…

The question festered all week, but Diana didn't know how to get a definitive answer. She hated to burden Matthew with her suspicion that Lori Fowler was pregnant when she died, because he had sunken neck-deep in the quicksand of his own worries. Ginny's lawyer, Geek Adams, had forewarned Matthew to be prepared to pay a sizeable bail, should the judge be inclined to release Ginny. Because Matthew didn't have enough in savings to pay the estimated amount in cash, he was investigating how long it would take to refinance his house. He was also talking to a bail bondsman, because he didn't want Ginny to stay in jail one minute longer than necessary.

Poor Matthew was under siege from every direction. His convenience store/garage was suffering from the economic downturn, so he was playing catch up at work, trying to pay bills and make ends meet. His early morning meetings with Ginny in prison were brief and depressing. Her spirits had sunken to the bottom of the gutter, and Matthew had confided to Diana that although he was absolutely convinced of his daughter's innocence, he was equally certain Ginny was holding something back. He described it as a black shadow in Ginny's heart, said she was suffering from a lie of omission, but Diana couldn't fathom what Matthew meant by that.

By bedtime, Matthew was unable or unwilling to make love, but Diana didn't take it personally. Instead they cuddled, often sleeping very little, each lost in his or her own obsessions, until the dawn birds chirped and they faced another day.

Only Lissa seemed blissfully unaffected by the adult angst, and thanks to the gift Vivian had bought her at the pet shop, Lissa remained distracted from the fact that Ginny was missing. When she asked about her mother, Diana followed Matthew's instructions and continued to tell the child that her mama was staying with friends, but she'd be home soon.

By Thursday afternoon, Diana was at wit's end when Lissa called her to see the new aquarium for the umpteenth time. "Look, my fish are kissing."

Sure enough, the matched goldfish were bumping noses as they fluttered in place above the multi-colored coral. Diana specifically recalled telling Lissa that night when she went to the pet store with Mama not to buy anything alive, not even *one* goldfish. So Lissa had purchased *two*, with Mama's approval. Mama delighted in undermining Diana's authority, and had returned to the restaurant looking smug after spending a small portion of her social security check on the two fish, a classic glass bowl, the interior accoutrements—including a plastic mermaid—and of course, that awful-smelling fish food.

"Do you think they're in love?" Lissa wondered.

"Maybe."

"Will they have baby fish?"

"I doubt it."

Lissa was disappointed. "Then maybe we can buy a turtle to keep them company?"

Diana sighed. "No need to buy a turtle, Lissa, when you can catch one out there in the lake."

"Honest?"

She told Lissa about the willow oak at the edge of Matthew's waterfront, how turtles sometimes sunbathed on the rocks underneath. Diana led the child to the boathouse and handed her Matthew's fish net. "Now remember, hold the net just under water, below the turtle's head, so when it jumps off, it'll land right in."

"But I don't see any turtles."

"Be patient. Sit really still, and they'll come."

Diana saw the child was skeptical. "Good luck!" she called as she walked away.

Once settled on the couch, where she could keep her eye on the girl, Diana realized she was alone for the first time all day. So she began brooding again. She could call Trevor Dula and ask him point blank if his fiancée had been pregnant when she died, but she didn't know him well enough. She had almost concluded that Paula Dula had killed Lori to prevent her from delivering a baby. Or maybe killing Lori worked no matter what? With Lori dead, Paula inherited everything even though she'd never birthed a child.

She watched as little Lissa crouched under the willow and lowered the big net into the lake. Matthew always said there were many ways to catch a fish, but Diana preferred the direct approach. She picked up the phone and dialed Wayne Bearfoot, who answered the third ring. When she expressed her theory and popped the big question, her old friend just laughed.

"Sorry to disappoint you, Diana, but the autopsy stated that Lori was no more pregnant than I am."

"Are you sure?"

"Yes, I'm sure. I've never been pregnant, just ask my wife. And neither was the unfortunate Lori Fowler."

TWENTY-NINE

Liz...

Liz tried to snuggle closer to Danny, who was driving his truck, but Amazing Grace kept nosing her way in between them. The greyhound was determined to lick Danny's new stubble of a beard and leave scratches on Liz's bare legs. They could have chosen Liz's Honda, but Danny insisted he didn't want to take their romantic vacation in what he described as her "real estate mobile." So they had compromised. If Danny agreed to leave Gracie behind with Diana for one short week, they'd travel in the truck. It helped that the campground they'd booked in Asheville did not accept pets exceeding fifty pounds, and since they'd been spoiling Gracie and she was getting fat, she'd tipped the scales too high.

Liz was grateful when they finally parked in Trout's driveway and let the beast loose. Gracie had not yet visited the lake, and when she bounded out the door and landed in the lawn, she was suddenly nose- to- nose with a suspicious canine stranger. Ursie approached slowly, her front lip ominously lifted to expose her frightening fangs.

"Gee, I hope they'll get along." Danny was already worried about his baby as Gracie tucked her long pencil tail between her legs and hunched up in fear.

"Don't worry, they're both sweethearts," Liz said. "They'll love each other like sisters."

"God, I hope so." He tried to smile as Diana came out the back door to greet them.

Liz gave Diana a big hug, then decided her partner looked pretty good, considering all the stress in her life. Like Liz, Diana wore shorts and a sleeveless string top. Her arms and legs were bronzed from the Lake Norman sun, and her sky blue eyes sparkled when she greeted Gracie.

Once Diana finished cuddling the greyhound, Danny moved in to give Diana his traditional full-mouthed kiss. It was a long-standing joke—sort of. Danny had always claimed Miss Prim and Proper Diana was the sexiest woman alive, so the kiss never failed to aggravate Liz with the tiniest twinge of jealousy.

"You know I still want to adopt your dog," Danny said when he came up for air.

Diana laughed. "In your dreams. C'mon inside."

Typically, Danny trotted after Diana like a love slave, leaving Liz to collect Gracie's stuff: bowls, food, collar, leash, and her favorite bunny play toy. Gracie followed Danny, with Ursie right behind. Ursie's ears were still pinned back as she dogged Gracie, trying to poke under her tail for a good solid sniff. By the time Liz lugged the paraphernalia into the kitchen and deposited it on the counter, Danny and Diana were already yakking it up, drinking iced tea. While the dogs continued to eye one another with deep suspicion.

"I hope it's okay to dump Gracie on you for one whole week." Liz helped herself to tea.

"Of course it's okay. Gracie's my dog, and I love her." Diana ruffled the greyhound's ears. "Besides, you guys need a good vacation. And Danny, what's with the beard?" She touched Liz's boyfriend's chin.

Danny blushed to the roots of his curly brown hair. "We're goin' campin', you know? Roughin' it. So I figured I might as well look the part."

"Well, you do." Diana giggled.

"Hey, Diana, where's Trout?" Liz interrupted their mutual admiration society.

Diana blinked. "He's working, remember? He's at his store."

"Oh yeah, that's right. So where's the kid?" Liz still hadn't met Lissa, the little girl Diana seemed to dote on. She followed Diana's gesture through the window out to the lake, where a child sat fishing on the dock. Even at that distance, Liz saw the child was adorable, with skinny arms and a head of curly red hair. "Cute," she commented.

Danny looked, too. "Jeez, Liz, that kid looks just like you. You could be her mommy. Do you think she'd like some iced tea? I wanna meet her."

"Lissa prefers lemonade," Diana said. "You'll find her sipper in the fridge, and I keep it full."

"Alright!" Danny fetched Lissa's drink, then called to Gracie. "C'mon, girl, it's time to meet your new little playmate." Seconds later, Danny and both dogs were out the door and headed for the beach.

"Sometimes I think Danny's the kid in this relationship. He acts like he's ten years old," Liz grumbled as she and Diana moved to the living room with their drinks, then plopped down on the couch, where they could watch the action at the dock.

"But that's what you love about Danny, right? All that energy?"

"Yeah, maybe so." Liz smiled. "We really do appreciate this, Diana. Danny and I haven't taken a romantic holiday forever, and it's not like there's anything happening at the office—except the Paula Dula deal, of course."

At the mention of Paula's name, Liz watched her friend transform from the happy-go-lucky creature who had hugged her out back to a worried, middle-aged woman. Diana's face wilted and her shoulders sagged. Suddenly Liz noticed the dark circles under her beautiful eyes. "Hey, what's wrong?"

"How is that Paula Dula deal coming?"

Was it her imagination, or did Liz detect a decided lack of enthusiasm about their one viable client? "It's going great. Super, in fact. After she saw the property, Paula signed on the dotted line. She gave me a check for twenty thousand to put in escrow, so it looks like a done deal. Paula's a great gal."

"Really? I'm not so sure..."

As Liz awaited Diana's explanation, she glanced out at the lake where a huge storm cloud passed over the sun, leaving Danny and Lissa in shadows as they sat side by side, sipping their drinks. But Gracie and Ursie had still not become friends, with Gracie pressed against Danny, Ursie standing protectively over the child. "Wanna tell me about it?" she asked at last. "What's your problem with Paula?"

About fifteen minutes later, Liz wished she'd never asked. The cock n' bull theory Diana had concocted was straight out of a B movie, and if she was anything close to right in her suspicions about Paula, it meant the biggest real estate deal she and Diana ever dreamed of was swirling right down the drain.

"I'm not buying it, Diana. You said yourself Lori Fowler wasn't pregnant, so all Paula had to do was bide her time, and they'd split the money at some future date."

"Not necessarily." Diana slumped deeper into the couch. "I feel sure Trevor and Lori would have had children eventually, but Paula and Maynard have been trying for some time to conceive, with no success. Maybe one of them has a problem. Maybe Paula knew she'd never have a baby."

Liz considered the possibilities. "I met Paula's husband at Lori's funeral, and he's a strange geezer, like some old Hippie, you know? I'm sure Maynard knew the terms of the Loveless Fowler Trust. His business was failing. Maybe *he* killed Lori to get the money sooner and save himself from bankruptcy?"

Diana frowned. "But you implied Maynard didn't know about Paula's inheritance. He doesn't even know she's buying a property at Lakeview Estates, right?"

"No, I never said that." Liz gave her friend a long, hard look. "Paula and I never discussed Maynard one way or the other. He could be aware of everything."

"Really?" Diana appeared stunned.

"Besides, why was Trevor's Jeep at Lori's house? I still say they had a lovers' quarrel, and her death was a crime of passion."

Liz wasn't about to tell Diana she also had suspicions about Ginny Troutman. The girl had been a bully at summer camp, and in Liz's experience, people seldom changed. Above all, she couldn't afford to lose Paula as a client.

"Also, who knows, Diana? The newspapers have been covering all the burglaries in Lori's neighborhood. The bad guys know those rich folks in Highland Gardens own lots of goodies they can pawn, so it stands to reason Lori's death was simply a robbery gone bad."

"You really believe Lori's death was a random killing?"

"I don't know, and neither do you, Diana. So let it go, it's making you crazy. And I do hope your problem with Paula Dula won't keep you from helping her while I'm gone. What if she wants another showing, what if she has questions? You'll work with her, right?"

Diana hesitated only a moment. "Of course I'll help her. It's my job."

Liz breathed a sigh of relief, then asked how Ginny was holding up. "You say Ginny's arraignment is next Friday, one week from today? How come they always hold these hearings so late in the week?"

"Beats me." Diana sounded utterly defeated.

"Do you want Danny and me to come home early? I can cover the office that day, or baby-sit for Lissa. Say the word, Diana, and I'll be here. It's no problem. Really."

Diana raised both hands. "Absolutely not. I want you two to go and have fun. Forget all this, we'll be fine."

Liz was ashamed by the relief that washed over her when Diana didn't take her up on the offer. She didn't want to cut her vacation short. Knowing she was a selfish bitch, she looked out and saw raindrops on the window. Shit. She imagined driving through the mountains in fog to a soggy campsite.

At the same moment, she saw Danny and Lissa jump to their feet and start running towards the house, hoping to beat the rain. Both dogs followed Lissa, who was fast on her feet. But then Ursie barked and lunged at poor Gracie, seemingly to protect the child.

"Oh my God!" Diana bolted out the door, screaming as the dogs got into an all-out fight. "Help me here, Danny!" she shouted as she picked up a bucket full of water.

184

Liz was horrified to see gentle Ursie baring her teeth, growling and snapping at Gracie's face. "Stop them!" she cried, not knowing what else to do.

Diana dumped the water, and in that brief moment, both animals froze. Diana grabbed Ursie's collar, while Danny tackled Gracie. Lissa stood at a distance, tears streaming down her face. Before Liz knew what was happening, Diana had pulled Ursie across the yard and locked her in the garage. When she returned, her face was blotched red with anger and her white shorts were grass-stained.

"Jesus, what happened?" Danny was devastated as he stroked the trembling Gracie.

"Is she hurt?" Diana eyed the greyhound.

Liz gave Gracie's body a once-over. "Nope, she's fine. What about Ursie?"

Diana scowled. "Ursie's fine, but she's in the dog house. By that I mean she's in deep doo-doo. The fight was about Lissa. Ursie has bonded with her these past two weeks, so now she thinks it's her duty to protect her, but she has another think coming."

"We can't leave Gracie here," Danny said. "Ursie'll kill her."

"No, she will not." Diana stomped her foot. "Gracie will stay in our bedroom. She and the parrot have learned to tolerate one another. In the meantime, I'll teach Ursie some manners. She'll learn we're all entitled to love Lissa, right, honey?" Diana called the scared child to her side.

Lissa dried her tears and popped a thumb into her mouth as they all stood in the rain. When she removed it, she said, "I love both the doggies."

"And they love you," Diana said. "Don't worry, they'll learn to play nice. Now, let's all go inside."

Liz was still shaking, but she marveled at Diana's ability to save the day. It wasn't the first time she'd seen the woman turn a bad situation around. She took Danny's hand, then looked at the weeping heavens. "We need to get on the road, Diana."

"Yes, I understand." After introducing Liz to Lissa, Diana gave Liz a quick peck on the cheek. "Now get going, and drive safely."

Danny was reluctant to leave, but Liz gave his finger a sturdy yank before he could reward Diana with a traditional goodbye kiss.

"Are you sure you'll be all right?" Danny asked.

"Right as rain." Diana rolled her eyes at the sky.

But as they left, Liz did not share Diana's optimism, and she feared for her friend.

THIRTY

Matthew...

As Matthew strode into the Mooresville courthouse, he wished to god Diana was with him, but as usual, she was stuck home caring for Lissa. And although Diana adored his granddaughter, Matthew knew the babysitting was taking its toll. This week she had taken Lissa with her to the office, so Diana could "sit her hours" in Liz's absence. But instead of accomplishing anything work-related, Diana had spent her time filling in coloring books and cutting out paper dolls.

Late afternoon shadows stretched across the hallway as he moved towards the tiny room where the judge would be waiting to arraign Ginny. In the meantime, secretaries cleared their desks and locked offices, eager to get on with their weekends. Why had his daughter's case been scheduled on a Friday, when everyone's tempers were frayed ragged by the workweek? When every last functionary wanted only one thing—to get gone.

Matthew tugged at the tie constricting his throat and perspired inside his suit coat. He hated wearing his church clothes, especially when the thermostat hovered at eighty-five in the shade and June was just around the corner. Yet he wanted to make a good impression. It was the least he could to do for his little girl. Far as he knew, everything else required to set her free had already been done, and if this hearing went as anticipated, he'd take Ginny home to the family for dinner.

"Are you Mr. Troutman?" A young woman with a bad case of acne touched his sleeve. "You're the first one here. Judge is runnin' late, but you can go on in and take a seat." She guided him into the little room, left, and shut the door behind her—leaving him alone in the claustrophobic space.

The cheap folding chairs and miniature tables seemed too small for his large frame, so he felt like an adult stranded in a child's classroom. The only window was set high near the ceiling, where the leaves of a poplar quivered in the light breeze. One large, noisy fly buffeted himself against the window glass. He was determined to escape, or die trying.

Matthew carefully unfolded his cotton handkerchief and mopped his face. Diana always made fun of his hankies, thought they were quaint and old-fashioned. Yet they'd come in handy a time or two, when his beloved Diana suffered a crying jag or a sneezing fit. She appreciated them then, all right.

As he thought of her, a familiar ache began somewhere near his heart and traveled down his ribcage. Their first three weeks of life together had not gone according to plan. He had imagined quiet dinners in the gazebo as they watched the sunset on the lake, companionable coffees on the deck in the morning, and long uninterrupted nights of love. As he thought of those pleasures, an unexpected longing replaced the pressing worries of the moment.

Diana and he had always been good together in bed, but lately Matthew had been distracted, so he mourned the intimate moments they had lost. Diana was always warm and understanding, a sweet comfort when he'd been paralyzed by worry about Ginny. Still, he preferred the nights of wild abandon, when he and Diana left their daytime skins and soared together like a single airborne creature. They flew passionately as one, shedding inhibitions until they touched the sun and melted into a hot and healing place.

She often described this place as an endless river, or cool pool, but he experienced it as molten, a fever broken to blessed relief.

"Hello, Trout. Sorry I'm a little late." The earnest young man with horn-rimmed glasses startled Matthew from his reverie, jolting him back to the troubled earth. The fellow extended his hand.

Matthew shook it. "No problem, Mecklin. The judge is late, too." He couldn't bring himself to call the lawyer "Geek," though Ginny referred to him that way all the time.

"Are you prepared, Trout? You know what to expect today, right?"

"Yeah, you already warned me that Ginny wouldn't be here." They both glanced at the monitor set on a large tray nearby. "The hearing will be conducted via video, but we'll pick her up afterwards, isn't that right?"

Mecklin removed his glasses and held them towards the window. He polished them with a small silk cloth he took from his breast pocket. "Yes, that's right. They're holding Ginny at the women's facility in Statesville, as you know. Your bail bondsman is already there. Did you bring your checkbook…?"

"I'm all set." Matthew patted his breast pocket. Inside was a navy blue wallet containing checks linked to his brand new home equity account. He was clear to spend up to one hundred thousand, the ten percent required if the judge set bail at one million, as expected. His bondsman would insure the rest, but if Ginny skipped town or failed to appear at any one of her court dates, Matthew would lose much of his equity—his nest egg. But that would never happen.

"Then we're good to go." Mecklin smiled. "Once we get a figure from the judge, your man in Statesville will get the ball rolling. They'll run Ginny's stats through NCIC to be sure there are no other outstanding warrants, then he'll cross the t's and dot the i's, and we'll pick her up. Okay?"

"Okay."

"The whole process will take about forty-five minutes."

"Okay." But Matthew thought the system was dragging its tail. By law, Ginny had received a "first appearance" hearing within forty-eight hours of her arrest. At that time, she had waived her right to a court-appointed attorney, and they had hired Mecklin Adams. Matthew had been told that under normal circumstances, bail would have been set back then, but due to the serious nature of the charges, and because Ginny wanted her lawyer present at her bail hearing, she'd been incarcerated one long week. To Matthew, it seemed a lifetime.

"I still don't see why Trevor Dula got to attend his arraignment in person, or why they released him on the spot." Diana had told him all about it, and the seemingly special treatment still rankled.

Mecklin loosened his tie and shed his topcoat. "I told you before. Lieutenant Sokolsky made those arrangements. He knew in advance that Trevor's release was a done deal. Surprised the hell outta me…"

Matthew frowned and wondered, not for the first time, if Mecklin was seasoned enough to handle a case like Ginny's. To Matthew, the kid looked like a "baby lawyer."

"It must be against the law to lower the thermostat in these public buildings." Mecklin complained. "Maybe they think they're impressing the taxpayers by saving on the energy bill, but I think it's a sin. Take off your coat, Trout."

Matthew scowled at the kid. "No thanks. Here comes the judge." The thirty-something man entering the room wore a black robe, yet the moment he moved behind a table facing the monitor, he shucked it off. He wore shorts and a pink golf shirt underneath.

"Please stay seated," the young judge said. "We're informal here, and it's been a long day." The woman who had greeted Matthew in the hall came in with a rolling cart bearing what appeared to be some sort of recording device. "This here is Mildred. She'll take the minutes." The judge dropped a file onto his table and sat down. "Turn on the monitor, Millie."

Static snapped briefly on the screen, and then Ginny's face appeared, larger than life. She looked pale, frightened, and nervous. From that moment on, Matthew could concentrate on little else but the sight of his daughter in distress. He was vaguely aware of the charges being read as Ginny nodded in miserable understanding. He realized the judge was reading from the file, citing evidence.

"Well, fingerprints, yes…" he muttered. "But that's a little thin, isn't it?"

Matthew's ears pricked when he sensed a sympathetic tone in His Honor's voice. Mecklin had prepared him to understand that all judges were different—a conservative might set an unreasonably high bail, while a more human specimen might read the evidence and consider Ginny's arrest an overreach.

Mecklin spoke up. "You are correct, Your Honor. Ms. Troutman's fingerprints are all they have."

191

Matthew saw a flicker of hope in his daughter's dark eyes as she listened. He felt the same. The judge's boyish pink cheeks were flushed as pink as his shirt as he ran a pudgy hand through his crew cut red hair. Suddenly this "baby judge" reminded Matthew of his dentist, and his dentist was a nice guy.

"On the other hand," the judge continued. "Ms. Troutman is a resident of Nevada. She has been in North Carolina less than a month, so she must be considered a flight risk."

Mecklin got to his feet. "But Ms. Troutman is mother to a six-year-old daughter, and her father, Mr. Matthew Troutman, is a pillar of our community. His family has lived here for generations, and…"

The pink judge raised his hand to silence the lawyer. "Yeah, yeah, yeah—I know Trout." He grinned at Matthew, who was sweating in his suit. "I've been in your store a hundred times. When I was a little kid, you gave me free ice cream. When I was a teenager, you refused to sell me beer and cigarettes."

Matthew blinked. For the life of him, he could not remember this man, but then again, his mind was a roller coaster of ups and downs. He hoped the judge's fond memories would serve Ginny well.

Mecklin seized the occasion. "We request that Ms. Troutman be released into Matthew Troutman's custody—on her own recognizance."

Again the baby judge lifted his hand. "Aw give me a break, Geek. This is a felony murder charge, so ROR is out of the question. But I'm tired and I wanna go home." He smiled at Matthew. "I understand you've already made arrangements to post bail. Are you listening, Ms. Troutman?" He frowned at the monitor.

Everyone stared at Ginny, who nodded her head.

"Then I hereby set bail at five hundred thousand dollars, and once it's been posted, you are free to go, Ms. Troutman—but not too far, you hear?"

He read Ginny the conditions of her release, and told everyone they would be notified of the dates of her upcoming court appearances by mail and by phone.

He stood and yawned. "That's all, folks." Mildred turned off the monitor and closed her machine. "Now go get your girl, Trout, and enjoy your weekend."

Matthew heaved a sigh of relief and peeled off his coat once the officials had left the room. "What do you think, Mecklin?"

"I think you were damned lucky, Trout. I guess the judge likes you, because that's a low bail, under the circumstances."

"He knew the evidence was shabby. They'll never convict my daughter with that garbage."

Mecklin Adams refused to meet Matthew's gaze. He got busy picking at his fingernails. "I'm afraid there'll be more for us to worry about by the time Ginny comes to trial."

"What do you mean *more*?" Matthew was sick and tired of legal games.

"It wasn't in the file, but it's coming."

"Spit it out, son."

"I'm sorry, but I can't tell you, Trout. That part is lawyer/client privileged."

"But I'm Ginny's father, and I pay the bills—including yours."

"If you want the truth," Mecklin said. "You'll have to ask Ginny."

THIRTY-ONE

Ginny...

Her favorite prison matron allowed her to dress in her wheat pants suit, the same outfit she'd worn to Trev's arraignment. The clothes weren't too disgusting, considering someone had balled them up and stuffed them into a locker along with her other possessions, one week ago. Ginny longed for her makeup bag, but hey, a girl couldn't have everything.

This matron, who'd been tending her during second shift, wasn't too obnoxious. She was a single mom, like Ginny, so they understood one another. Best of all, the woman looked the other way when Trev's visiting period ended and always let him stay an extra ten minutes. And he'd come to see her almost every afternoon.

Once she'd finished dressing, the matron took her into a holding room where a stranger with a briefcase was waiting.

"Miz Troutman? I'm your bail bondsman." He smiled, exposing two gold caps where his incisors should have been. "I've done all the paperwork. The criminal database burped up your conviction in Vegas, but the cops already knew about that. So as soon as your daddy gets here and writes me a check, you're good to go." He blew his nose and fidgeted in his seat.

Ginny understood his discomfort. The whole place stank of disinfectant that never quite covered the odor of a bunch of women locked up together—their sweat and their fear.

"You're lucky to have a daddy like Matthew Troutman. He's coughing up fifty thousand for you today."

"Yeah, I know." Ginny inspected her fingernails, where bits of chipped polish clung like lichen on pink bark. She'd die for an emery board and some remover. Thing was, she was humbly grateful to Trout and needed her daddy. She'd cried stupid tears each time he'd come to visit, but they'd always been separated by a Plexiglas window, when all she wanted was one of his big, comforting bear hugs.

The bondsman continued to fidget. "Miz Troutman, will you excuse me a couple of minutes? Call of nature…"

"Yeah, sure." Once he'd left to take a leak, Ginny wandered to the heavy metal security door and peered through the chicken wire glass to the lobby. The usual collection of scared-looking family members and tacky boyfriends were assembled to visit with their loser loved ones. But then, sitting ramrod straight in his chair in the corner, she spotted Trev.

Her heart stopped. Did he realize she was about to be released? How the hell did he know? He was so handsome in his crisply ironed tan shirt and casual kakis. His brown dockside deck shoes looked clean and new, like military spit n' polish. In general, Trev was always excessively neat, while Ginny was a slob. She seldom made up her bed, but visualized Trev bouncing a dime on his tightly made cot, like they did in those boot camp movies. They were an unlikely pair.

She liked how he'd allowed his curly black hair to grow out like it was when they were kids, but she hated the expression he wore in those unguarded moments, when he thought she wasn't looking. His deep blue eyes stared straight ahead, like he was watching ghosts, and similar to those other lost souls assembled in the waiting room, he also looked frightened.

Ginny tapped the glass, got his attention, and his haunted stare dissolved into a broad smile. His eyes focused and danced as he strode to her window, where he pressed one large hand against the glass. She spread her fingers against the glass, inside his handprint, which would have been a no-no before she'd gotten her walking papers. But at the moment, no guard was there to stop her.

He took his hand away and gave her the V for victory sign and mouthed the word "congratulations." She mouthed "thanks." They couldn't hear one another through the sound-proof barrier, so Trev ambled over to the dour receptionist, who was also behind security glass, and charmed her out of a pencil and some paper. He made a sign for Ginny, held it to the window:

"Have dinner with me?"

Her heart stalled again. She knew damned well that Trout would have a celebration planned back at the lake. Ginny had visualized it a million times—ribs on the grill and a big "welcome home" cake. Next to Daddy's bear hug, the party idea had kept her putting one foot in front of the other as she'd sleep-walked through the prison routine. She shook her head "no."

Trev tapped again. He scribbled a second note in much larger letters.

"PLEASE?"

Oh God. She searched his expectant eyes and realized they still needed to talk. Under the watchful gaze of the blasted guards, Ginny had avoided the one topic she most needed to discuss with Trev. He held up a third sign and rapped harder.

197

"PRETTY PLEASE?"

Sweet Jesus, the man was persistent, and she was crazy. Surely Trev was still deeply in love with his dead Lori. That had been clear each time they met. He bled his pain from a big hole in his heart, so she was insane to agree. Yet she had traveled halfway across the country to do this thing.

So Ginny lifted her face and said, "Okay."

THIRTY-TWO

Matthew...

Matthew feared his swollen heart would explode if they made him wait one minute. The bondsman met them at security, then took them into a stuffy office where Matthew signed the check and the release papers.

"Are we done?" He tossed the pen on the table.

"Sure thing, Mr. Troutman." The bondsman's golden incisors sparkled.

Matthew stared. "So what are we waiting for?"

Mecklin placed a calming hand on his shoulder. "Ginny is ready. They'll meet us in reception."

Matthew led the double-time parade to the waiting room, then all three men rushed the taciturn clerk behind the window and passed her the papers. While she lifted her glasses and took her sweet time reading each line, Matthew thought he'd gag on the ammonia stench. He was sick to the gills of the jailhouse smell. Finally, the infuriating clerk climbed to her feet and exited the back of her cubicle through a sinister steel door.

"They'll bring Ginny out now," Mecklin assured him.

Matthew's vision blurred and his pulse raced. The others waiting in the sad room became watery, unrecognizable shadows. He heard the door open, then both Mecklin and the bondsman rushed past him to greet his daughter. They pumped her hand, then parted so she could break through.

Suddenly she was in his arms. "Daddy!" she sang into his ear as he crushed her in a hug.

Ginny felt so tiny, like a frightened, trembling creature come in from the wild. He felt her warm tears on his neck, then he buried his face in her soft hair. No more jailhouse, only the smell of his sweet little girl. His Ginny.

"You okay, honey?" he whispered against her ear.

"Not really. Are you okay, Daddy?"

"I'm okay now." He extracted himself and looped his arm around her waist. "Let's get the hell outta here."

As they moved towards freedom, Matthew heard several people in chairs clap and cheer. Some woman in a uniform called out to Ginny and wished her good luck, while Mecklin and the bondsman followed them into the parking lot.

He took a gulp of fresh air. The sun had begun its descent in the western sky, and the oppressive heat of the day had given way to the cool of evening as Matthew guided his daughter towards his truck, with Mecklin and the bondsman close on their heels. The two men wanted more congratulations, more handshakes. They couldn't seem to get enough of the magical reunion, so Ginny thanked them both and sent them on their way.

"You ready to go home, honey?"

"God yes, Daddy!" Yet she lagged behind.

"So hop in the truck…"

Only then did Matthew spot the lone figure standing several paces away, his face obscured by the long shadow of the prison wall. He realized this man had followed them out, and Ginny tensed as the stranger approached.

"What do you want?" Matthew demanded. "If you're a reporter, go away."

"No, Daddy, it's Trev Dula, don't you see?"

Matthew didn't see. Not at all. He squeezed his moist eyes and looked again. The fellow was straight and tall as a flagpole as he walked closer.

"Hello, sir, it's good to see you again." The man held out a stiff hand.

Matthew ignored it. He saw the man was uncertain. "Get lost, Dula. You're not welcome here."

"Please don't say that, Daddy." Ginny gripped his arm. "I know it's hard, but Trev has invited me to dinner tonight."

A sudden anger rose up in Matthew. His hands involuntarily clenched. "But you said 'no,' didn't you, Ginny?"

Ginny started to cry. Her sobs came from somewhere too deep to fathom, and all at once Matthew glimpsed the black shadow in her heart, the one he'd try to describe to Diana. He now knew for certain that Ginny was hiding something—a secret, a shame, something to do with Trevor Dula.

Matthew's hands relaxed, He was terrified for his girl, yet he couldn't abide her tears. Ginny's mother had once told Matthew he possessed a "woman's intuition" when it came to their only child. At the time, he hadn't known whether to be flattered or humiliated by her remark. Yet over the years, long after his wife's death, her instinct had proven to be true. Unfortunately, Matthew had used his power poorly. In Ginny's difficult teenage years, he had seen through her schemes—the drugs and the alcohol—and used his intuition to punish her, not help her. And in the end, he'd driven her away.

"I promise to bring her home early, sir," Trevor said.

Matthew didn't want to make the same mistake twice. "Is this what you want, Ginny?"

"Yes, Daddy," she pleaded. "So long as you save me some cake. There is a cake, right?"

He would have laughed, but it hurt too much. "Yeah, it's chocolate, your favorite."

"Then please tell Lissa I love her, and I'll be home in time to tuck her in. And tell Diana I love her, too." Ginny dried her tears. "Will you do that, Daddy?"

Too much emotion. The last thing Matthew expected was his daughter's declaration of love for Diana. Far as he'd seen up to then, their relationship had been one of mutual tolerance at best.

"I'll tell them." He almost choked on the words as he felt Ginny's hand slip away.

"Thank you, Mr. Troutman. I appreciate this," Trevor said.

Was it his imagination, or was the tough-as-nails soldier blushing? Matthew remembered only bad things about Trevor, but people did change. Lord knew Matthew was trying to change. But it was a challenge. He almost called Ginny back as she gave him a shy little wave, took Trevor's hand, then walked away towards her date's Jeep, which was parked at the opposite end of the lot.

She did not look back.

Matthew experienced an ache behind his breastbone as he climbed into his truck and opened the glove box. Diana had insisted he take her cell phone, to call her the second Ginny was free. He glanced at the sun falling into a stand of pines in the distance and made the call to tell Diana he was coming home— empty-handed.

THIRTY-THREE

Ginny…

Being in Trev's Jeep again messed with her head. It was like being time-warped back to high school with a horny boyfriend at her side. Back then the car smelled like pot and suppressed sex. Trev kept rum in the glove box and a six-pack of Cokes on the floor. The interior had been littered with fast food bags, and once when Ginny was contorted on her back across the uncomfortable front seats, with Trev on top of her, she remembered focusing on an abandoned French fry lying stiff on the rubber floor mats.

No more. Today the Jeep was like the man, neat and polished. It smelled of Trev's subtly spicy aftershave and car wax, and the windows were spotless—as opposed to being fogged up from heavy breathing and smudged with both fingerprints and footprints.

But what really tripped her out now, as they rode through the peaceful countryside, was that the Jeep had become a symbol for Lori Fowler's murder. Ginny couldn't drive the image away: Trev's car in the dead girl's driveway. And it was the damned car that had gotten them both in trouble.

They had been shy with one another, not spoken one word as they left the town limits behind and drove through darkening fields. But Ginny had to ask. "Trev, were you at Lori's the morning she died?"

He eased up on the accelerator and pulled off to the side of the road. When he cut the engine and rolled down the windows, she heard tree frogs singing and the faraway droning of a private plane cruising above the lake.

"I told you before, Ginny. I wasn't there. You know I loved Lori. Why would I harm her? And why won't you believe me?"

She wanted to trust him, yet she couldn't erase the horror. "Then please explain why your car was there. Your alibi from the VA hospital doesn't work, and you know it. After you dropped off your friends, you had time to return home, pick up the Jeep, and drive to Lori's house before Diana and I arrived."

Trev's body tensed. She felt his frustration even though she had attached herself to the passenger door, out of accidental touching range.

"You're right, Ginny, but you're also dead wrong. After I left the guys at the pancake house, I drove around to clear my head. Seeing my buddy James go into convulsions, then miss his own birthday party, put me into a bad place. Brought back memories I'd just as soon forget.

"I drove to Lake Norman State Park and just sat there, maybe two hours. When I drove my station wagon home that day, the Willy's was parked in my driveway, just where I'd left it."

She searched his face for lies, but saw only truth. "Okay, so who took your car?"

Trev exhaled, loosened the top two buttons of his shirt. "God knows it could have been anyone. Hate to say it, but I always leave my keys in the ignition. Everybody knows it—my army buddies, even the kid who mows my fields."

Ginny sighed. "Like an open invitation. So who usually borrows it?"

Trev gazed out the window. "Well, Paula sometimes takes it grocery shopping when Uncle Maynard's using their old Cadillac. But Paula hates the Jeep, claims it's so bumpy it knocks her tailbone up her ass. Sorry, her words, not mine. I guess Maynard uses it most, though. My uncle loves that car. Says it takes him back to the sixties. He even threatened to paint a daisy on its hood, or some such nonsense."

So Paula and Maynard had access to Trev's Jeep, but why would either one of them want to kill Lori? They were both kinda weird, especially Maynard. But she shared history with Trev's uncle, and although he was eccentric, he'd always been kind to her. Paula was another story, the bitch. From the get-go, Ginny had sensed Paula had a thing for Trev.

"Was Paula jealous of Lori?" she blurted it out.

Sweat broke out on Trev's brow. "What happened between Paula and me is past history," he answered sheepishly.

OMG. She should have known. Paula had said that every young girl in the county had a fling with Trev, so obviously Paula was on that list. "Jesus, did you have an affair with Paula *before* or *after* she married your uncle?"

"Before, for Christ sake." He blushed to his curly black roots. "It was a huge mistake. And to tell you the truth, I wish to god it never happened."

"I bet." Ginny slumped in her seat. She knew all too well that Trev was a powerful narcotic, a hard habit to break. She'd been trying to kick her personal addiction for years. But even now, as they sat so close together, her ex-lover's allure was a heady drug. "Did Maynard know about you and Paula?"

Trev nodded miserably. "Yeah, he knew. Paula still uses me to punish him. She's always comparing the two of us. When she's really pissed, she tells him I was better in bed. Makes him feel like a piece of shit. Makes me feel even worse."

"So I guess Maynard was thrilled you were marrying Lori. What about Paula?"

Trev rolled his eyes. "Look, far as I know, they were both really happy for Lori and me. I'm sure neither one would ever hurt her."

Yeah, right. Ginny placed a mental bet on Paula as the killer, but she couldn't imagine her motive. After all, killing Lori wouldn't bring Trev back to Paula's bed. She glanced at the man beside her and noticed his eyes were moist.

"I'm sorry, Trev. Let's change the subject."

He reached out and took her hand. "Okay, but first I need to ask you something. It's been troubling me, and I want to know the truth. That morning when you went into Lori's kitchen, did you see her body, Ginny?"

The brutal memory gripped her gut and squeezed hard. Right after she'd borrowed the cold bottle of water from the fridge, she had seen the dead woman lying on the floor, her long, tan legs contorted in an unnatural position, her crotch exposed—her twisted white terrycloth bathrobe, gaping open to feature the silver carving knife buried between her breasts, and all that blood soaking her soft brown hair. Worst of all, Lori's terrified blue eyes had been frozen in disbelief, staring at the ceiling, her lips stretched open in a silent scream.

"Well?" Trev pressed.

Thus far Ginny hadn't told a living soul what she'd witnessed that day. Maybe someday she'd have to tell a shrink, if the pain wouldn't go away.

"Yes, I saw her," she confessed.

"Please tell me…"

"Lori looked peaceful," Ginny lied, refusing to plant that seed of horror in Trev's heart.

"So how come you didn't call the cops?"

She stared into his stricken eyes. "Why do you think?"

The question expanded between them in the humid air, sucking all the available oxygen until Trev's eyes expanded in understanding. "Good God, Ginny, you were trying to protect me!"

"I saw your Jeep, so I thought you were in the house, maybe upstairs. I didn't know what else to do."

He took both her hands into his and held them to his heart. "I am so sorry."

THIRTY-FOUR

Trevor...

After Ginny explained, he was relieved to be back on the road again, feeling the familiar shifting of gears, deciding when to go fast and when to slow down. And he was especially glad to be off the subject of his beloved fiancée—how she had died. Since Ginny had told him that Lori looked peaceful, he could breathe a little easier. Yet even when the killer was brought to justice—and Trevor was determined to see that happen—he knew he'd never be completely at peace again.

He glanced at Ginny's strong profile and wished he could ease her pain. He hated how she'd taken the heat for him, and he wouldn't rest until she was acquitted of all charges. He should apologize for dragging her into his drama, but mostly, he wanted to forget all that unpleasantness for one blessed evening. Maybe the best way he could thank Ginny, was to show her a good time.

"By the way, where are we going?" she asked from the far side of the front seat. "I hope no place fancy, because I feel like I've been dragged out from the bottom of a dirty clothes hamper."

He laughed. "You look great, and don't worry, I don't do 'fancy.' Remember the old Juke Joint?"

"No way! Is that place still up and running? By rights the kudzu should have swallowed it up years ago."

Trevor felt a weight lift off his chest as he visualized the bar and grill he and his pals were renovating. Before Lori died, it had been his pet project, the first venture to capture his imagination since he'd returned from the war.

"You won't recognize it, Ginny. We've been fixin' it up—new roof, new walls, even a stage and dance floor. We call it *Buffalo Guys*."

"We?" Her dark brows arched in a question.

"Yeah, two other guys and me. I provide the money, they provide the elbow grease and design. I think you'll approve. It's all about the music."

Ginny's soulful brown eyes expanded in surprise. "*Live* music? You're kidding, right? That was always your dream, Trev."

"Your dream too, remember?" During his brief visits to the jail, she'd told him she'd kept up with her guitar, even played a few gigs in Vegas. He was curious to know if she was any good. "Tonight is Open Mic Friday," he told her. "A chance for all the locals to strut their stuff. Maybe you could..."

"Don't even go there, Trev. You won't get me up on that stage."

He turned onto Buffalo Crossing Road and drove towards the lake, while Ginny retreated into a place he could not enter. When he looked closer, he saw she had aged, yet she was even more beautiful in her new maturity. The lightness in his chest left him giddy with memories. They say you never forget your first love, and Ginny Troutman definitely held that dubious honor. He recalled those hours of obsessive, almost desperate lovemaking in his lonely farmhouse. Then the aftermath—lying in one another's arms and listening to the radio: blues, rock, and star-crossed country ballads. Back then they were Ginny and Trevor against the world, a cruel world that took her mother, killed his parents, and left Ginny as his only sanctuary.

But they had both moved on. As he pulled into the gravel parking lot, already crowded with everything from dirty pickups to expensive BMW's and Lexus', he experienced an unexpected tug of loss when he stared at Ginny. She had been married, given birth to a kid, yet she never talked about it. And he had been poised to get those same things for himself before some crazed killer stole them away.

She turned to him, utterly defeated. "We're different people now," she said, reading his mind. But then she brightened and tried one of her famous smiles. "But hey, this place rocks!"

Her gesture included the customers' cars parked in the lot, the Tiki torches burning a path to the entrance door of the clapboard club, and even the rustic deck built out over the lake, the tables already filled with laughing diners.

"Looks like you done real good, Trev."

"Hope you like it." He was planning to open her door, like a proper escort, but she was out before the engine stopped and halfway up the path before he caught her. "Hey, wait up!"

She slowed and tucked her hand in his arm as they entered the dim club, where a raspy-voiced blond woman in a cowboy hat was singing "Stand By Your Man," causing Ginny to wrinkle her nose.

"Oh, she's a regular. We've got better talent comin' as the night wears on," he half apologized.

"It's not her, it's the sawdust." Ginny rubbed her shoe on the floor. "Nice touch. Love the smell. You got peanuts in little tin buckets, too?"

Trevor flushed with embarrassment. "'I'm afraid so. Those were Chip's idea."

Right on cue, Charles "Chip-off-the-old-block" Hinson sashayed up to them and gave Trevor a big kiss on the cheek. He yanked Ginny into his muscular arms and planted a sloppy one on her mouth. "Oh, my God, it's lil' Ginny Troutman. Where you been keepin' yourself, gal?"

"Chippie? Is that you?" Ginny squealed with delight and danced Trevor's manager around in a tight circle. "You're still the handsomest man in Iredell County."

"Ginny's a celebrity," Trevor said. "She lives in Las Vegas now."

Trevor was grateful Chip hadn't mentioned Ginny's trouble with the law. Yesterday, when Trevor had confided that he hoped to bring her to the club, Chip had made a joke about the two of them—*felons' night out*. But in fact, Chip had been Trevor's comfort and support throughout the whole sad affair. He was the best friend a man could want.

Chip winked at Ginny. "What happens in Vegas, stays in Vegas. Maybe my partner and I should get married in California, then honeymoon in Vegas. What do you think, doll?"

Ginny laughed. "Your *partner*? I'd love to meet him."

"Stick around, and I'm sure you will." Bypassing the woman at the reception stand, who flirted shamelessly with Trevor, Chip ushered them straight past the busy booths and dance floor, then out the back door to the deck. "Saved you the best seat in the house." He seated them at a secluded table near the railing. It faced the lake, where the moon and first stars filled a cobalt sky.

"So, I'll leave you guys alone." Chip signaled a waitress, then quietly left.

"Chip was in my high school choir," Ginny said. "Back then some of the kids gave him a hard time."

"Not anymore. They don't call him Chip for nothing. Ever seen his daddy? That man could win the Tough Guy competition, and since Chip's been working out, he can put the fear of God in any ignorant redneck looking for trouble."

After their waitress served them cold draft beers in iced Ball jars and took their dinner orders, Trevor began rambling on about the club, and how it got started. He told Ginny how Chip had come up with the design, their plans to expand, and how much he enjoyed fostering new musical talent. He explained how he had used his military pension to finance the place, and how he much preferred running a club to farming his land.

In short, he talked about everything except what he really wanted to say—like how the stint in Iraq had made him crazy, about his crushing depression since Lori's death. And most important, why was Ginny suddenly back in his life?

She looked up from her catfish platter. "I hate to eat and run, Trev, but you know I promised to be home in time to tuck my daughter into bed."

He cursed himself for running off at the mouth, wasting precious time. She'd mentioned several times that she hoped to return to Vegas, providing she didn't spend the rest of her natural life in prison for a crime she didn't commit—a subject Trevor was emotionally unable to discuss. So he knew time was short. He sensed he would lose Ginny after tonight.

"I know you have to get home, but can't you stay for coffee? We'll go inside and check out the talent."

"I need to tell you something, Trev." Suddenly Ginny was dead serious and excessively nervous. Her long fingers trembled as she reached for her last sip of beer.

Her tone frightened him, but he saw an opportunity. "Okay, I'll make you a deal. You can tell me whatever you want, but first I insist that you perform." He pushed his uneaten steak sandwich aside. "There's a decent band up now, and they have both electric and acoustic guitars. I reckon you could borrow one. They'll back you up, Ginny. Sing if you want, but I definitely want to hear you play."

"That's blackmail, Trevor Dula."

"Yeah, I know." He grinned. "But I hold the car keys."

THIRTY-FIVE

Ginny...

If she weren't already nervous enough, Trev's insistence that she perform turned her knees to jelly and set the butterflies knocking around in her belly like marbles in a pinball machine. If she hadn't just been released from jail, wasn't about to confess the darkest secret of her screwed-up young life, then maybe she could do this thing. Maybe even enjoy it.

She felt his warm hand on the small of her back as he guided her inside the noisy barroom. They wove between tables filled with raucous drinkers who were not entirely attentive to the crossover band delivering a hyped-up version of James Taylor's "Goin' to Carolina in My Mind." And Trev was right about one thing—the sweating musicians were giving a solid performance, yet they failed to capture the audience—not a good sign. With her luck, they'd throw peanut shells at her.

"Is Ginny gonna play?" Chip fluttered to their side, if a big man like Chip could be said to *flutter*.

Trev smiled and nodded, and as soon as the band finished their number, Chip put two fingers to his mouth and catcalled, startling the room to attention. Ginny's throat went dry as Chip began an effusive introduction, billing her as a Vegas headliner. In the meantime, Trev approached the musicians gesturing, whispering, and pointing in her direction.

Dear God in heaven, they were setting her up for failure. She wiped moist hands on her pants and practiced deep breathing.

Because tonight failure was not an option. She'd faced worse crowds than this. In some of the dives in Vegas, she'd played to wild, drop-dead drunks falling off their stools. But these folks were her folks, fellow North Carolinians who'd likely give a hometown girl the benefit of the doubt—at least for the first stanza. So as she approached the small stage and greeted the musicians, she summoned her two muses: Janis and Melissa, and decided to go with "Bobby McGee," a proven favorite, if she could pull it off.

"What's your pleasure, Miss Ginny?" The lead guitarist offered two instruments, and they were good ones. After a quick inspection, she decided to go unplugged and borrowed his acoustic Fender.

She whispered her song choice, and the guy passed it on to the others, who grinned and jabbed their thumbs up. So far, so good. She sat on the edge of the stage, hunched over the instrument, and began tuning it. In the meantime, she saw Trev take a seat in the corner, while two excited waitresses in Buffalo Guys T-shirts hustled orders for fresh drinks.

Ginny tuned them all out and went to her quiet place, closed her eyes and imagined Lissa sleeping with her thumb in her mouth. She listened to waves slowly rolling ashore. The waves hissed in, then sucked back out. As they got larger and stronger, their ebbing more powerful, Ginny stretched, stood up, and moved to center stage.

She closed her eyes again, and with both arms, reached for the sky—left hand clenched in a fist, right one gripping the guitar. She felt the heat of the spotlight on her face, and once the crowd was totally quiet, she hugged the instrument in position against her body, tucked under her breasts like a lover, strummed a few chords, opened her eyes and made slow, intense contact with key corners of the room. She smiled, rolled her neck, and began.

Soon she was lost in the famous road trip with Bobby McGee. As the rhythm built, Ginny strummed, plucked, slid on the strings, and tapped the soundboard. She was busted flat in Baton Rouge, waiting for the train, and while she never intended to sing, she felt her throat opening and heard the deep, slightly husky melody pouring from a voice she barely recognized as her own.

Windshield wipers slapping time, and holding Bobby's hand in mine—by the time the music rolled her all the way to New Orleans, Ginny knew she'd hit her sweet spot. She knew this not because she was aware of her fingers moving or her feet dancing, but because she heard clapping and shouting through the buzz in her ears. Freedom's just another word for nothin' left to lose, and by the time she lowered her instrument, she was exhausted, exhilarated, and knew she'd been good enough not only for her and Bobby, but for everyone else.

And luckily, she felt Trev's arm slide around her waist, supporting her in that moment when she always felt like collapsing—but never did. His hot breath tickled her ear.

"You are smokin', girl! Just listen to them. They want more. Give 'em an encore."

She blinked, licked a bead of sweat from her upper lip. "No can do, Trev. I'm done. And we made a deal, remember?"

So she shook hands with the musicians and thanked them, lowered her head and hung onto the back of Trev's belt as he pushed a path through the appreciative patrons and eventually shuffled them out to their original table by the lake.

"Everyone wants a little piece of your heart," he said once they were seated.

"Well, *I* sure as hell do." Chip appeared out of nowhere. "Let's hire her, Trev. Think we'll have good receipts tonight? Imagine if Ginny were on the ticket every weekend? Our profits would soar through the tin roof."

"Want a job?" Trev asked.

She saw he was serious and recognized the old need in his eyes. Once upon a time, his offer would have sent her over the moon, but Ginny knew it was too late. It was like the dark water of the Catawba River flowing under the proverbial bridge just upstream. There were so many things she wanted to ask him, like why the hell had he enlisted in the damn army at a time when she needed him most?

But back then, Trev didn't know her issues. He was too busy dealing with his own. She had seen his restlessness and understood the crushing hopelessness of small town life, especially to those who had big dreams. And they'd both had super-sized dreams.

She turned to Chip. "Thanks, I appreciate the offer, but once the courts find me not guilty, I'm outta here, back to Vegas."

Chip emitted an exaggerated sigh. "I hate that. Can't you get her to change her mind, Trevor?"

"Well, maybe I can if you leave us alone, give me some quality time with the lady."

"Okay, I can take a hint." Chip winked at Ginny. "Catch you later." And then he was gone.

Trev and she settled back in their seats and gazed out at the black lake, where a pencil-thin reflection shimmered across the placid water, connected to a slice of melon moon. The stubby candle in the round, red glass dome had melted down into a puddle of itself, yet its flame stretched straight up from the wax like a proud soldier. Frogs chattered, and somewhere along the shore an angry blue heron squawked in alarm, but otherwise they were alone.

When Trev took her hand, Ginny shivered in the hot, humid night. Now that this moment had arrived, after seven long years, she feared the words wouldn't come.

"So, what did you want to tell me?" Trev's voice faltered.

She took a big gulp of the night. "I need to tell you about my daughter, Lissa."

THIRTY-SIX

Moment of truth…

Diana lowered more plates into the sudsy dishwater and looked out the window to the dark driveway. Damn Ginny! How could any mother break her promise like that? Ever since Matthew had returned without her, Diana had feared Ginny would be a no-show. And now, as the hands on the clock inched towards ten, Lissa's bedtime, Diana's anger boiled over.

She ducked her head to wipe the sweat off her chin onto her shoulder sleeve, then cursed under her breath. To top it off, the air conditioner was malfunctioning. Matthew's ancient heat pump couldn't keep up with the unprecedented heat wave, and since it was Friday night, the repair guys wouldn't come until Monday. They had placed antique fans in crucial positions. They cranked, clattered, and helped a little—but in the end, the adult members of the family's emotional thermostats quivered in the red zone.

The welcome home dinner had gone well, considering the guest of honor was missing in action. They'd eaten barbeque on the deck while they still had a breeze off the lake. Afterwards, she'd put the chocolate cake in the fridge to keep the icing from melting, and then began praying Ginny would come home in time to tuck Lissa in bed.

Damn her. Diana rinsed the last dishes and stacked them in the drainer rack. She dried her hands and listened to the frenetic romper room music coming from the living room. Matthew was playing a video game with Lissa. It involved remotes mounted in small, white plastic steering wheels and featured wacky-looking cartoon characters racing through exotic graphic landscapes—not Diana's idea of fun. But Matthew and Lissa were laughing, so that was good.

Matthew had not been laughing when he returned home alone. Indeed, Diana had seldom seen him so upset or depressed. He gave her the briefest of explanations, when she was hungry for details about the hearing, and then he stomped away to brood in the shower. Again, not Diana's idea of fun. When he finally explained that Ginny had opted for a date with her old boyfriend, rather than a celebration with her family, Diana decided the girl was beyond redemption.

She turned on the cold water spigot and filled Amazing Grace's steel drinking bowl, set it down on the linoleum for the poor greyhound, who had been panting and cowering all evening. Ursie was holding forth in the living room at Lissa's feet, still guarding the child—another bad situation. The dogs had not yet made peace with one another. No more fights, thank god, but Matthew's Ursie continued to growl at Diana's Gracie whenever the two were in close proximity. She chose not to believe the animals' inability to live together was a metaphor for her relationship with Matthew. Instead, she hoped the dogs would eventually work it out when life returned to normal.

But when would that be? She drifted out the back door to see if the humidity of the night was better than the oppression in the house. As she stood on the porch, unimpressed by the air quality, she saw headlights coming up the road.

The Jeep turned in, its beams briefly blinding her before the driver cut the engine. Ginny slid out the passenger door and headed in her direction. Trevor exited slowly, remained several paces behind as they approached. A melon slice of moonlight illuminated their tense faces, and to Diana, the two looked like pale, unhappy ghosts.

Ginny fell into her arms and gave her a tight, desperate hug. The girl smelled like sweat and fear, but Diana hugged her anyway.

"Hello, Mrs. Rittenhouse." Trevor's eyes remained downcast, so she couldn't decide if he was shy, ashamed, or both.

"Is Lissa still awake?" Ginny gripped Diana's hand.

"Yes, lucky for you, she insisted on waiting up for her mommy." Diana didn't want to sound angry, she just couldn't help it.

"What about that chocolate cake?" Trevor was still unable to make eye contact. "Ginny figured you'd save a piece, or two."

"Forget the cake, Trev," Ginny snapped. "We'll talk first, then decide about the damn cake."

Diana extracted herself and held the door open. As the couple passed into the house, tension shimmered off their bodies like shock waves. The electrical disturbance tingled against Diana's skin and lifted the soft hairs on her arms. Not good. Had they been fighting, or was the static caused by something far more elemental? They were together, yet apart, and when Trevor finally glanced at Diana through his troubled blue eyes and offered a jerky smile, she sensed his fear. Whatever had happened between them had cast the tough war veteran into a state of sheer panic.

Even Gracie felt their vibes. She whined, tucked her tail between her legs, and tried to hide under the kitchen table when the strangers entered.

"What's with the dog?" Ginny asked.

Diana realized Ginny had been in prison when Gracie arrived at the house, so they'd never met. "She's my dog, and it's a long story. I'll tell you later."

"It's mighty hot in here." Trevor mopped his forehead with his hand.

As Diana explained that the air conditioner was on the blink, Lissa flew into the room.

"Is Mommy home?" she squealed.

Ginny dropped to her knees and gathered her daughter into her embrace, while Trevor froze like a marble statue.

"I'm home, honey. Lord, I missed you so much!" Ginny's tears flowed freely into Lissa's curly red hair.

"It's about time." Matthew hovered in the crowded entry like a storm cloud. He frowned disapprovingly at Trevor. "But at least you brought her home."

"Yes, sir." Trevor gulped, finally thawing from marble to mobile as he shifted nervously foot to foot.

"Let's all move to the living room." Ginny kept tight hold of Lissa's hand. "Time for a family conference."

Diana's heart seized up. The tone of Ginny's pronouncement set blood charging through her arteries, spreading dread through her veins to the extremities of her toes and fingertips. She sensed that whatever they were about to hear would be life-changing. It could be anything from a sudden announcement of wedding plans, to confessions of murder, or something Diana had suspected all along, had she bothered to listen to that erratic heart of hers.

But she held her peace, because this was Ginny's show, God help her. Diana followed quietly and sat in her favorite armchair as Matthew settled into his recliner. Ginny and Trevor chose opposite ends of the sofa, with Lissa between them. It was a moment of truth, and one look at Matthew told her he knew it, too. His tanned face had taken on the same sickly pallor as his male counterpart on the sofa. His mouth had compressed to a thin, grim line.

Diana listened to the ticking of the grandfather clock, which was disturbingly much slower than the rhythm of blood pulsing in her ears, and absurdly, she found herself imagining a scene from the Tom Dooley legend—an idyllic interlude with Tom's pregnant Laura riding horseback through a peaceful mountain forest—before all the violence.

"I remember you." Lissa pointed at Trevor. "You came to visit Mommy on my birthday. I asked you to watch me ride my new bike, but you got in your car and drove away."

Lissa's high, piping voice brought Diana back to reality. She braced herself.

"That's right, Punkin." Ginny hugged her daughter close. "This man is Trevor Dula, and he was a dear friend of mine before you were born."

"Really?" Lissa reached out and grabbed one of Trevor's fingers. "Can you eat some cake with us tonight?"

Trevor stared at the child, an expression of stunned disbelief on his face as he tentatively patted her hand.

Ginny cupped Lissa's face in her palm and forced the child to focus. "Now pay attention, Lissa. Are you listening?"

Lissa nodded. "Yes, Mommy."

For a moment Ginny hesitated, glanced at Matthew and Diana, then at the ceiling seeking what—divine intervention?

223

Finally she fixed on her daughter. "This man, Trevor, is more than my old friend, Lissa. Once upon a time, we were in love, and he is your real father."

THIRTY-SEVEN

Pillow talk…

"I knew it all along," Diana said as Matthew crawled in beside her.

"No, you didn't. If you'd known, you would've told me." He reached up and turned off his bed light.

"I wasn't sure," she admitted truthfully. "But I sure enough suspected."

Ever since that morning when she and Ginny drove into Davidson to deliver Lori's wedding present, Diana had wondered about the bridegroom, Ginny's ex-boyfriend. Ginny had said she'd driven all the way from Las Vegas to "give him a hard time," and even then, Diana had thought it was an extreme measure to take for some guy from the distant past.

"But the timing was right, Matthew, do the math. When Ginny ran off almost seven years ago, she was already pregnant. She hooked up with that oilman, Charley Harkin, and they got married in Galveston. Then six, maybe seven months later, Lissa was born."

Matthew groaned and turned his back to her. "Give it a rest, Diana. From what Ginny told us, her husband was a drunken roughneck, but she never said he was a fool. He could do the math, too, so he had to know Lissa was another man's child."

"Yes, but maybe Charley didn't care. Ginny was a good looking young woman, a real catch. He accepted Lissa because he wanted Ginny."

"Or maybe he abused Ginny because he resented Lissa." Matthew pulled his part of the sheet around his shoulders, encasing himself in a cocoon. "Turn off your light and go to sleep. I don't want to talk about it."

Diana was losing him. This was not her idea of pillow talk, so she stared at the ceiling and began counting acoustic tiles. Okay, she got it. Matthew felt desperately guilty about what he termed "driving Ginny away," so it went without saying this latest twist, driving a *pregnant* Ginny away, was almost intolerable. She could only imagine his pain and longed to comfort him.

"Well, I think Lissa took the news pretty well, don't you?" She reached down and touched Matthew's mummy-wrapped hand. No response.

In fact, Ginny had done a credible job selling a new "real" daddy to Lissa. Naturally the child was confused, and Ginny's metaphors were somewhat convoluted. She had compared her love for Trevor to Lissa's love for her very first toy—a raggedy monkey, then compared her love for Charley to Lissa's love for a later toy—a Barbie doll. Ginny reminded her daughter that it was okay to love both toys, and that both toys loved Lissa. Or some such thing. But it was brilliant, because it worked.

Matthew mumbled. "I'm not sure Trevor appreciated being compared to a ratty old monkey."

Diana was relieved that he was listening. "I know, did you see Trevor's face?"

"I think he was in shock," Matthew chuckled from his shroud.

"But he managed it well." Clearly Trevor had been handed the surprise of his young life, and although he remained tongue-tied through much of his brief introduction to his daughter, he'd cracked a couple of jokes and put Lissa at ease. "Did you notice how Lissa was watching him? She's really curious."

Matthew turned onto his back, glanced at Diana. "Lissa laughed when Trevor dropped his cake onto his lap, but it will never work out for the three of them, and you know it."

She watched his eyes shifting and realized Matthew wanted a response—confirm, or deny. But Diana had no idea. Just because Trevor loved Ginny once, didn't mean he'd love her again. Indeed, she believed it would be a very long time before Trevor got over Lori, and if that ever happened, likely Ginny would be long gone, home to Nevada.

"Well, Trevor did agree to visit again tomorrow. Ginny and Lissa are taking him on a boat ride, then a picnic."

"That's a mistake," Matthew grumbled. "In the end, Lissa will get hurt. I'm glad I won't be around to watch them today."

Diana counted more tiles and listened to a motorboat speed by the dock in the dark. Its drunken passengers were laughing and shouting, and as their waves crashed ashore, she wondered if Matthew was right. For Lissa, Trevor could easily become more than a shiny new toy. He was, after all, her father.

"I won't be here either," Diana said. She had to put in an appearance at the office, so when Liz returned sometime that weekend, she could pretend she'd done some work. "But who cares if we're here? Ginny and Trevor don't need a chaperone."

"They should've had a chaperone seven years ago." Matthew rolled out of his sheet and vigorously kicked it to the foot of the bed. "And they shouldn't be seen together now."

Diana understood guilt, but she didn't understand his anger. It burned through his skin and shimmered between them. "What's your problem?" she demanded. When he faced her, she saw both wrath and desperation.

"Remember when I told you Ginny had a secret, that she was hiding something?"

"Sure, I remember." His intensity frightened her.

"Turns out Lissa is Ginny's dark little secret—the fact that Trevor is her father." Matthew pulled upright. "Ginny's lawyer implied the cops had more evidence against her, and this is it."

"I don't understand."

Matthew picked up his extra pillow, tossed it up in the air, and punched it across the room. "Seems like Ginny's a pretty good liar, don't you agree? She travels halfway across the country because her old boyfriend's getting married, brings their lovechild along for leverage to change his mind, and then confronts his fiancée, who winds up dead."

"What are you trying to say?"

He flopped down on his back beside her, took her hand, and helped her stare at the ceiling. "I'm saying now the cops have a motive for murder."

THIRTY-EIGHT

Back at square one...

By the time Diana woke up, Matthew had already left for work. By the time she showered and dressed for the office, Ginny and Lissa had finished breakfast and were frantically preparing for Trevor's visit.

"Are you okay, Diana?" Ginny was slicing hoagie rolls for a picnic. "Looks like you could use some more sleep, or maybe you got up on the wrong side of the bed."

"Do I look that bad?" Fact was, Matthew had gotten up on the wrong side of the bed. They'd argued late into the night about Ginny, Trevor, the evidence—you name it. Diana found herself projecting an optimism she did not feel in order to balance Matthew's premonitions of doom. Granted, Ginny was his daughter, so perhaps he was entitled to be judgmental about the choices she had made. But Diana resented being cast in the role of Pollyanna, so bitter words had passed between them.

"Daddy's pissed, isn't he?" Ginny slathered the rolls with mayonnaise and stuffed them with ham and cheese. "It's about Trev, isn't it? Dad hates me for getting pregnant and splitting."

"No, it's more than that. Where's Lissa, by the way?" Diana felt compelled to clear the air, but not in front of the child.

Ginny laughed. "She's changing her outfit for the third time. She wants to look extra pretty for her new daddy."

Diana grunted. Like Matthew, she was unsure how much Lissa should be encouraged to bond with a father here today, gone tomorrow. If Lissa came to love the man, then got dragged back to Nevada, her emotions would spin like a yo-yo.

"Lissa couldn't sleep at all last night," Ginny merrily continued. "She was already on a sugar high from the cake and she couldn't stop asking questions."

"Well, who can blame her? It's a lot to lay on the kid." Diana knew she was grumpy because she hadn't fallen asleep until just before dawn, then woken up alone with a splitting headache. As she watched Ginny place pickles and peppers on the sandwiches, her stomach did flip-flops.

Ginny frowned and looked up from her task. "Don't start in on me, Diana. Let me worry about Lissa, and I promise I won't let her get hurt. You know Dad will read me the riot act when he gets home, so I need you on my team."

Diana poured herself a cup of hundred-proof caffeine from the bottom of the coffee pot. "Matthew's worried about you. He's afraid your relationship with Trevor, the fact he fathered your child, will work against you in court. He thinks it'll give the prosecutor a motive, and they'll try to make a case against you based on jealousy."

"Yeah, I've heard it all before. Geek, my lawyer, says the same thing. Did you know that asshole, Lieutenant Sokolsky, searched my records back in Galveston? He dug up Lissa's birth certificate and saw I named Trev as the father."

"Stop right there." Diana was incredulous. "You actually named Trevor?"

Ginny shrugged dismissively. "Sure, why not? My loser husband didn't give a shit. I knew I'd tell Lissa the truth someday, because I didn't want her going through life thinking Charley Harkin was her daddy."

Diana took a long gulp of coffee and held her tongue until the caffeine hit her bloodstream. At some level she understood Ginny's reasoning, but it seemed a bitter irony that the mother's good intentions had come back to bite her on the butt.

"And you know what else?" Suddenly Ginny's expression took on a dreamy aspect. "You should've seen Trev when I told him. At first he was in shock, but soon he started to cry, he was so happy."

Diana took another sip and waited.

"In fact, he confided in me." Ginny glanced towards her bedroom to be sure Lissa had not yet emerged. "Would you believe Lori was pregnant?"

Diana choked on her coffee. Bearfoot had made it perfectly clear and she remembered his exact words: *Lori was no more pregnant than I am.* "There must be some mistake."

"No mistake. Trev and Lori were ecstatic, already designing the nursery, and they didn't give a rat's ass what people thought."

"Did they tell anyone?"

"Well gee, Diana, who cares?" Ginny began folding the hoagies into plastic wrap. "I know he told his uncle Maynard, so I'm sure Maynard told his wife, Paula. What does it matter?"

Diana slumped deeper into her chair. "You better sit down, too, Ginny, because I need to tell you a story about a bitter old man named Loveless. It's all about the trust fund he set up for the nieces he adored…"

231

As Diana told the tale, Ginny's mouth sagged in disbelief. Diana paused only long enough to greet Lissa, who had settled on an emerald green shorts outfit that made her look like a feminine Peter Pan. Lissa explained how they were taking her new daddy to their secret island for a picnic, and then she and Ursie went down to the dock to wait on the boat.

Once the child was out of earshot, Diana concluded, "So you see, with Lori pregnant, Paula had about ten million reasons to kill her."

"Holy shit!" Ginny's fingers trembled as she shoved her black bangs off her forehead. "Only one problem with your theory, Diana. Lori wasn't pregnant when she died. Tragically, she had a miscarriage last month. She and Trev were devastated. Don't you get it? That's why he was so stunned to hear about Lissa. He'd pretty much given up on ever having a child."

All right, that made sense and it jived with Bearfoot's statement, but Diana was still troubled. "Did Trevor tell Maynard and Paula about Lori's miscarriage?"

"I don't know," she answered slowly. "Maybe not. Trev had a terrible time telling me about it. He was so torn up, it's possible he kept it to himself."

So Diana figured they were back at square one. Another irony. What if Paula, or Maynard, had committed murder because they were ill informed? Diana's headache returned with a vengeance. As she fished a small bottle of aspirin from her purse, she realized Ginny might have just revealed another relevant clue.

"You told me both Maynard and Paula had access to Trevor's Jeep that morning, right?" Diana asked.

Ginny seemed thoughtful. "Right. Believe me, I'd love to pin it on that bitch, but Maynard's been acting weird, too. He's very protective of Trev and thinks I'm a bad influence. He thinks I'm gonna hurt his nephew. Trev claims that lately Maynard's been moody. One minute he's angry at the world, next minute he's drunk and crying in his beer. I don't get it. Maynard and me used to be friends."

Diana didn't get it either, and the effort was making her ill. For all she knew, the murder had been a simple robbery gone bad, as Liz had suggested. At the moment, she lacked the strength to speculate, so she swallowed two aspirins and climbed to her feet.

"Hate to run, Ginny, but I must go to the office."

"Oh, don't tell me you won't be here to say hi to Trev?" But Ginny's eyes betrayed her. She wasn't at all sorry Diana was leaving. Then she and Lissa could have Trevor all to themselves.

"I hope to be home in time for supper, but tell Matthew not to wait, okay?'

"What about Gracie?" Ginny pointed at the greyhound lying under the table. "What if she and Ursie get into a fight?"

Well, Diana had been dragging Lissa to the office to help cut out paper dolls, so why not take Gracie? "C'mon, girl…" The dog tucked her tail and skittered out the door after Diana. She jumped into Queen Vic, and then Diana waved goodbye.

"Okay, sweet one," she cooed to the animal. "It's just you and me."

THIRTY-NINE

Practicing apologies…

Diana spotted Trevor's Jeep as he turned off River Highway onto their road. She noticed his tense profile as he stared straight ahead. He was going to a picnic, but truth be told, these recent weeks hadn't been a picnic for anyone. Moments later she passed Matthew's store, saw his truck parked out back, but resisted the temptation to rush inside to kiss and make up.

Instead, she patted Gracie's sleek head, which was already cradled on her lap. "Let's let him stew awhile, what do you think, girl?"

But Gracie had nothing to offer regarding the battle of the sexes, so Diana tuned to classical music and tried to sort out her emotions. It proved impossible. By the time she reached the junction of I77 and was poised to merge onto the expressway, heading south to Davidson, she had decided to call Matthew. She pulled off at a gas station, killed the engine, and took the cell phone from her purse.

She paused to come up with the right words to apologize and gazed down at the highway, where a steady stream of high-speed traffic rolled by in four orderly lanes, moving half and half in opposite directions. Diana reflected on the hundreds of drivers, each with his or her own agenda—separate lives, joys, tragedies—all hell bent on getting somewhere at seventy miles per hour. She noticed a storm cloud gathering on the horizon and hoped it wouldn't spoil Ginny's picnic.

When she was ready, her mind focused in spite of the buzzing whine of traffic, she held down button one and saw Matthew's name and number pop into the lighted digital display, but still she hesitated. How did one apologize when one felt no remorse? In that moment of indecision, the phone rang, vibrated in her hand, and Gracie leaped up from her lap.

What the hell? Diana stared at the incoming name and number on her screen. As she struggled to place the person, she suddenly realized who was trying to connect across the miles. She pushed the green "talk" button, stated her name, then listened as the caller began her tirade.

"Hello, Mrs. Rittenhouse, can I call you *Diana*?" Paula Dula said. "I've been calling your office, but no one ever answers. All I get is the damn machine."

"I'm so sorry." Diana had met Paula briefly at Trevor's arraignment. She recalled her hard green eyes and imagined them now, sparking with anger.

"This is ridiculous. Liz told me she was going on vacation, but she promised you'd be there to help me," Paula ranted.

"Yes, I know, and I'm sorry." Diana was ashamed. Selfishly, she had powered off her cell for too many hours during Liz's absence. "But I'm here now, Paula, so how can I help?"

"When is Liz due back? The stupid construction guys at my lot in Lakeview Estates are sitting on their butts. Nothin's gettin' done, and we're set to close in less than two weeks."

"Liz'll be back sometime this weekend, and I'm sorry the men are goofing off." If Diana had been practicing apologies for Matthew, she was getting plenty of experience with Paula.

"You can bet your sweet ass those jerks are there now, sittin' around, crackin' jokes, and eatin' tacos." Paula fumed. "I can't wait for Liz. I want someone to light a fire now."

Diana sighed, looked at the storm cloud. "I understand. What would you like me to do?" She hoped Paula wasn't getting buyer's remorse, because Liz would kill her if this deal fell through.

"I'm at Big Jay's Mall and my fuckin' car won't start. I figure my retard husband left the lights on, and the battery's dead. Can you pick me up, Diana? We can visit the property together."

Diana glanced at Gracie, who cocked her head and gave her a mournful look. Why hadn't she brought Gracie's leash along, why hadn't Liz returned one day sooner, and what had she done to deserve this? The last thing she wanted was to spend a day alone with a pissed-off potential murderess, but Diana swallowed her self-pity and adjusted her attitude.

"No problem, Paula. I'll be there in a half hour."

FORTY

Moral fiber…

As promised, Paula was waiting outside Big Jay's. She was leaning against the long hood of a gold, vintage sixties El Dorado that listed to one side, as though the white wall tires on the driver's side were slightly deflated. What was it about these Dulas—Trevor with his Willys, Maynard with his Caddy? It seemed they were stuck in a former decade, maybe a happier time for both.

Paula hugged a large shopping bag in her arms, and by the huge grin on her heavily made-up face, her mood was much improved. "Check it out…" she called as Diana approached. "Look what I bought on sale." She pulled a black leather Harley Davidson jacket from the bag, then a pair of rhinestone-studded cowgirl boots. "Pretty cool, eh?"

"Pretty hot for this weather," Diana commented. She wouldn't be caught dead in such a getup, but hey, it was perfect for Paula. "Did you call someone to come fix your car?"

Paula shifted her long legs and scooted off the hood. She wore obscenely tight jeans shorts and a clinging pink top to enhance her generous figure. "Sure, Triple A's on the way."

"Shouldn't we wait until they get here?"

"Hell, no. I left my keys, and they know what to do. We'll swing by and pick my up car later."

It seemed these Dulas also made a habit of leaving their keys in their cars. "Don't you need to pay them?"

Paula offered an amused, cross-eyed response. "I gave 'em my card number, and I reckon my credit's good."

I reckon. Diana kept that thought to herself. It stood to reason a multi-million dollar heiress could pretty much write her own ticket. "Ready to go, then?"

"Gimme a sec…" Paula tossed her purchases into the Caddy, then fished out a carton of cigarettes. "You smoke?" She held the carton out towards Diana.

"Nope, I quit."

"Now why don't that surprise me?" Paula removed a pack for herself, then tossed the carton back in her car, through the open window.

As the woman trailed Diana across the lot to Queen Vic, Diana was tempted to tell her to roll up her car's window, in case it rained. Typical Diana, always trying to be someone's mother. She suppressed her maternal instincts and allowed herself to relax, because maybe Paula wasn't the monster she had originally supposed. The woman had offered her a gift of cigarettes, and although in politically correct circles the gesture was akin to offering someone lung cancer, Diana appreciated her generosity.

"Hop in…" When Diana pressed her key remote, unlocking the doors to Queen Vic, Gracie howled in surprise to see a stranger.

"What the fuck?" Paula recoiled when she saw the greyhound cowering in the front seat. "You expect me to ride with that animal?"

Diana groaned inwardly, quickly revising her positive impression of Paula. "She won't hurt you. Gracie's a gentle soul." Yet Paula wasn't buying it. "Okay, get in back, Gracie." She snapped her fingers, and for once her pet obeyed and jumped into the back seat. "Good girl!"

Once convinced Gracie wouldn't attack, Paula pointedly brushed dog hair off the upholstery and slid into the car. "Where I come from, dogs compete for food. It's one thing to keep livestock, but a damn dog ain't good for nothin' but huntin'."

Diana gave Paula a hard stare.

"I like cats, though," the woman quickly amended.

Oh God. Diana wanted to call Paula a few choice names, none of them complimentary, but she knew the world was made up of dog people and cat people, and the two groups seldom cross-pollinated. It was interesting, though, that Paula presented herself as such a country girl, when her dead cousin, Lori, had been just the opposite. As she peeked at the woman's tough profile—long, dishwater blond hair framing her thin, cruel mouth—Diana couldn't tell truth from fiction. Maybe the backwoods persona was a clever act.

A few raindrops fell on the windshield as she steered out of Statesville and into the suburbs. Diana wondered if she should broach the subject of real estate. After all, that's why she was here. But the woman seemed intent on discussing Big Jay's, the store where she'd just been shopping.

The place was famous for selling discount cigarettes, cheapest in the nation, and several years ago a group of young, Islamic terrorists had actually purchased vanloads of cartons there. They were smuggling them north, selling them at a huge profit to finance Jihad, until they were finally captured at the Canadian border. Paula seemed impressed by their cunning.

"You admire those terrorists?" Diana wondered.

"Hell, yes. Maybe they were a gang of ignorant rag head shits, but they knew how to get what they wanted. Ask me, their plan was brilliant."

Diana scowled at her passenger, who was seriously lacking in moral fiber. "They got caught, Paula."

"Yeah, but sometimes the prize is worth the risk."

Diana let it go. She'd have plenty of time to reflect on Paula's ethics, but at the moment she was entering Lakeview Estates and trying to recall how to find Paula's property. The huge, gated community was still in the planning stages, with lot numbers posted on fragile, temporary signposts and very inadequate maps to distinguish one rutted red clay road from another. Diana paused at a crossroads. "Help me, Paula. I'm lost."

"That's easy." Paula grinned. "Soon as you smell a bunch of beaners sittin' on their butts with their hands up their ass, you'll know you've found my lot."

FORTY-ONE

Bad mistake…

Paula's bigoted remark was beyond disgusting, so by the time they entered the wooded dogleg leading to the property, Diana was ready to call it a day.

"Ready to kick ass, Diana?" Paula unclipped her seatbelt.

They rounded a bend and climbed a steep promontory. On the crest of the hill stood the soaring framework for a mini-mansion. The bruised purple sky served as a backdrop for the wooden skeleton, with fast-moving gray clouds racing high above the turrets. The scene had the surreal quality of a stage set for a horror movie, and as the car bumped onto the gravel lot, Diana saw they were alone—not a workman in sight.

"Shit. What did I tell you?" Paula beat the dashboard with her fist. "Lazy mother fuckers."

Once Paula had exited the car and stomped angrily up the grade towards the project, Diana eyed Gracie, who was whining in the back seat. She again regretted not bringing a leash. She suspected Gracie needed to answer a call of nature, and thus far her dog had never attempted to run away, so she let her loose. Sure enough, Gracie sneaked into the bushes, squatted and peed, an embarrassed look on her face.

"Are you coming, or what?" Paula hollered.

"Be right there!" Diana whistled to Gracie, who sped to her side. "What do you think, girl? Shall we get this over with?"

Paula was pacing the perimeter when they joined her. "I swear they got these studs wrong. The damn kitchen's supposed to face west, so I can watch the sunset on the lake while I wash the stupid dishes."

Diana was unfamiliar with the floorplan, but she was determined to do her best. She knew something about construction and saw that much of the plumbing was in place. If she could locate the well and septic, then follow the pipes, perhaps she could determine where they'd made plans for the bathrooms and the kitchen.

She noticed the concrete block foundation was in place on all four sides. It was built of twin walls running parallel, about two feet apart. These walls were approximately three feet tall at the rear of the structure and much higher in front, where the land fell away to a magnificent lake view across a deep valley.

Paula had already found her way in through a future doorway, so Diana and Gracie followed carefully, avoiding the piles of two- by- fours, stacks of rebar, and other dangerous rubble. She said a silent prayer that Gracie wouldn't step on a stray nail.

"Why the hell aren't they working?" Paula sheltered against the foundation, cupped her hand, and lit up a cigarette.

"It's Saturday, Paula, and a storm is coming." Diana glanced at the angry sky. "Maybe they figured it wasn't worth it?"

"Bullshit. Liz promised my house would be done by August. At this rate, I'll be lucky to move in by Christmas."

Diana was at a loss to comfort this woman, who was obviously coming unhinged. She saw tears in her eyes as she sucked at her cigarette, and Diana wished she could give Liz a piece of her mind. Clearly the construction was way behind schedule, so it was irresponsible for Liz to misrepresent, no matter how badly they needed this sale.

"What the fuck am I supposed to do? I just checked into a hotel, but I can't stay there forever. I feel like a god damned gypsy."

Diana did a double-take. "Aren't you living with Maynard anymore?"

Bad mistake. Paula dropped her cigarette and ground it viciously into the dirt with the toe of her sandal. She wiped at her eyes with the back of her hand. And when she raised those eyes and stared, Diana felt like she'd been penetrated by two lasers. The woman's pent-up fury cut deep, filling Diana with dread.

"You ask too many questions, Diana. What the hell do you want?"

"I don't understand...?" Diana retreated several paces and looked around for Gracie, but the dog had her nose buried in a discarded white paper bag, obviously enjoying someone's lunch scraps. She was definitely not in protective mode.

Paula lit another smoke and advanced to where Diana was backed against a partial retaining wall. "Did you really think I wouldn't find out? My lawyer, Geek Adams, told me you'd been asking about the terms of my uncle Loveless' Trust. What's that about, bitch?"

Suddenly Diana knew she was in serious trouble, but she couldn't think of anything to say in her own defense. Plus, what ever happened to lawyer/client confidentiality? But then, Diana wasn't Mecklin's client, was she? It stood to reason he'd have to check with Paula before releasing the particulars to Linc Davis, and then on to her.

"I'm sorry," Diana stuttered. "I wanted to be sure you had sufficient assets to afford this property. My mistake."

"Nice try." Paula moved so close Diana coughed on the smoke exhaled in her face. "Then I understand Ginny Troutman asked Trev last night if *I* had borrowed his Jeep the day my ignorant cousin Lori died. Obviously Ginny passed his answer on to you."

"We were just curious…"

Paula's harsh laugh echoed through the bones of the building, and thunder clapped nearby. She ground out the second cigarette and ran her fingers through her wild blond hair. "Why did that slut show up after all these years? Did she seriously think my Trev would lie down and roll over just because she bore him a bastard?"

Diana's heart pumped adrenaline so fast she feared she'd faint. "How did you know?"

Another maniacal laugh. "My loser husband and Trev are like this…" She twisted her hands together. "Soon as he got home last night, after hearing the glorious news, Trev called Maynard and spilled his guts. Trev was equally thrilled when my stupid cousin got pregnant, but that didn't work out so well for Lori, did it? And you solved the case, didn't you, Diana?"

The fear coursing through Diana's system escalated to sheer terror. So this was it, no more speculation. In the end, a few loose tongues and the small town grapevine had answered every question too late, and Paula had lured her here knowing all the answers in advance. Diana could tell the crazed woman she'd made a terrible mistake by killing Lori, since Lori had already miscarried when she died, but likely that revelation would only serve to further enrage her.

"It won't work out well for Ginny, either. She'll go to jail for the rest of her life." Paula bent over and picked up a short length of rebar. "Did you hope that little slut would become your new daughter, Diana? Then you'd all live together like one big happy family, including my Trevor?"

Paula was clearly insane as she tossed the thin, heavy bar back and forth in her hands. Absurdly, Diana noticed the woman's well-muscled arms and how the violent wind lifted her mass of hair like a golden halo around her contorted features. Diana reached back and groped along the rough concrete wall, hoping for what? To lay her hands on a weapon of her own? A shaft of lightning cracked against a tree in the nearby forest, and torrential rain cried from the heavens.

Diana felt the support of the wall disappear and the hard edge of the lower foundation pressing against the back of her knees. When Paula lifted the rebar to strike, Diana's scream was joined by Gracie's furious barking. Another lightning bolt exploded inside Diana's head.

And when she stumbled backwards, her world went black.

FORTY-TWO

Matthew…

Lissa was mighty proud of the fried chicken she'd helped her mommy make, but Matthew wasn't hungry. Using her tiny fingers, she lifted a crispy drumstick onto his plate, then spooned out a mound of potato salad.

"Please try to eat. We made this just for you, Grandpa."

"Thanks, darlin'. It looks delicious." He glanced at Ginny, who was also anxiously awaiting his approval, so Matthew took a big bite and licked his lips. "Umm, yummy."

He had come home physically whipped and emotionally exhausted, kicking himself for every harsh word he'd said to Diana last night. He wished he could take it all back. He remembered how she'd lain beside him, holding his hand and telling him everything would be all right, but he'd turned a cold shoulder and behaved like a petulant child.

"Are you sure Diana didn't call?" he asked for the third time. "You checked the answering machine?"

"No, Daddy, she didn't call. And yes I checked the machine. In fact, she said we should go ahead and eat without her. She expected to be late."

He trailed his spoon through a pool of baked beans. He'd expected Diana to contact him at the store. He wasn't proud of it, but generally when they argued, even when it was his fault, it was Diana who always made the first move towards

246

making up. But today—nothing. When he finally broke down after lunch and dialed her cell phone, he got a message saying the subscriber was *unavailable*, which meant she'd turned the phone off.

"She probably worked late at the office. You know how far behind she was with all her work." Ginny added as she slid a hot biscuit onto Matthew's plate. "Stop worrying and eat."

He pushed back from the table. "You're right. I'll try the office again." Ignoring their protests, he stepped outside onto the deck to make his call. Normally he'd use the landline in the living room, but he didn't want Ginny and Lissa listening when Diana answered and he apologized. He'd grovel, if necessary.

But he returned to the kitchen more worried than before. "Nope. She must've left for the day. Got their blasted answering machine."

Ginny shrugged. "So sit down and finish your supper before it gets cold. Maybe Diana went out to dinner, or decided to go home to her condo to eat?"

Matthew scowled at his daughter, who thought she knew all the answers. Naturally he'd been trying Diana's condo all afternoon, with no luck. No harm trying again. This time he stepped onto the back porch to make the call. As he leaned in the shadow of the roof's overhang to dial, the oppressive heat of late afternoon filled his lungs and glistened on his forearms. As he listened for her to pick up, he visualized the little princess phone ringing in the foyer of her apartment. His imagination roamed through the cool emptiness of Diana's rooms, but he didn't see her there.

His brain started to panic. He let it ring and ring as he watched a mockingbird chase a terrified squirrel across the street. He didn't hang up until the animal found safety in the bushes.

"Please come in, Grandpa." Lissa tugged at his trousers. If you don't eat your supper, you don't get dessert."

"Is that how it works?" He grinned at the child even as an odd sense of dread settled in the pit of his stomach.

"Yeah, stop worrying, Dad." Ginny appeared at his elbow. "Maybe you did something to piss her off? Maybe she figures you guys need a vacation from one another?"

Matthew sighed. Likely Ginny was right. He'd been distracted lately, and sometimes surly with Diana. He wouldn't blame her if she decided to take a breather, and yet…

""Who's that?" Lissa squealed, interrupting his train of thought. She pointed down the road to where a pickup truck was driving fast, kicking up dirt. It swung into Matthew's driveway, and the driver honked the horn.

Seconds later, Liz McCorkle jumped out with a huge smile on her face. Her sunburned arms were dotted with new freckles. "Hi, guys, we're home!"

"Yeah, did y'all miss me?" Her boyfriend Danny leaped out and began scanning the yard. "Hey, where's my dog? Where's Gracie?"

"She's not *your* dog, silly." Liz punched his arm, then she too began searching the premises for the one missing person. "And by the way, where's Diana?"

FORTY-THREE

Bad dream…

The pain in her head was intolerable, but when she tried to wake up and climb out of it, it got worse. She took deep breaths, but something was covering her mouth, so she inhaled through her nose and smelled the loamy wet earth, human sweat, and the metallic scent of blood. She tasted the same metal at the back of her throat, and when she tried to scream, the rag compressing her lips muffled the sound.

She remembered nothing and decided she must be dreaming, except for that pain. If only she could open her eyes, the nightmare would go away. She lifted her lids slowly, blinked away grains of dirt, but saw only black. Or brown. Thin lines of light ran parallel along the length of her body. The lines two feet apart, just above her face. Late afternoon. When she tried to lift her head, the pain exploded in a cacophony of jagged red stars, so she closed her eyes again.

Dear God in heaven, where was she? When she tried to move, she felt two walls—cold and rough. Concrete pressed against her shoulders, arms, hips, and legs. Her back ached from lying on something round and hard. Pipe. And when she tried to shift position, she found she was pinned.

Sweet Jesus. She flexed her ankles and realized she'd lost one shoe. She tried to move her hands, but they were bound together at the wrists with flat wire. She lifted her arms, pounded against the ceiling, but nothing moved. Exploring the lid with her fingers, she found it was heavy, wooden, and unyielding.

As her panic escalated, she told herself this was only a bad dream. The oxygen she sucked through her nostrils was foul and dense with sawdust. When she moved her bound hands towards her mouth, her left elbow was trapped, could not reach the gag. Would she suffocate? Her eyes flooded with tears.

Couldn't think. Couldn't remember. She pounded against the ceiling, tried again to scream, but the pain was like knives spinning inside her skull. She tasted more metal as blood drained from her head, and she fainted to blessed unconsciousness.

FORTY-FOUR

Liz...

Liz saw immediately that something was wrong. "Where is Diana?" she repeated.

"She's not home yet," Ginny answered. "Why don't you come inside? We were just eating supper."

"I'm starving," Danny said.

Liz punched his arm as they trailed the Troutmans into the kitchen. "I didn't hear anyone inviting *you* to eat."

This wasn't the homecoming she'd expected. After a week in the mountains, she was eager to describe all the adventures they'd shared, especially how she'd saved Danny from sliding down a waterfall. But tension hung so thick in the air, she decided to save her stories.

"Don't look now, Grandpa, but Ursie's eating your chicken!" Lissa charged the table, shooing the Doberman away, but the dog already had Trout's drumstick clenched firmly in her jaw. She slinked away with her prize and hid behind the sofa.

Trout exhaled in exasperation, then clapped Danny on the back. "You could've had my dinner, son, but Ursie beat you to it."

When Lissa ran after the dog, chasing her out from behind the couch, onto the deck, then down into the yard, Ginny sighed and dished up a plate for Danny.

"There's plenty more where this came from. Are you hungry, Liz? Apparently Dad's not eating tonight."

"No thanks. I'm still full from the burgers we ate on the road. "She gave Danny a sour look as he sat right down and began stuffing his face. Far as she could tell, his stomach was a bottomless pit. She returned her attention to Trout and Ginny, who were clearly in a funk. "Okay, someone wanna tell me what's going on?"

Trout lumbered into the living room and sank into his favorite recliner. Ginny explained the situation to Liz as they followed him. "Bottom line? We have no idea what's happened to Diana," Ginny finished.

Liz plopped down beside Ginny on the sofa, then turned to Trout. "So, what did you do to piss her off?"

But Trout wasn't in the mood for jokes. "We've tried her cell phone, called the office and her condo. I don't get it," he said.

"Dad's really worried," Ginny added.

Liz looked from one to the other and decided they were over-reacting. Naturally Trout was upset. He loved Diana and sometimes got too protective, but Ginny was another story. When they were children, General Ginny had been tough, nothing fazed her, so if she was concerned now, maybe there really was cause for alarm.

"You say Diana planned to work at the office all day?" Both nodded. "Okay, let's check it out. I'll call in and review the messages." Liz took out her cell.

"You can do that?" Trout perked up.

Ginny rolled her eyes. "Of course she can. Honestly, Daddy."

252

As Liz scrolled through a week's worth of voice mail, she realized only one client had attempted to contact her with annoying persistence, and that person was not a happy camper. "Paula Dula was calling every ten minutes this morning," she told them. "And she sounded hopping mad. But since she's stopped, I assume Diana got in touch with her."

Trout frowned, slumped deeper into his chair. "So how do we find out for sure?"

At the mention of Paula's name, even Ginny seemed distressed, and Liz had a hunch it had something to do with Lori Fowler's murder and the trouble Ginny'd gotten herself into. So far Liz hadn't brought the subject up, hadn't even congratulated Ginny for being out on bail. Truth was, she hadn't yet figured out how to relate to her childhood friend, the summer camp bully.

"I could call Paula," Liz offered half-heartedly.

"Then please do it," Trout snapped.

His tone startled her so much that Liz actually flinched. She got to her feet, stomped into the hallway for a little privacy, then dialed Paula Dula. Shit. It was one thing to help out an old friend like Trout, quite another when that friendship put her in an awkward position with her only viable client.

She paced nervously, glanced back into the kitchen where Danny was still gobbling chicken, and almost hoped Paula wouldn't answer. Unfortunately, the woman picked up on the tenth ring. She sounded breathless and irritated when Liz stated the reason for her call.

"What's the big deal, Liz? So I talked to Diana on the phone this morning, and she answered all my questions. Then she drove to her office and went about her business. End of story."

After their short, unpleasant conversation, heat crawled up Liz's neck. She felt like a complete fool, yet she resented Paula's attitude. All eyes were upon her when she returned to the living room.

"What's up?" Danny wandered in munching a cookie.

"Everybody chill." Liz held up both hands. "Diana's fine. Paula talked to her on the phone this morning, just like I thought, and there's absolutely nothing wrong."

"Oh yeah? Paula Dula's a bitch," Ginny grumbled. "I don't believe one word she says."

Trout stood up, walked to the window, crossed his arms, and scowled out at the lake.

"Anybody want a cookie?" Ever the peacemaker, Danny trotted back to the kitchen to fetch the tray of chocolate chips, but on the way his cell began playing the theme from Star Wars. Everyone was startled as Danny fumbled the phone from his shirt pocket.

Liz watched her boyfriend's face change from happy-go-lucky to wide-eyed surprise. He kept saying, "Are you sure? Are you sure it's *her*?"

By the time he hung up, pale and shaken, Liz was certain something awful had happened to Diana. "Was that the police?"

Danny blinked and leaned against the nearest wall. "No, it was Iredell County Animal Control. Seems they found Gracie wandering around in an abandoned land fill up in Statesville."

The room was dead silent for what seemed an eternity as everyone processed this shocking bit of news. Finally Ginny broke the spell.

"How come they called *you* about *Gracie*?" she demanded of Danny.

254

He blushed. "I couldn't resist buying her one of those fancy dog tags, you know? And since Gracie lives with me so much of the time, I put my phone number on the tag."

Suddenly Trout walked to the back door. On the way he grabbed his truck keys from the hall table.

"Where are you going?" Liz called.

But clearly Trout was not in the mood for conversation as he turned to his daughter. "How do I find Paula Dula's house?"

Ginny saw the determined look in his eyes and hesitated only a second before giving him directions. "Let me come with you, Dad."

"Absolutely not. You stay here with Lissa, and please call Wayne Bearfoot. Tell him Diana is missing."

Ginny opened her mouth to argue, but changed her mind.

"Then let *me* come with you, Trout." Liz stepped forward, but Trout placed a firm hand on her shoulder, stopping her in her tracks. "No, why don't you drive down to Davidson. Check the office and Diana's condo. Maybe she's there, after all."

"No problem."

"But what about Gracie?" Danny whined.

"Oh hell, you can borrow my Subaru," Ginny told Danny. "But please make sure Gracie sits in the back of the wagon. No tellin' what kind of shit she's been wallowing in."

In spite of her gruff tone, Liz could tell Ginny was worried sick, so she actually felt a teeny weenie spark of sympathy for her old nemesis as Ginny's father backed out the drive. And when she glanced again at Ginny and Danny standing together on the back porch, they looked for all the

255

world like a pair of frightened, white- faced owls in Trout's
headlights.

FORTY-SIX

A distressed animal…

She remembered waking up and hearing something—or someone—scratching at the ceiling of her tomb. She hoped it would claw its way through the plywood, or whatever barrier held her prisoner in this living grave, but now it was gone. And when she swam painfully back into consciousness, she saw the thin bars of light had grown dim as the sun moved west across the sky, shifting afternoon towards evening.

Her hole was still hot as hell, she could barely breathe through the rag in her mouth, but at least the pain in her head had receded to where she could think straight. She decided the stiff substance dried on her forehead was blood, and she recalled the crazed face of the woman with halo hair as she lifted the bar to strike. And before fresh terror overpowered her reason, she put a name to that face—Paula. The creature clawing at her roof had surely been her own dear Gracie.

Sweet Jesus. As the truth of her predicament hit home, she mourned for herself and her beloved dog. Surely Paula had not hurt Gracie. Why would she? But then, why would she attack Diana? How could she possibly hope to get away with a second murder? Didn't the woman realize the workmen would discover her trapped in this disgusting foundation first thing Monday morning?

But what if Monday morning was too late? As her panic mounted, so did her anger. She writhed against the plumbing pipes digging into her back and fingered the bindings on her wrists. The restraints were fashioned from those flat aluminum bands used to bind bales of brick. She'd seen them on the site. And as Diana began picking at them with her nails, she felt the tension lessen as her fingertips began to bleed.

She didn't care about the blood, kept picking and flexing her wrists, panting for air as the bonds gave way. She tried to block out the pain, her aching ribs, and the very pressing need to use a bathroom until suddenly, her hands was free. Dear God, thank you!

She rested, gave thanks, and once the numbness left her freed right hand, she reached up and started tugging at her gag. She tasted blood on her lacerated fingers, but kept working. When she finally got it loose, she realized she'd been muffled by her favorite scarf, the one she'd chosen to wear to work this morning. Somehow this ultimate indignity fueled her fury.

When she opened her throat to scream, her voice was so hoarse no sound came out. So she tried again and again until her vocal chords produced the raspy, inhuman cry of a distressed animal. She screamed and gasped for oxygen, beat against the ceiling until her lungs gave out. When she wet herself, tears of self-pity rolled down her cheeks and she lapsed once again into a deep, unconscious sleep.

FORTY-SEVEN

Matthew…

Matthew slowed when he saw the crooked oak tree Ginny had described, then made a sharp right onto Dula Road. He passed the old, two-storied frame farmhouse on the left, Trevor's place. He noticed lights in the windows and his Jeep in his drive, but kept on driving towards the dead end.

He hadn't been down this lane in years, so everything looked different, especially the high chain link fence erected on both sides of the road. He read the sign: Dula Construction, and saw aging lumber, rock, and concrete blocks piled inside. An abandoned forklift was silhouetted against the setting sun, with its claw lying palm up in the dirt, like a hand at the wrist of a broken steel elbow. Even at a distance, Matthew noted the rust peeling off the machine's body.

By the looks of it, Maynard's business was not thriving, so clearly his wife's whopping inheritance would come in handy. Unless, as Diana had suspected, Maynard knew nothing about Paula's fortune. Since the eerie yellow security lights had just begun to glow, Matthew estimated he had a good hour of daylight left, so he had better get a move on.

But why? As he approached the simple brick ranch house at the end of the street, parked and walked up a short sidewalk bordered by flowers, he had no clear idea why he was there. He hesitated at the aluminum screen door decorated with

259

the letter "D," and wondered what on earth he'd say to the woman. He didn't even know these people, although he had a vague recollection of them visiting his store a time or two. Still, Matthew had a bad feeling about Diana's disappearance, and his gut told him Paula and Maynard Dula were involved up to their eyeballs.

He squared his shoulders and knocked with his knuckles, then listened as an ungodly yowling started up from somewhere in the depths of the dark house. The agonized crying put him on edge, and he wondered fleetingly if he should have brought a weapon. But Matthew didn't hold with violence, had never owned a gun, and had always figured most disputes could be settled with human reason. Maybe not this time.

He took another deep breath and realized the sound was familiar, only a cat in heat. He laughed at himself for reacting like a nervous Nellie. But then he heard a crash inside, followed by a loud curse, and before Matthew got a handle on the nature of these new threats, the aluminum door flew open.

"What the hell do you want? You fixin' to sell me something?"

The man swaying in the doorway was drunk and stank of beer. His long gray hair was matted. It hung loose on his bony shoulders, and he was shirtless, with a silver crucifix dangling against his scrawny chest.

Matthew stepped back a pace. "Maynard Dula? I'm Matthew Troutman. I'd like a word with your wife."

The man's odd gray eyes were unfocused, yet they fixed on Matthew. "Yeah, I know you. You're lil' Jailbait's daddy, ain't that right?"

Matthew let it go. He knew Ginny had visited this hovel not long ago. The stench from inside—cat box and cigarettes—was overwhelming. "Is Paula home?"

Maynard raised both skinny arms and hung onto the doorjambs for support. His body sagged with his weight, and thanks to an odd red illumination backlighting him from within, Matthew was struck by his perverse resemblance to Christ on the cross.

"No, man, Paula's gone." Suddenly Maynard's eyes brimmed with tears.

Matthew was startled by the depth of the man's grief. "I'm sorry. I don't understand…"

"Ain't you hearin' me? Paula done left me. She moved into a damn motel."

Matthew's hopes plummeted. No use telling Maynard his story, or asking about Diana, because no words would penetrate his drunken despair. "What motel?"

"Shit, man, you think she'd tell me? She wants a fuckin' divorce."

Matthew retreated another step. "You have no idea where I'd find her?"

Maynard stumbled as the afflicted feline who'd been making the racket escaped between his legs and raced off into the darkening yard. Once he regained his balance, Maynard held up a shaky arm and pointed down the road. "You might could ask my nephew. Him and Paula's real close, so maybe she told that son-a- bitch."

Matthew flinched as Maynard fell back, then slammed the door in his face. His legs felt wobbly as he strode back down the flowered sidewalk and spotted the cat streaking down the road, looking for her Tom.

261

As he climbed back in his truck, the image made him uncommonly sad because it conjured up a conversation he'd had with Diana that day they'd visited Tom Dooley's schoolhouse in Whippoorwill Village. It seemed a lifetime ago. They were standing together in the parking lot. Diana's face was lit by an aureole of sunlight, and he'd pointed out what had happened to Tom when he tried to balance three women at once.

"They should've called him *Tomcat*." Diana had laughed. "Laura, Ann, and Pauline…three cousins. Like juggling three balls in the air."

Matthew's heart ached as he worried about Diana, so he started his truck and drove down the road to confront Tom's present-day ancestor. Dooley was dead, but Trevor was very much alive, and somehow he had managed to insinuate himself and the horrors of that accursed legend into what used to be Matthew's happy family. The time had come, after nearly a century and a half, to put those old ghosts to rest. To make it right. And before the night was through, Matthew was determined that Trevor would help him do just that.

FORTY-EIGHT

A sad and shallow grave…

Diana knew she was fading faster than the thin lines of light defining her prison ceiling. This last waking she knew time was short, and although the excruciating pain in her head had become a dull throbbing that kept precise time with her slowing pulse, she also knew she was losing all grip on reality.

She required air, water, and final escape from her numb body, along with the stench it left behind. Her voice made no sound when she screamed, her hands were dead from pounding. And although she struggled to hang onto all the good moments of her life as they streamed backwards through time, her brain kept snagging on the regrets—those moments she could have done much better with Mama, her children, and mostly with Matthew. Why had they parted with angry words? Would that final argument be the memory that lingered above all others when all memory passed into eternity?

As she slipped deeper into delusion, she found herself sleeping at the base of a mountain. Above ground, the laurel bloomed, a gentle breeze bent the leaves of a willow tree, but a jealous lover had buried the blade of a mattock in her skull. Diana longed to drive the legend away and pull herself back into her own life—or death—but one line from the story kept repeating like an old phonograph needle stuck in one groove;

"They found Tom Dooley's woman buried in a sad and shallow grave."

FORTY-NINE

Matthew…

He rapped hard on Trevor's door, and unlike the reception he'd received at Maynard's, Trevor opened immediately, a wide grin on his face. "What a surprise. C'mon in, Trout."

He ushered Matthew down a floral hallway, past the requisite parlor and dining room, and directly into the kitchen, the heart of any farmhouse. The space was brightly lit by a new white ceiling fan and smelled of freshly brewed coffee.

"What's your pleasure, coffee or beer?" Trevor exuded hospitality. "I had a great time at your place today. Ginny and Lissa took me for a boat ride, then we picnicked on an island. Too bad that storm came up."

"Please stop, Trevor." Matthew held up his hand. "I'm glad you had fun, but this isn't a social call. As the young man's smile drooped, Matthew searched for the right words. The deeper he committed to this course of action, the more his mind told him he was on a fool's mission. But his heart told him something entirely different. As he studied Trevor, standing ramrod straight and respectful in a bright blue T-shirt that matched his eyes, Matthew realized that under different circumstances, this man might have been his son-in-law.

On the other hand, from the beginning everyone, including the police, had fingered Trevor for Lori Fowler's murder, just like in the Tom Dooley legend. Yet the women in Matthew's life had always believed in his innocence.

Trevor pulled out one of four antique pressed wood oak chairs and offered Matthew a seat. "I don't know what this is about, but why don't you sit down and tell me about it?"

Matthew hesitated, but then sat down. Trevor sat across from him and pinned him with those probing eyes as Matthew explained his concerns. As he spoke, he was mindful he was likely hitting quite a few nerves by dredging up details about Lori's murder. After all, the woman had been Trevor's fiancée. As he told about Loveless Fowler's Trust—all the money at stake—the young war vet shook his head.

"Sure, I knew about the money. Lori talked about it all the time, but we didn't need it. Not now. We could've lived just fine on my pension. For awhile."

Matthew sensed his companion was becoming agitated. His large, powerful hands rested flat on the table and his fingers began to tremble.

"What about Paula Dula?" Matthew pressed. "Did *she* need the money?"

Trevor's heavy brows dipped in a frown. "God knows what Paula needs. The woman is crazy."

"Crazy?"

"Unstable." Trevor attempted to pick up his coffee, but his hand shook too much. "She always had this insane fantasy about me, but it was bullshit, and she knew it." He climbed to his feet and started pacing. "Even so, she'd never hurt Lori."

"Are you sure?" Choosing his next words carefully, Matthew revealed that Paula had already claimed all the trust money and was about to purchase an expensive property at Lakeview Estates. "Did you know about that?"

"No, I did not."

"Did your uncle Maynard know?"

"I doubt it." Trevor's pacing put Matthew in mind of a caged lion.

"I just saw Maynard. He's drunk. And Paula has left him, moved into some motel."

Trevor stopped abruptly, his face turned ashen and his clenching fists went slack. "Jesus Christ." He sighed. "I knew this would happen someday, but not so soon." His gaze shifted wildly around the room but refused to light on Matthew's face. "I'm worried about Maynard. He'll kill himself. We need to go up there and check on him."

Matthew noted Trevor's distress and wondered briefly if he was on drugs, some sort of psyche medication. He sensed the man swinging between extreme highs and lows and feared not only for him, but for himself. Still, Matthew had an agenda and needed Trevor's help.

"Don't worry," he offered soothingly. "By now Maynard's passed out. He'll sleep through 'til morning." Matthew hoped with all his heart that it was true, because he didn't want a suicide on his conscience. He waited until his words sunk in, seemed to have a calming effect, and then he told Trevor about Diana—how she'd gone missing.

Trevor seemed to be listening. He ceased his pacing and poured the leftover coffee from the pot into the sink. He now stood above that sink, both hands braced on its rim, and contemplated whatever wisdom he saw in the brown liquid swirling down the drain.

"What motel would Paula choose?" Matthew asked when the time was right.

Trevor laughed bitterly. "I could've answered that question back in the day, but now Paula has more choices. I'm sure she'd choose something more upscale than the fleabags we used to inhabit, but I don't know where she's staying. Besides, it doesn't matter."

Reading between the lines, Matthew realized that once upon a time Trevor and Paula had had an affair. "Why doesn't it matter?" he demanded.

"Because she won't be sitting around in any motel room." Trevor backed away from the sink and wiped his hands on his jeans. "What's that you said about Diana's dog? Where'd they find her?"

"They found Gracie wandering around in an abandoned landfill." Matthew wondered what the hell the dog had to do with the problem at hand.

"Listen, Trout, you said Paula's buying property in Lakeview Estates, right? Well, there used to be a landfill adjacent to that land. If Gracie was with Diana, then that's where she got lost."

The implications hit Matthew hard. Gracie had been the key all along. "So you think Paula was lying? Do you think she and Diana got together after all, and they went to the site?"

"What other explanation could there be?" Trevor continued excitedly. "And I hate to say it, but if Gracie got lost, then something happened to Diana."

Something bad. Matthew filled in the blanks and the fear he'd been feeling all evening congealed like a hard knot in his stomach. Why hadn't he put it together sooner? "You know the way to Lakeview Estates?"

But Trevor had already left the kitchen. Matthew followed him into a bedroom just down the hall and found him rummaging through the top drawer of a dresser. "What are you doing?"

"We'll take my Jeep," Trevor said. "I haven't been up there in years, but the land used to be rugged. Four-wheel drive will come in handy."

Matthew was impatient to leave, but he needed this man. As his eyes roamed around the space, he saw an austere single bed made up military style and clothes hung neatly in the closet, the hangers spaced at perfect intervals. Precisely what one would expect from a Sergeant Major.

"This might come in handy, too." Trevor located what he'd been looking for.

Even in the dim light, Matthew saw the gun in Trevor's hand and his body tensed.

"This is my baby." Trevor stroked the gleaming pistol with a corrugated black grip. "Beretta M9, standard army issue."

"Put it away, we don't need it."

But the man ignored him. Instead, he removed a small holster from the drawer and tucked it inside his pants, took out a clip and loaded the weapon. "Okay, are you ready, Trout?'

Trevor tucked the gun out of sight, and then Matthew trailed him out the door.

FIFTY

Matthew...

Trevor made a couple of wrong turns along the way, but Matthew held his temper and prayed they weren't on a wild goose chase. What if Diana and Paula had completed their business at Lakeview Estates hours ago, then gone out together, for dinner or shopping? Not likely. Considering the suspicions Diana had about Paula, not to mention the fact that she'd never leave Gracie behind, convinced Matthew that the last thing Diana was up to was a girls' day out.

"This is it..." Trevor made an abrupt left through a pretentious stone entryway to the future gated community. "Hope we can locate Paula's lot fast, it'll be dark soon."

Matthew felt helpless as the light faded from the sky and Trevor made more wrong turns. The development was illuminated by incongruously ornate, newly constructed streetlights—yet there were no streets or sidewalks. The would-be neighborhood looked oddly sinister in twilight, with homeless foundations lifting like tombstones from the red clay and the wooden bones of residences waving their naked skeletons against the sunset.

"How will we know Paula's lot?" Trevor asked.

"Beats me, but why don't you turn here and drive up that hill?" When they reached the crest of the promontory, they saw the soaring framework of a mini-mansion. "This is it," Matthew stated with certainty.

"How do you know?"

"Climb out and I'll show you." They parked in the gravel lot. Trevor handed Matthew a flashlight, then both exited the Jeep. Matthew led Trevor to a fragile temporary signpost. "See, this one is sold."

"So what?"

Matthew pointed to the "Rittenhouse-McCorkle" logo attached. "So Diana and Liz sold it, this has to be the place."

"Good work, Trout."

The men smiled at one another and started up the hill. When they reached the top, Matthew turned on the flashlight and beamed it into the large foundation. The light jumped along the concrete walls, then flew into the rafters, but much to Matthew's disappointment, they saw not one sign of life.

"If they were here, they left." He struggled to keep the desperation from his voice.

"Yeah, but they *were* here." Trevor squatted and trailed his hand across the earth. "I saw fresh tire tracks down below, and these are footprints. Near as I can tell, we've got us a pair of medium sized flip-flops and a pair of larger, sensible sandals."

"So now you're an expert tracker?" Matthew was skeptical.

Trevor grinned. "It was way harder in the deserts of Iraq, where the blasted sand kept filling in the evidence. This here's a piece of cake."

Matthew wanted to believe, because if he knew anything about Diana, it was her longtime love affair with her all-purpose sandals, and these prints looked to be her size. "What else do you see?"

Trevor took the flashlight and beamed it up and down the hillside in a grid pattern. "Okay, here we go..." He scrambled halfway down and Matthew followed. "Those first impressions were made by two people walking forward, up to the site this morning. This set was made by the person in the flip-flops sometime this afternoon, and she was coming down the hill. Alone."

Matthew didn't want to believe this. "How can you possibly know all that?"

Trevor's forehead creased with worry. "The morning prints were made before the big storm, which hit around noon. They've been partially washed out by the rain flowing down the hill. These flip-flop prints, with the toes pointing down to the car, are deep and unaffected by the downpour."

Matthew didn't need Trevor to draw him a map. He understood that Diana and Paula had visited the site together, but only Paula had left. "We'd better get up there and have a look."

Trevor fetched a second flashlight, and wordlessly they returned to begin their search.

FIFTY-ONE

Angels...

From deep inside the bowels of the earth, she heard the animal return. Even in a fugue state, suspended on a precarious tightrope stretched like the flat line warning on her own heart monitor, she had expected them to come for her body with shovels. Instead she heard a desperate scratching sound at the ceiling of her tomb.

She knew she was dead because when she opened her eyes, she saw no more thin strings of light, only black. She felt only numbness. No more sensation of a corporeal being, except that insistent sound. She had expected them to bring a wagon from the village, the clip clop of horses' hooves like from the stables of her childhood. Instead, she heard the heavy thudding of objects hitting the earth so hard they vibrated her walls, causing friction on her shoulders, and the skin she'd thought was gone.

Then came the loud shattering of wood splintering above what used to be her face. Next the sharp, painful rush of cold oxygen through her nose, then mouth. It expanded her lungs and sent the old message of pain to her brain, but when she tried to scream, she heard the animal. It had gained its final, long-sought access to the carrion of who she used to be.

She dragged her eyes open to witness its attack, but saw only cool cobalt sky, clouds, and pinprick stars. As she gulped

273

air, she heard a familiar human voice, and through what surely must be her own tears, saw the dark outline of a beloved face.

"Diana?" he said.

Next his hands, warm and remembered, became the cup under her head, the hammock under her shoulders. Then more hands, not his, sliding under her legs and hips.

"Easy, don't hurt her," the stranger said.

She was moving up and up, easing towards heaven. She guessed these angels were worried as they labored, trying to be gentle, but she could have told them, if she'd had a voice, "Don't worry, it doesn't hurt."

Down and down onto the damp earth, with her upper body cradled against the intimately known contour of his chest. She recognized the rough angle of his chin against her forehead, but didn't find her way through until the butterfly-soft flutter of his lips against her parched mouth.

"Matthew?" She tried to smile.

FIFTY-TWO

Trevor...

"Good, she's coming to." Trevor exhaled a deep sigh of relief as he carefully lowered Diana's legs to the ground. "Stay with her, Trout. I keep a blanket and some bottled water in the Jeep." He rose up to run.

"Fine, but first call 911. We need an ambulance pronto!"

Trevor began his downhill sprint, ignoring the pain in his left knee, the reminder of that roadside bomb with his name on it. Thank God they'd found one of Diana's sandals wedged under a pile of boards, otherwise they'd have never found her. He'd seen the tears in Trout's eyes, along with the terror, as they'd resurrected Diana from what could have been, by all rights should have been, her makeshift grave.

He envied those tears and wished he could shed his own, but since he'd been home from the war, those emotions were blocked, at least outwardly. As he scrambled into his vehicle and retrieved his cell from the glove box, he sensed that if only he could cry, he could heal. At least that was what the shrinks had told him.

He dialed 911, got an immediate pickup. After giving directions and a short briefing of what had gone down, after requesting the ambulance, Trevor signed off. And in those moments after hanging up, he was breathing hard. Hyperventilating. Reliving too many emergencies from his former life. As if those years of exploding IUD's and sudden death would ever be *former* in his injured mind.

He touched the hard outline of the pistol holstered in his pants to reassure himself, then practiced deep breathing until his sanity returned. All that blood. He reminded himself that Diana's injury looked worse than it was. Scalp wounds were always dramatic, but seldom life threatening. Shock and dehydration were the bigger threats, so he snagged two bottles of water and the blanket from the boot.

He seriously doubted Diana could swallow any liquid. Likely she'd have to wait for the IV she'd receive in the ambulance. But the water might keep Trout occupied, allow him to be useful by cleaning her wound and touching the moisture to her lips while he waited for help.

Trevor envied the man. He'd seen the look of loving recognition in Diana's eyes. Soon she'd regain lucidity and embrace Trout like the hero he was. Yes. Trout was the hero, the steady one. Even as an ignorant, badass teenager, Trevor had known this about his first girlfriend's father—the grandfather of his only child. Trevor felt moisture on his cheeks. Tears were too much to hope for, but he knew reconnecting with Ginny and meeting sweet Lissa had brought him closer. Perhaps there was hope for him, after all?

As he lingered with that thought, he heard the distant cry of a siren. That was fast. But then, just when he was about to run up the hill and tell Trout that help was on the way, his cell phone rang. He had forgotten to power it off, as was his habit, and when he checked the caller ID, the name displayed there sent Trevor's brain kicking back into high gear.

He recalled the half dozen concrete blocks that had been piled deliberately on the sheet of plywood sealing Diana's prison. Saw the baling wire the assailant had used to bind her wrists, and of course, the bloody rebar lying in the dirt. Then, as now, Trevor knew that the person who could commit such an act was a monster, a stone cold killer. And she was on his line.

"Hello, Paula." He fought to keep his voice neutral, then listened as the woman came on to him, flirting and insistent, requesting a meeting.

"All right," he told her. "I'm on my way."

His goal was to leave before the ambulance and cops arrived with some argument to detain him. He rushed up the hillside, gave Trout the water and blanket. Much to Trevor's relief, Diana was smiling and holding Trout's hand. She didn't seem to recognize him, though, as he told her goodbye.

"Where are you going?" Trout demanded. Clearly he wanted Trevor to hang around for moral support.

"Did Diana tell you who did this?" Trevor had to be sure.

Trout nodded grimly. "Paula Dula."

Suspicions confirmed, Trevor decided to share the truth. "Paula's waiting at my house, Trout. And I agreed to meet with her."

Blocking out Trout's shouted protests, Trevor ran back down the hill. He believed this was his moment, his one shot at redemption, absolution, closure—whatever psychobabble the shrinks would throw his way. Basically, he needed to confront Paula before the cops got to her.

He had no choice.

FIFTY-THREE

Trevor...

Trevor passed the ambulance heading in as he was heading out. An unmarked police unit followed the emergency vehicle. The driver, who appeared to be Wayne Bearfoot, had attached a portable cherry light to his roof. It spun as his siren hiccupped, and for once Trevor was glad to see the tenacious sheriff.

Matthew said he'd asked Ginny to call Bearfoot, so Trevor wasn't surprised to find the man in the vicinity, far from his regular beat. And clearly the sheriff had spotted him, recognized his Jeep, and for a few seconds their eyes had locked as they sped in opposite directions. Trevor took it as a good omen when Bearfoot chose not to pull a U-turn and chase him. A positive sign, perhaps, that the cops had come to their senses and Trevor was off the hook, once and for all, for Lori's murder.

As he neared the turnoff to Dula Road, he realized his hands were strangling the steering wheel. How would the cops feel after tonight? After he had finished with Paula? Refusing to dwell on those consequences, Trevor wiped the sweat from his eyes. His blood hummed with the same numbing electricity that once mobilized him forward into combat. He wasn't nervous or frightened, and he'd learned not to overthink a mission. No, the sensation was more robotic, like his body was moving on autopilot, without a specific plan.

Turning left at the landmark oak, all his senses were heightened. He saw clouds skidding across the sliver moon as stars vibrated in an inkwell sky. When he switched off the air and powered down the window, the sudden humidity glazed his skin and a cat in heat yowled somewhere nearby. But when Trevor pulled into his driveway and parked beside the truck Trout had left there, he saw no signs of an additional visitor. The only light burning in his farmhouse was the lamp on the hall table, the one he'd lit when he left with Trout.

Okay, so maybe Paula had changed her mind and left. The speculation didn't alter his momentum one way or the other, he was too pumped. His heart thudded with the heavy strokes remembered from battle, with only the pulsing in his bad knee connecting him to present reality as he pushed at the front door with the toe of his shoe.

It swung inward, as he knew it would, although he had definitely locked it. Paula had a key. As he moved into the dim hallway, her scent permeated the air, the same strident, exotic perfume she'd worn when they were kids, when he'd made the tragic mistake of taking her to bed.

He moved through the shadows, past the parlor and dining room into the kitchen. Nothing. Had she been here, then left? Without turning on the overhead light, Trevor tried the back door. It was locked. But then it would be, because the screen door was also locked, and no one had a key to it. He switched on the wall toggle to the barn light and peered through the dark yard. At first he saw nothing, but then spotted the gleaming golden fin of his uncle's El Dorado parked deep inside the barn.

The short hairs prickled on the back of his neck, heightening his hunter's instinct. He had been here so many times before. In Iraq, he'd tracked the unseen enemy hiding right behind the door with a club, knife, or gun intended to end his life. He thumbed open his holster and drew his weapon as his eyes became accustomed to the dark. Paula was on his territory, his killing field, but where was she hiding?

Unlocking the safety on his Beretta, Trevor was ready as he retraced his steps to the staircase leading upstairs. To the bedroom he'd once shared with Ginny Troutman, but no other woman. By now Paula knew he was in the house, had heard his Jeep drive in, so why was she waiting?

Putting one foot above the other, he mounted the stairs, and with each riser her scent got stronger. Taboo...he remembered its name as the smell lined his nostrils. Reaching the top of the landing, he saw the bedroom door was ajar, with a single candle glowing from the dish on his parents' dresser. Its wobbling flame illuminated his folks' framed wedding portrait and reminded Trevor of the happy days, before the automobile accident stole their young lives.

And when he entered the room and stared at the bed, where Paula was sitting cross-legged, a smug, seductive smile on her face, he lost his famous objectivity. The woman wore a tight pink tank top under a black leather Harley jacket—and denim shorts with ridiculous rhinestone cowboy boots.

"You took your sweet time getting here," she crooned.

Her crass violation of this sacred space where Trevor had been conceived, where he had planted the seed that had miraculously become Lissa, unleashed a violent rush of fury. The anger caused his finger to twitch dangerously on the trigger, so he lowered his right hand, let his arm dangle at his side as he struggled to regain his equilibrium.

"We found Diana Rittenhouse," he told her in a deadpan voice that in no way reflected his turmoil. He knew she heard him because even by candlelight, he saw her face grow pale beneath the layers of makeup, and her pink lips quivered as she processed the information.

She stood up and inched closer as her mouth spewed a flood of explanations and excuses. Through his rage, Trevor tried to make sense of her tirade as she told him about the money, begged him to run away with her, described a future fashioned by her madness, and not one word made a lick of difference.

When she touched his arm, her heat sent shock waves. "You killed my Lori." He accused her.

More explanations and excuses. As Paula tried to tell him Lori's death had been a tragic accident, an unpremeditated moment of insanity, Trevor visualized his beloved fiancée lying in a pool of blood, Paula's knife buried in her chest. He decided the monster standing before him must die.

He shoved her away, raised his gun, and pointed it at her heart. In a moment of brilliant clarity, Trevor felt time stand still. He saw his prey, her green eyes stretched wide with fear, her hands fluttering like wings on a broken bird. He saw her lips twisting, pleading for her life, but heard nothing but the blood of revenge roaring in his ears as he took aim.

Mostly Trevor imagined the bullet streaking through the air, as in a dream. He saw it enter her breast and the blood blooming like a red rose on her pink top. But the dream was frozen, like a movie stuck on a single frame as the film disintegrated from the projector's heat.

"You can't do it, Trev," Paula taunted. "You don't have the guts to kill me."

Sweat poured down his face and pooled under his collar as Paula backed away and walked to the door. His hand trembled, his knees shook, but his feet remained bolted to the floor as she called him a coward and an idiot.

Trevor agreed. He was a coward and an idiot, but he finally managed to swivel and draw a bead on her retreating back. He imagined the same bloody red rose blooming between the shoulder blades of her black leather jacket, but it never happened. He listened to her boots clipping down the stairs, heard the back door slam as he gasped to catch his breath. Even as his heart beat outside his chest and he struggled for air, Trevor was unable to move while the Cadillac El Dorado fired up and left the barn.

Only then did his feet break loose. He took the steps two at a time and flew out the front door. But by the time he stumbled into the front yard, his pistol hanging like an impotent appendage in his right hand, Paula's car was halfway down the road. He ran into the street, chasing her taillights, but then he saw the police blockade.

Trevor fell to his knees as the patrol cars and one unmarked unit brought Paula's Caddy to a shrieking halt. He saw the spinning red lights. He heard her tires skid as she hit the brakes, the sirens and muffled shouts.

And then he carefully laid his weapon on the hot pavement as the moving picture played on without him, and when he lifted his eyes to watch, he found he could no longer see, because he was blinded by the long-awaited tears of redemption.

Epilogue

One month later…

Diana captured Matthew's hand as they exited the small rustic cabin that replicated the schoolhouse Tom Dula had attended all those years ago. Liz and Danny were right behind them, and next came Ginny, Lissa, and Trevor.

If she'd had her way, Diana would have skipped this visit to Whippoorwill Village. She was more than ready to leave the legend behind, but the younger generation had never seen the place, so they were curious. Especially Trevor, who had developed a fresh interest in his long-dead ancestor.

Diana sighed and lifted her eyes to the hazy foothills looming beyond the parking lot. The doctors had to shave a portion of her hair to put in the stitches, but it had all grown back in now. And except for the usual forgetfulness she'd experienced even before Paula's attack, Diana was none the worse for wear. These days she feigned amnesia only when it suited her.

The police had found her car, Queen Vic, parked in the last row of a used car lot near Big Jay's. Evidently Paula had driven it there after burying Diana alive. Paula had abandoned Diana's car, and then simply walked across the street to the shopping center where her Caddy, which had never required repair from Triple A, was waiting and ready to go.

"Can I sit up front with you, Grandpa?" Lissa asked as they approached Queen Vic.

"Sure, Punkin." Matthew winked at Diana.

Lately they'd noticed how crafty little Lissa was conspiring to pair her mama with her newfound daddy. At every opportunity, like now, Lissa tried to get them alone together. The child was determined that the wish she'd made on her birthday would come true: "I never want to go back to Nevada. I want to stay here forever."

Diana glanced to where Trevor had paused to pick a yellow daisy from the edge of the lot. He tucked it behind Ginny's ear. Far as Diana could tell, Lissa's chances were fifty/fifty of having her wish come true. Ginny was playing her life day by day. Although she still claimed she'd return to Vegas someday, for now she had accepted a job playing guitar and singing at Buffalo Guys, Trevor's nightclub. And while Trevor seemed attentive, he wasn't quite ready to commit to Ginny. But Diana, always the romantic, had her fingers crossed.

She hoped in time they'd be half as happy as she was with Matthew, whom she loved more every day. She wished the same for Liz and Danny, who were halfway there already. They had come here today in Danny's truck, and Amazing Grace was riding with them.

Soon after her recovery, Diana had been so grateful she'd made one impulsive gesture—her way of thanking her Creator for sparing her life. She had finally, once and for all, awarded custody of Gracie to Danny, because the man loved the greyhound with all his heart. Not only had it made Diana's life at home with Matthew easier by restoring Ursie as the once and future queen, it was the right thing to do.

But she'd regretted not adding her voice to those of Trevor and his uncle Maynard, after Paula Dula had been convicted of Lori Fowler's murder. Paula was also convicted of the attempted murder of Diana Rittenhouse. Even though Paula had victimized Trevor and Maynard, the men had found it in their hearts to recommend that she be treated gently and receive psychiatric counseling during her imprisonment. They both had detected a kernel of goodness in Paula, a seed that could be nurtured towards eventual rehabilitation. At least Trevor believed this. He claimed he had experienced such an epiphany himself.

But Diana had seen the essence of pure evil in Paula's eyes as she raised that rebar to strike, and she had known the horror of a living death. Gentle Matthew claimed Diana would someday find a way to forgive her attacker, and she believed him, because his love would lead her there.

But in the meantime, as Danny and Gracie rushed up to say goodbye, she wondered aloud as she looked out at the fields where Tom Dooley's ghost still roamed. "Did any good come from this whole stinking mess?"

Danny instinctively understood as he patted his greyhound's sleek head. "Well sure, Diana. I got me a good dog."

Kate Merrill is an art gallery owner and real estate broker with a lifelong passion for writing. She lives with her family on a lake in North Carolina. When she is not writing, working with the art community, or selling real estate, she enjoys swimming, boating, and allowing her two strong-headed Golden Retrievers to take her for a walk.

Diana Rittenhouse Mystery Series
A Lethal Listing
Blood Brothers
Crimes of Commission
Dooley is Dead
Buyer Beware

Amanda Rittenhouse Mystery Series

Murder at Metrolina
Homicide in Hatteras
Assault in Asheville
The Mayberry Murders

Mainstream Romance
Northern Lights (as Christie Cole)
Flames of Summer

www.katemerrillbooks.com